VOYAGE OF THE
ARROGANT

by Norm Gibbons

Table of Contents

TUNA BOAT "ARROGANT"

Inclining Test — July 5th 1945

at Benson's Shipyard.

3/4" = 1 Foot

Expansion Trunk

2 Bait Tanks thus.

Weight inc! water 7½ long tons
placed aft on raised deck.
Water level always within
expansion trunk.

M.G. reduced from 12¾" to 8½"
in worst condition of lading;
with bait tanks installed.

Mean draft with bait tanks & water

Mean draft as tested

Water plane Areas 1" = 100□"

6'-3" mean
5'-9" mean

5'4" Fore
7'-1" Aft
5'-10" Fore
5'-6" Aft

Condition on Test
Vessel complete
Fuel tanks full
Lower watertank empty
Top water tank full
Hold empty
6 men on board (4 on deck & 2 in hold)
1½ tons iron ballast under hold floor.
2000# shifting ballast on Main deck abreast hatch.

Moment to alter trim 1" = 3·065 Foot Tons at 6'-3" mean draft
Tons per Inch at 5'-9" mean draft = 1·018 tons & at 6'-3" mean draft = 1·044 Tons

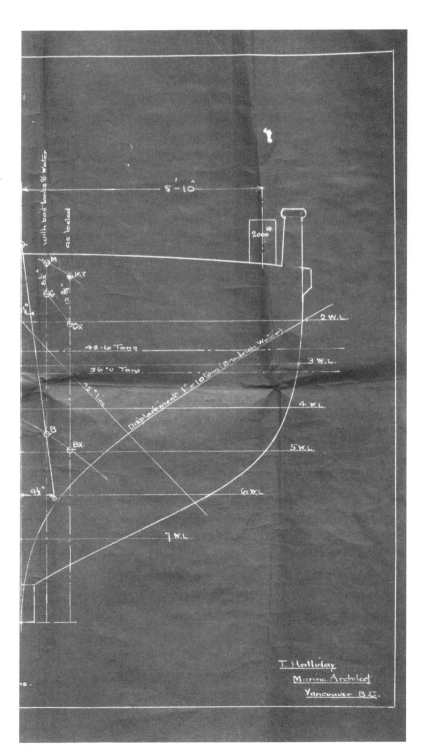

with ballasts & water

as tested

5'-10"

2000#

6¼"

12⅞"

M

Jr.x

G

Gx

2 W.L.

42.6 Tons

36.0 Tons

3 W.L.

4.5 line

Displacement 1" = 10 tons (Brackish Water)

4 W.L.

B

Bx

5 W.L.

9½"

6 W.L.

7 W.L.

T. Halliday
Marine Architect
Vancouver B.C.

To Denise

Shipmates of the Arrogant
R.I.P.

Captain Perry Jenzen
Jimmy-James (JJ) Ballentyne
Robert (Bob) Archer
Darwin (Dar) Wilkes

CORTES ISLAND FAMILIES

THE JENZENS

Colin and Mable Jenzen

Sons: George (Georgie) and Wesley

Wesley and Madeline Jenzen

Son: Perry

Perry and **Marlene** Jenzen

Sons: Bradley and Jim

THE BALLENTYNES

Crawford and Marie Ballentyne

Son: James (Jimmy-James, JJ)
Daughter: Martha

James (JJ) and **Meredith** Ballentyne

Son: John

THE ARCHERS

Joseph and Mary Archer

Son: Robert
Daughters: Marlene and Maddie

Robert and **Margaret** Archer

Son: William

William (Will) and Marne Archer

THE WILKES

Samuel and Melissa Wilkes

Sons: Darwin and Adam

Darwin (Dar) and Mercy Wilkes

Rock of Ages, cleft for me,
Let me hide myself in Thee;
Let the water and the blood,
From Thy wounded side which flowed,
Be of sin the double cure,
Save from wrath and make me pure.

Augustus Montague Toplady

replenish the curative for man's ills...please

1919

ON A SUNDAY MORNING, when others paid lip service to their Lord Almighty, the bushwhacker lolled on a cot in his flop hotel room overlooking the banks of the Fraser River. He heard a persistent church bell clang and boom, begging for worshipers. That's a wretched noise, he thought.

Through his mouse hole window, he watched the river glide at a molasses pace, and for a tedious time he gazed at a derelict craft drift on the sluggish water, revolve slowly, going nowhere, motionless but for the slow twirling, captured in the clutch of an enormous eddy. He wished he was aboard.

A few months earlier the old man had strayed over an imaginary line drawn across the continent into Canada. So far, he could find no excitement in the alien land, or the city of New Westminster, and on that account had entered a vile state of boredom.

Simply stated, life had lost its luster.

Drinking did not help his condition. Nor did the soiled doves, who frequented the back alleys and doorways of his favoured dives. Neither did gambling. If truth be told, he was a poor loser, always had been, and recently played an all night poker game with dull-witted men who insisted on Canadian rules - dreamt up from game to game, card to card and bet to bet. Due to the perceived injustice, as well as a menacing atmosphere around the table, he inclined himself to fabricate an altercation: loud accusations of marked cards followed by overturned tables and chairs. For encore, he revealed a weapon and threatened a certain flimflam fellow with his uncertain life.

In retrospect, best not draw attention to oneself, he thought.

Since family and friends were dead, probably, or at least dying bit by bit and painfully too, though he had no idea which or what was the case, to distract the chatter in his skull, he often took to practical occupations such as sharpening his scalping blade on a worn whetstone carried the many years and long distances from his Missouri home. Sitting on the edge of his bed, each time the stone dried from his skillful honing, he spit more lubricant and then continued the monotonous grinding. Calming like a meditation, he thought. His smart brother made the knife - for the handle, a deer antler fitted glove-wise into a dark tough hide, and for the blade, a tempered steel buckboard spring. To achieve the aesthetic appeal of a great work of art, the bushwhacker added tassels of human hair, which, remarkably, had thinned and greyed over the years. Whose they were, he couldn't say or care. The patch of hairy scalp sprouted from the handle, a decorative addition many noticed, though few dared comment. Due to overzealous honing through the decades, the weapon now looked more like a fish fillet knife than the original design engineered by his brother.

Soon his mind wandered from the task even as his clever hands persisted with their chore. A voice, speaking from the depths inside his head, that had been vocalizing for the last number of years with a persistence which had finally gained his attention - not just persistent, but with frightening authority too - announced that the moment had come for his final fling, a last utterance to magnify an unbroken string of triumphs catalogued under "life's greatest achievements." The gist of the message went something like: In this wasteland, your last chance for a big splash in this rotten world has arrived, which, if you are crafty, and I know you are, will grab the attention of generations into the long arc of time.

Tacked lopsided to a wall in his room hung a mariner's chart of the southern coastline of British Columbia, which he had studied intently during recent months. One night he and his voice had decided, whilst alcohol inspired many wild notions, that somewhere on that map lay their ultimate destiny. Where exactly, they were unsure. Since the day was Sunday, and a day to think, his voice said, I got a idea, let the knife decide where we go. The old man threw the blade and bullseyed an island. Not a bad throw. He lifted off his cot and approached his target. Upon study he liked the shape. Not regular, but not raggedy either. More than anything, he liked where it sat secretive, nestled in a cluster of likeminded others, protected by Vancouver Island from the wild and raging Pacific Ocean, close to the snow capped mountains and reaching out to beautiful blank spaces of nothingness. He liked the name too – after an historical figure like himself. And he liked that the island brushed up against a watery world called Desolation Sound, perhaps, he imagined, the gateway to a wonderful wilderness where he could finish his days, stop the wandering, stop the evading – just stop. For the rest of the afternoon, he watched a spider weave a web across his one broken windowpane, but his eye kept tacking back to his knife, which had pierced the heart of Cortes Island at the top of the Strait of Georgia.

Beside his flop hotel stood a ship's chandlery. Over the course of a few more months he provisioned up in preparation for the great journey. More charts, a big rowboat and anchor and chain – clinker, deep-drafted. Like a miniature freighter, he thought. Two sets of oars. To get the hang of sea life, to locate the whereabouts of his sea legs, he watched others, saw how they tied their boats, stowed their gear and he practiced rowing on the river, but, unlike the others, stood and pushed.

Sitting back to front is an invitation to ambush, his voice correctly observed.

And then added, From now on your boat is your horse.

I ain't had no horse in lots of years, he said.

Think of them oars as stallion legs, said his voice.

On one of those practice runs, still refining his technique, getting his muscles and fibres accustomed to the instability of a watery life, a fellow on the riverbank yelled out, "I ain't never seen nobody row like that before." The idiot clutched his gut like he had never enjoyed a decent laugh in a sordid lifetime. If the bushwhacker could have rowed to shore fast enough, he would have smashed the fellow over the head with both oars and then set to work creating a permanent sense of cataclysm and ruination.

He bought a miner's tent. And tools – shovel, pick, axe, saw, hammer, screw drivers and chisels, nails and screws and nuts and bolts, fish line, hooks and lures and sisal ropes of various gauge and length. He didn't know or care if he'd ever use any of his equipment. And he bought food - cases of canned peaches and beans, spuds, two pails of lard, salt, two full slabs of bacon, sugar, flour, and four big buckets of strawberry jam. Then he bought necessaries - matches, tobacco, papers, candles, lots of candles, coffee and whiskey, lots of coffee and lots of whiskey. With each purchase the energy of youth surged into every one of his musty corners. Maybe I got a second wind, he thought. His voice agreed, You sure do. He bought a new fry pan, new pot, and a real good American rifle, Winchester 44. Rounds for it too. He still had one patch ball for the old .36 revolver - a concession to nostalgia was all it was. Or maybe he would use it one last time. You never know, said his voice. He packed his moth-eaten Confederate flag because he could not imagine not having it, could not imagine the stars and stripes flying over Missouri, and could not forgive the murderous North and never would. He bought a lantern and coal oil. He bought those new rubberized boots. He rejected the need for a compass as his internal bearings had always behaved adequately, but acquired bushels of empty medicine bottles from an apothecary at a penny apiece - the bubbly lilac coloured kind - for he had an entrepreneurial idea learned from a medicine man at a carnival show down in Oregon though the method should be amended slightly now that he lived on foreign soil. He paid the proprietor the grand sum of fifteen dollars in advance for future deliveries and said he would send shipping instructions later.

The man asked, "Don't you need no stoppers?"

"No I don't," said the bushwhacker.

Then he asked, "What you going to do with all them bottles?"

"Tain't your business."

To tell the truth, his profitorial idea was vague - not conceptual either - but for certain genuinely creative. Nor could one say this venture was motivated by need as his stash of loot – hoarded and fondled over the decades - looked just as tall and just as pretty after the spending spree.

On April 19, 1919, he said good-bye to civilization, though no one heard his farewell, and oared out the mouth of the Fraser River passing sawmills, fish canneries and never ending trains of log booms lined with tranquil grey gulls and their splatterings of slippery white shit. Troller boats and gill-netter boats chugged to he-didn't-know-where, as did coal tugs puking black billows at an innocent blue sky. The muddy water turned light green. Soon an actual line divided the sea from the river - the blue from the green. When he reached over and tasted salt, he knew he had entered the Strait of Georgia. The idea was to get over there, where the mountains stood tall and toothy, and keep following the shoreline, but keep refusing to go up the mouths of inlets until you got to the top of the chart; then you could sort out the jumble of islands until you got the right one. To celebrate his life change he rechristened himself with a new alias, Frank Waterman: Frank to honor his older brother, and Waterman – well that was obvious. So went the business of his mind. An American legend fitted with a new spring for an old life. Three score and ten - plus or minus. Impervious to the ravages of time.

TWO MONTHS OF ROWING: calluses on calluses, sore legs and sore ass, minor mishaps, bailing, loafing, fishing - they leapt into the boat like on the Sea of Galilee when Jesus came along for the ride - and wrong turns, and once he becalmed in the deafening quiet of fog for three full days and three long nights, when he heard the ghostly jabbers and bleeps of sea birds who could care less about where they were or if land were near or far. His voice said, Little peculiar out here. He agreed, Peculiar yes, but one hell better than what we come from.

Avoidance of citizenry was another practicality, especially difficult since those he encountered were too damned friendly, and offered him shelter, hot cooked meals, work, directions, none of which he needed or wanted. He engaged in seabird hunting, but learned quickly that the charlatan gourmands of the citified upper crust of New Westminster had overrated the tender delicacy of sea ducks. Those .44 slugs don't leave a whole lot for munching, said his voice. All in all, his journey turned into a kind of holiday.

The windy day he entered Lewis Channel with Cortes Island on his portside and Desolation Sound to starboard was miserable, dark and gloomy. As Frank neared the shoreline at the southern tip of the island, he saw a protected and abandoned bay. An old shed with moss-covered shakes crookedly stood at the highest tidemark and a lanky-legged, black wolf snuffled along the gravelly beach occasionally looking to sea at him or so Frank thought. He called out, "Hey, Lobo," but the wolf did not hear him.

Frank could do his arithmetic better than most men and knew immediately that an abandoned shed, plus a lone wolf, plus a protected bay added up to the invitation he had secretly yearned to receive for a lifetime. Looks a whole lot like we arrived at Destiny, said his voice. Maybe so, he answered, and then repeated, Maybe so, with every push on the oars. Unfortunately the southeast picked up and swept him by his chosen resting place, a mile further along. He landed at Seaford – that's what the chart said.

Seaford: a poor excuse for a harbour – shallow, boulder-strewn, wave tossed, not more than an indent in a crummy shoreline. Three wire strapped logs thrashed at wretched pilings and Frank presumed this an excuse for the wharf. At anchor, three fishboats bounced and two small rowboats rested ashore upside down. He dragged his clinker up the cobbly rocks where there was some calm. The lively swell gave an assist and he was savvy enough to anticipate each wave as it levered the boat further onto drier land. He then commenced to bail the ocean from the stern with a rusted three-pound jam tin. After considerable labour, he pulled on his boat again; lighter, it moved a few feet up the beach.

A fellow had watched him work. He smoked a long stemmed pipe discharging astonishing volumes of blue smoke. The man had extremely large ears and stained buckteeth. Made for cropping coarse sedges, thought Frank. More like saplings, said his voice.

The man ambled up and said, "Tide's falling." He could get more smoke out of that pipe than a street full of chimneys in the great city of San Francisco.

Frank said, "Maybe when the wind sighs down you might offer a shove."

"Sou'east be up fer days."

"That means you ain't offering no help, right?" Not wanting an answer to his question, Frank turned his back and stared out at Lewis Channel and the gateway to Desolation Sound.

The fellow wandered back up the hill. The southeast blew harder, but it did not rain. The tide dropped and came back up and dropped another time, never once touching the stern of his boat. He wondered, How does the sea do that? He slept ashore under a maple, the clinker tied to the tree on a long line. The evening redness in the west dwindled until the frogs from a nearby pond chanted a twilight song giving his mind a deserved rest. During the night the wind shifted to northwest, clouds cleared before daylight and pale stars speckled the dew-grey morning sky. When the sun breached the mountains on the mainland, it blasted the shore so swiftly Frank thought he had woken into a bold and brilliant dream. This is nice, said his voice.

He had beans and peaches for breakfast and thought about his discovery. The shed, the bay, and the wolf had become his just by thinking. He planned to chisel Wolf Bay into a giant granite rock by the deserted shed as soon as he got there. That act of permanence would grant him inextinguishable title. Frank considered walking the shoreline for a scout, but feared leaving his possessions to the inquiries of the fool or any of the other citizens in the hamlet of Seaford. He decided to wait for the tidewaters to reach his boat and then shove off.

The path the fool had taken led to a red miniature post office. Beyond, a gaggle of homes nestled on the cleared land – outbuildings, coops for chickens and ducks, three barns, vegetable gardens, fruit trees, and limited pasture where sheep grazed. The postmistress busied herself in the cramped quarters of the building loading sacks with parcels and bundles of letters. She came out onto the little porch and they introduced themselves.

"Hello, I'm Mrs. Archer. You can call me Mary."

"Frank Waterman, ma'am." He tipped his hat and positioned his profile in such a manner that only his unblemished side could be seen by the postmistress. The healing process had not gone entirely well.

She pointed. "That's my husband, Joseph; see him logging up the hill. And that fellow over there is Georgie Jenzen who looks after the sheep. He is a little simple, but the rest of his clan are the best fishermen in these parts. And the Ballentyne people live in that house, they're fishermen too, and the Wilkes live over to the right and keep to themselves, but they are very nice."

He asked, "Is that all the folks on this island?"

"Oh, no," she replied. "People are scattered here and there, but there's lots of us."

He asked, "How often do you get mail?"

"The freighter comes once a month." Mary looked a wiry woman, but he thought that did not detract from her appearance. "We expect it today or tomorrow; that's why I'm so busy."

He said, "I'm thinking of settling permanent-like in the bay south a piece...the one with the beat up shed beside that big rock."

She said, "Be my guest. No one lives at that end of the island. You should just go and set up shop."

She then speculated that whoever built the shed had not really been interested in settling down. It was government land probably, or it might be Indian land, but he could check. Getting title would be easy, especially if he homesteaded to gain, as she put it, "the rights of occupation." Mary said it was always good to have new people come to the island. He learned that a barn served as a hall for neighbourhood functions and her little post office was the only one on this side of the island though a larger community was a mile further north, the Klahoose Indian village at Squirrel Cove.

She asked, "What happened to your face?"

He lied, "Logging accident."

He pulled his cowboy hat further over his brow.

Perhaps not wanting to dwell on his imperfections, she asked, "What do you plan on doing on our island?"

"Into business speculations."

While they talked, he watched the fool tending the sheep in the fenced pasture of struggling grasses. Uphill, behind the field, stood a tall forest. He heard a sledge ring against a metal wedge and a Swede saw biting its way through a tree. As the postmistress seemed friendly, but more importantly, as she would talk to everyone on the island, he told her about his business plan.

Frank pointed to the logging show where her husband worked. He said, "You see them tall trees yonder?"

She said, "You mean the firs?"

"Yeah, the firs."

And then added, "They is your salvation."

She said, "I don't get your meaning." Perchance she thought he was a preacher.

At that moment, the metallic ringing amplified and multiplied, as if many sledges hammered on many wedges, and the sound caused them both to look toward the forest. They heard a slow aching moan and then the hinge of a fir barked out a series of loud cracks and the tall tree fractured itself from its base describing a long pensive arc through the silent sky. The earth shuddered where they stood and alarmed crows flew from the peak of a barn.

Soon the silence invited them to continue their conversation.

Frank said, "That tree that just come down is worth more on its feet than on its belly." He kept positioning his profile to best advantage.

Mary said, "Pardon?"

He reached into his pocket and pulled out a lilac-frosted, medicine bottle. "This here's the future for the whole dammed island." He gave her the empty container and proceeded with the explanation of his long rehearsed scheme.

"Certain highly intelligent persons have experimented with a bunch of different samplings and narrowed it down to the juice from fir trees."

"You mean sap," she said.

And he said, "Yeah, sap."

"It appears," he continued, "that due to coldness and lines of longitude, maybe its got something to do with the magnetics and the up-pushing and the surface leaking of powerful energies from the earth's core-centre, and other more complicated causes, like the light passing through these specialty coloured bottles to give the sap a kind of boost, which makes Cortes Island about the best place to collect the best sap in the whole world. They get it other places from other trees, but figure it'll be ten times more potent from yours. This island is a whole bit more rare than the other ones if you didn't know it." He reckoned that was the longest speech he had made this century.

"It looks like a regular medicine bottle to me," Mary said, now holding the glass to the sun. A splintery light electrified the bottle and magically washed her fingers in a cascade of pretty rainbows.

"That's where you're wrong ma'am, if you don't mind me doing some contradicting, the bottles may be regular but the lilac colour is extra unusual and they got non-duplicating patents on all of it."

"Well, what's the sap for?"

"It's a remedy to just about anything. There's nothing better for headaches, skin diseases, bruises, knife slashes, stomach ailments, bullet wounds, brain pustules, carbuncles, tumorous cancers and it can be taken by rubbing it on or pouring it down the hatch."

She said, "It would be too sticky and taste terrible."

"The scientific types got that figured too, and make it quite presentable in their production factories in Chicago and New York City. Soon they'll be opening a branch in my home town of San Francisco."

"My goodness," she said.

"I already sent samples back on my last trip up this way, just a scouting mission mind you, where I didn't introduce myself to nobody, and they proved up more potent than the scientest people had figured. Now I been commissioned by headquarters to source out the island and get the people's cooperation."

Frank noticed that the wind had lulled and the tide washed the stern of his boat. He had given her enough information to distill anyway. When they parted, she commented, "It must be difficult for someone your age taking on a new adventure."

He waved her off as if to say, "I may be shot up some ma'am, but I still got a lively brain."

A FEW NUDGES AND his boat floated. He started his row the mile south to Wolf Bay, at one point passing an eagle's nest in a fir snag near the shore. He watched the birds, by turn, forage out into the channel, dive to the water and retrieve glistening silver fish for their screeching young. He recalled how he and his brother had used the birds for target practice back in Clay County, Missouri. He fretted during his row though. What if someone staked my claim? During the remainder of the short trip, he invented various evils in the event of a hasty requirement to regain his imagined loss. When he arrived, the bay looked calm and deserted. But no wolf. Damnation, said his voice, Where's that wolf?

During the next weeks he amassed a respectable woodpile and thought little of Seaford and his crazy scheme. Frank made minor repairs to the shed. The door required new hinges, strap leather. He left it open most of the time to let in light. He planned, maybe, a window at some point in the future. The dirt floor was dry and easily excavated. In a corner, he encountered a large boulder and tunneled underneath it to bury his loot in three big buckets, but kept a wad of pocket change for show. He had no furniture, made none, and slept on a pile of soft cedar bows with his guns nearby. He liked the smell of cedar. He hung his food and gear on ropes from rafters. He built small cook fires on the floor and smoke poured through the many channels to the outside world. The lilac medicine bottles lay in their sacks in another corner. Some nights he wondered why he had started the sap caper as he had enough money to last ten lifetimes times ten times ten. He drank his whiskey, but not extravagant amounts, and rolled cigarettes whenever time moved like the slimy green slugs crawling in the forest - slow. He hung the tattered and mildewed Confederate flag on one wall and plastered another wall with nautical charts. On the crossbeams he displayed his tools on nail hooks like he was a regular fella with regular ambitions. The shed had a homey feel, more so than all the hideouts from his past, especially at night when his coal oil lantern ate the cavelike gloom.

Get up you sleepy creature, said his voice. A habit of a lifetime, he rose before the eastern light, splendid in its ecstasy of ascension. The clear mornings he enjoyed a grey granite ledge near the shore and there sat and smoked quietly, a contemplative emulating the stillness in the rock, the quiet smoke drifting into a world coming to life one more time. He would shiver slightly until the big bright eye breached the walls of the coastal mountains and catapulted him into startled wakefulness. Then he absorbed the glittering pink light tinting the calm waters of Desolation Sound, and softening too, the wild jagged peaks on the mainland – enough combustion to get him going for the remains of the day.

At dusk the wolf started. Plaintive, melancholic and lamenting. Filling the cool still nights with notes of remorse.

Sadly, none returned its call. Frank thought he heard desperation in those howls, perhaps the anticipation of an end lurking around a corner or behind a tree. On rock bluffs Frank found its droppings mingled with shards of bone and tuffs of fur. Colonies of crawly insects had made temporary homes there. I bet it inspects my sign too, he thought. In the forest, wandering along deer trails, he saw its tracks on mud puddle shores. Big prints on long legs, said his voice. He inspected under logs and stumps where it had dug in the rank humusy earth retrieving stashes of previous kills. It has a fondness for venison and so do I, he thought. He imagined they both entertained a curiosity for the other and that they recognized in the other a secret kinship due to their commonalities. Delight in solitude. Confidence in inner strength. A piquant taste for alienation.

When the peaches, beans and spuds gave out, he survived quite nicely on a new diet. He had learned the rudiments of fishing during his voyage from New Westminster to Cortes Island, and of course, knew how to hunt. Soon he feasted on red snapper, lingcod, rock cod and salmon. He browsed huckleberries and salmonberries in the early summer and the sweeter blackberries later on. He found the salal berries bitter, as were Oregon Grapes, and certainly didn't know the names of any of these fruits. With the Winchester, he shot a three point buck near Mary Point, the southeast tip of the island. He smoked and dried the meat into long thin tasty strips. He discovered a beach loaded with littleneck clams and butter clams and horse clams and tiny familiar oysters enjoying the warmth of the shallow intertidal pools. In the late gold rush days, he had eaten "Ollie's," as they were then called - a dollar a piece, twelve to a plate - in the fancy bars of San Francisco, always a gear up to a succinct, but strenuous, encounter with a soiled dove. Though he tried to conjure these stimulating memories, the youthful juices were rarely unlocked by the Canadian oysters resulting in disappointment and a waste of warm lard.

ONE MORNING THE SIMIAN fool arrived on a rising tide. He let his rowboat crunch on the pea gravel shore and then tied a long tether to a large boulder. He carried a bucket.

With his scalping blade, Frank gutted a salmon on a smooth rock, the silvery scales gyrating in the early morning light. He made not to notice the haze of smoke drifting over the beach.

The shepherd came up and took the pipe out of his mouth. "I got a bucket of sap." He flopped it down beside the salmon.

Frank, well knowing the habits of mountebanks, loafed his time before viewing the contents.

Georgie let out a smoke cloud and said, "How much fer it?"

Frank said, "It's spoiled."

"Pitch don't spoil," said the fool.

"Yes, it do."

Georgie nudged the bucket of sap closer to Frank's base of operation and Frank moved the salmon so it maintained the original distance from the bucket.

"Didn't Mary tell you about them bottles?" asked Frank.

Georgie said, "What of 'em?"

Frank launched a long explanation. "They's specialized bottles made for the specialized purpose. If the sap don't sit in the bottle straight from when it drips in, then the healing properties ain't released."

The fool looked at his bucket and said, "It don't look spoiled."

"Well it is." Frank threw the guts and gills of his salmon all in one go at the feet of the fool.

"Well, give me some bottles then."

"Ain't no giving. A dollar fer each," said Frank.

The shepherd learned it was necessary to charge a dollar deposit for each empty because of the extreme expense in manufacturing the lilac bottles. He was relieved to learn, however, that he would get the dollar back plus a fiver for each full one, but he must first fasten the bottle to the tree and let the sap drip until it was full. Being careful and patient was essential during the collection process.

"Corks ain't necessary. The sap dries and corks itself," said Frank.

It seems Frank could only accept bulk shipments, a full bag of full bottles, which would probably net in the neighbourhood of one hundred dollars plus all the deposit money returned. He had a huge order for the new factory in San Francisco and had to stockpile the stuff and ship it all in one go.

Georgie wanted a bag of deposit bottles, but didn't have any money. Frank thought for a long moment. He threw his scalping blade into a nearby log. The knife twanged while he manufactured his thoughts.

Frank said, "Wait here. And don't touch nothing."

He went into his shed and came out with five bottles. "Here's five empties, but come tomorrow with the deposit money…or else."

Georgie took the empties home and returned the next day with five dollars. Frank took the bill and reached inside his jacket pocket and pulled out a wad of American hundreds secured with a shiny gold money clip. He said to the fool, "I'll put this little fella longside his big American cousins."

WHEN HIS NECK HAIRS shuddered, he knew the wolf watched him. Kind of a thrill feeling. He felt the eyes before he saw them. Sometimes Frank scanned the trees and brush for hours before he finally picked out the unblinking still-ness staring through those yellow incandescent globes, seeing all before others could, seeing what others would never see. Soon the wolf took to using the intertidal beach as a short cut and often lingered pushing at pebbles and even bigger rocks, pushing and pushing, digging in the gravelly substrate, quickly springing off all fours like a startled puppy if a clam squirted, and then giving a single yip.

That wolf's a pusher and a digger, thought Frank.

As they felt more comfortable with the other, Frank found that he could walk out onto the beach flats, get within a hundred feet of the wild canine, and tease with scraps of last night's dinner. The wolf would not touch the offerings for two full weeks, but one sunny afternoon snatched a generously meated thighbone of a buck deer and from then on it turned into a chore feeding the animal plus himself. He noticed the wolf had a slight limp, favoured his front left leg, and his jaw bore a long scar much like his own. He amended the bay's name and for three days chiseled, Long Legs Bay, into the large rock behind the shed – the letters a foot high and nicely spaced. For all time, the bay would be theirs, two of them sharing it, but the wolf getting the credits, which, oddly, was okay with Frank, the concept of sharing a new and enjoyable experience.

Frank always sat on the same log by the sea and Long Legs always flopped close on piles of dried seaweed stranded high on the shore. Each day the animal sat a little closer, but remained wary testing the wind with his quivering nostrils, jumping at unfamiliar noises, perking his directional ears, fretting with the quivers and trembles of the wild, but never spooked enough to leave the beach and disappear into the darkness of the forest.

Frank's voice said, Why don't you talk to him?

The conversations were one-sided at the beginning. Frank commenting on the weather, the boat traffic in the channel, the young eagles learning to fly, whatever caught his attention. On occasion, he shared details of his past, stories he had never admitted to anyone, which could have sounded like boasting to the untrained ear.

He said, "Once in awhile I wonder if what I done is shameful and try to feel the feeling of shame, but it will not come no matter how hard I try."

And then he asked the wolf, "Do you ever feel that way, for all the killing you've done?"

Long Legs did not respond, but his ears perked up extra high as though he was formulating a thought and preparing an answer. Because Frank was impatient and because he did not yet have faith like his voice had faith, he replied to his own question. To the shame query he said, "I know it don't bother you. I think we are quite alike, a little shot up, but cunning and quiet and content."

Dreams started. Bright moon-night dreams, repeater dreams, the worlds of sleep and wakefulness latticed into a lavish tapestry, the doors of perception opening fully to the marriage of heaven and hell and Frank lost and stumbling into a bone-white clearing where the wolf guarded his latest kill. A rank familiar smell of death. Snow bloodstained. Foggy icy crystals panted from both their tongues giving a tinkling chime as bits of their fossilized breath careened each off the other, initiating the eternal trip through the cold and quiet universe. Near the end of these nightly visions, his faithful companion, Long Legs, would always ask the same question, "Old man, why we are here in the white forest with the pale moon shining?"

Frank had been thinking much on the query himself and came up with a plausible answer. "Maybe we come on a paradise for the ones what don't deserve it."

Their dialogue had begun.

THE SHEPHERD ARRIVED WITH his bottles of sap, crusted nicely on top, full to the brim, and had turned from a pale translucent liquid to a dull white crystalline paste. Frank gave him thirty dollars.

He said, "Here's a fiver for each full one and here's a single for each deposit return."

Greedy Georgie gave him the thirty dollars back and coughed up another twenty. He said, "Give me fifty empties."

Frank warned him. "Listen up. I can't pay every time the sap is delivered. This here payment is made as a one-time-only consideration."

The shepherd learned that from now on he could deliver the bottles full, take more empties, but only if the deposits were paid. Frank explained that he must have the whole order filled before releasing all the funds. That meant hundreds, hell, thousands of bottles full of the magic paste.

"That goes for anybody else who wants to get in on the basement floor of this new industry," said Frank. He reached into the depths of his jacket pocket and flashed his wad again and said, "The Company makes the rules."

The fool left for Seaford with fifty empties. As they parted on the beach, he invited his new employer to a dance in the barn the next night. Frank said he'd come, as it had been a long while, decades actually, since he'd done a proper socialization.

FRANK WATERMAN ARRIVED AT dusk for the dance, a warm summer evening. A golden glow loitered on the mainland peaks. Desolation Sound looked steel grey, benign, moody, quiet and still, but ready to speak. Bats flew about, erratic flight, pecking at flying insects, taking on the chores of daytime birds. Workboats and fishboats anchored in the bay. Rowboats and dugout canoes lined cheek to jowl on the rocky shore. Frank carried a case of whiskey and headed for the barn. When he passed the post office, Mary stood by the door talking with friends. She grabbed him immediately to do the introductions. They all knew about the old man and the fir sap. Unlike a noble southern gentleman, he did not remove his hat, wishing the weakness in the evening light might pass over the blemishes of past transgressions.

They made their way to the improvised community building. The Klahoose men from Squirrel Cove village had assembled outside the open barn doors, hoping for an opportunity to partake in forbidden firewater. They shuffled shyly when Frank and the women approached, heads bent, eyes catching nothing but crickets, spiders and dust mites, silently shuffling as the white folks pattered by. The loft was filled with hay and that's where the children played, swinging on ropes, digging tunnels and jumping from bales. The women had provisioned the tables on a potluck arrangement with casseroles of every concoction: roasts of chicken, duck, pork, venison, lamb and beef, bowls of gravy, and plates of steaming vegetables, peas, carrots, potatoes; then baked salmon, steamed clams, butter, bread, buns, pickles, baked apples, cakes, pies, milk and a punch bucket. The men stood at the punch bucket, smoking, drinking, and discussing what they always discussed - a whole lot more people than Frank had anticipated. Just for show Frank opened a bottle of whiskey and poured it in the punch. He displayed the other bottles on the table.

"Compliments of the sap people," announced Frank.

He hadn't eaten a proper meal in a lifetime and ate like a ravenous hog until he could only sit and stare. Georgie made a point of introducing him to the men. Each in turn approached cautiously and then they talked small about the weather, logging, fishing, you settling in okay, ever need a hand just walk over, and so on. They would talk-the-talk of sap later.

Musicians struck up, an accordion player and two fiddlers. Still too early in the dawn of time for a piano. The crowd danced and drank and laughed. Frank sat on a chair in a corner and refused all invitations. "Never learned," he insisted. He kept his hat on and fluffed up his collar. The children cautiously grouped up near him and only one was brave enough to ask the questions that might be on their minds. Wesley Jenzen's son, Perry, ventured, "Can I see that there knife of yours?"

Frank smiled crookedly at the boy. He stroked the tassel of hairs crowning the sheath. "Boy, no one sees this knife, especially those that wished they hadn't." That was that. Young Perry ran back to his friends to report on the conversation.

In this friendly sea of confusion and delight, Frank followed the trail of memory - a thing he tried not to do even though he was good at it – one hot day in an Arizona town, he had discovered that he was still a famous man. Not that he doubted. The five cent yellow novels, now costing a dime, told the most awful truths - wild hunches that he might still be alive. They speculated the one bullet grazed through his jaw and the other ripped off an ear. They got the ear wrong, it was the left one - they got the whole damned story wrong. Nearly. And they forgot how the patchball lodged above his heart tasted leadlike when the weather dampened. One savvy writer mentioned he would never be taken except on his own terms. Where, when and how I please, he thought. Exactly, said his voice. Frank wished he had written the stories himself, so he might punctuate more fully the dazzling flare-ups of his youth. There was a certain joy wrung from incarnating himself as a mystery. Watching the story grow. A hoax here and wool over the eyes there.

Near midnight, the men approached with a nonchalance that fooled no one but themselves. They would all be down to "get them deposit bottles," said Crawford Ballentyne, Georgie's brother-in-law.

"It would be a good thing for the island," said Wesley Jenzen, Georgie's brother. "And the children and women might get in on it too. Young Perry keeps pestering me to get them funny bottles you got."

| 21 |

"Be a nice pastime when the fishing's off," said Colin Jenzen, Georgie and Wesley's father.

One of the shy Wilkes joked, "Gosh, we might have to forego logging."

By now, Frank was a little drunk and his mind moved to his lower desires.

He said quietly to Georgie, "I ain't interested in yer wife, it's them sheep I want."

Georgie laughed and laughed. "I ain't got no wife." They both laughed.

Frank excused himself. "Nature calls."

On the way out of the barn, he passed off a whiskey bottle to a young Klahoose buck hoping it might encourage a knife fight and slashed bellies. He soon found the flock of sheep. The drought for his passion had been too long, but he could not stiffen himself no matter which ewe he mounted. Too much dinner, too much punch. Or Georgie had done something awful to the sheep. He slunk from the party and rowed home listening half the way as the natural and happy sounds sadly tumbled over the still waters, his oars protesting, squeaking and clunking in their leather collars. Once he stopped for a minor sabbatical and shipped his oars. In the white moonlight he watched drops of seawater slowly roll along his paddle blade, fall like beads of steamy liquid mercury into the sea's quiet embrace creating a series of ever-expanding, pewter rings. After the last drop had fallen and after the last ring had melted into the immensity of time, he resumed the journey to his home in Long Legs Bay.

DAYS AND NIGHTS PASSED like they always do. Eventually the men showed one by one with their dollars and departed with their empties. Some were skeptical but they still came. Frank reinforced the notion that full payment could only be made once the entire shipment was filled and loaded on the freighter. He flashed a wad of hundreds to each of his new employees to reaffirm the concreteness in their arrangement. The swindle money piled high and he now hid it separate from his American loot – another hole in another corner of the shed under another rock. He had to strain mightily to move that rock and make room for the bucket of colourful Canadian dollars. He thought, Me and the wolf is pushers and diggers now. Increasingly he wished the people would leave him alone. The interruptions were too frequent. He couldn't get his work done and Long Legs would skitter and be gone for days until he knew the coast was clear. Business and responsibilities and bookkeeping were not the lark he thought they would be. He realized that soon more bottles would have to be ordered up on the freighter.

Some nights he melted little chunks of sap and applied it to his ear, neck and jaw. Sticky like Mary said and lacking the potency of a lasting cure.

The greatest annoyance of all was the fool and his pipe who kept arriving with full bottles and when Georgie had run out of his own money and exhausted all the sucker loans he could wheedle, then he begged and begged for deposit advances from Frank.

"When you going to send the shipment?" he said.

"Don't forget I got first dibs."

"Can't you loosen up the cash...sheepin' ain't that full of profit you know."

Whatever friendship had sparked on that one party night went out for good. The thought thickened as a frightening possibility that he would have to leave Long Legs Bay before they all caught onto the swindle.

IT WAS LATE SEPTEMBER when the leaves come falling down. Desolation Sound looked like it was called. Sunrises refused to energize. He slept longer as days grew shorter. The mornings were fog filled – giant cotton balls careening each off the other, lost and meandering over the highways of Lewis Channel, bouncing from bluff to bluff, shrouding miniature islands, battalions of sea smoke awaiting ascension skyward. Afternoons lived without purpose. The maples turned colour – red, yellow, orange. Clutters of alder leaves washed in zigzag windrows along the shoreline. The firs, cedars and hemlocks looked greener. Arbutus peeled their ochre skins; splitting, curling and falling in slivers and scrolls. Another forsaken opportunity for Nature to record her shrewdness - the papyrus unwritten. The snow line crept down the coastal mountains. He noticed the clams had fattened and turned creamy, tasted sweeter. Same with the oysters, but the change made no difference to the dehydration in his passion. Eagles went to the rivers for the salmon feast. And ducks flocked up in great gibbering colonies over the waters of Lewis Channel. Geese honked overhead. For America, he thought. Berries were finished, picked by the birds, stripped by the bears, over ripe and insect filled, desiccated, moldy, fertilizing the soil from which they came. Buck deer did not spook so easily, as their minds had migrated to their nethers. He saw fragments of their velvet rubbings at the base of scrub trees and scuffed up places on moss bluffs where they had jousted as practice for the fecund odor of the upcoming rut. Crisp nights. All in all, truth hidden in the sad unbearable beauty.

Long Legs howled longer, louder, and lonelier through the nights. Howls to the ends of the universe, shot straight passed the moon, beyond the planets and stars, to the gathering place for all life's howls, shattering the infinite, crushing the infinite, demeaning the infinite. Frank stayed up with the wolf, smoking, drinking and answering as best he could with his newly learned language of wails and yelps and yowls. Shrieks and screams whenever the whiskey overwhelmed. Only the desolation in the sea could hear their nightly songs and translate their hymns of sorrow as man and beast bonded in the notes of each other's declarations of remorse. Now and forever - nothing more or less than howling.

During the daylight times, Frank studied his charts on the wall. The vast godforsaken spaces on the mainland need discovery, he thought. Why in hell are them names so damned Mexican? his voice wondered. Marina, Malaspina, Redonda, Raza, Quadra, Senora, Hernando, Texada, Cortes and then that Frenchie one, Rendezvous. The old marksman threw his scalp blade and now he opened a big slice in Desolation Sound.

LATE ONE MORNING A rowboat rounded the point into Long Legs Bay. That pipe is worse than a coal tug, thought Frank. It sure is, said his voice.

The shepherd was desperate. A wolf had killed four of his sheep. He shot the wolf right off, but now he had to have his pay.

Frank, understanding completely the stealth required when an idyllic act of retribution presented itself, said, "Was it black and old?"

The fool said, "Yeah."

"Did it have a white sock and a white patch on the side of his neck?"

"Yeah."

"I seen it around here," Frank said.

Georgie dragged on his pipe and soon a dark cloud formed over them. He said, "What about my pay?"

"You got full ones done up?"

"Yeah."

"Go get 'em and you'll get your money."

"Full up?" said the fool.

"Yeah, full up. We'll tote the whole shebang."

"Be back real quick." The happy man rowed home.

He rows back to front, said his voice.

I noticed that.

TWO DAYS LATER A native boy clamming on the beach found the rowboat wedged between two boulders on the shore beyond Squirrel Cove village toward Turning Point. Georgie Jenzen lay in the bottom face down in an expansive pool of dried blood. Clutched in one hand was the stem of his pipe and the shattered bowl lay piecemeal in the sanguine mess. A bullet had lumbered through his jaw so there wasn't much left of the lower face. He had not died quickly however, and therefore had time to write his concluding remarks on the only parchment available. The native boy could not read, but when Wesley Jenzen arrived, he deciphered the letters scrawled into the darkened layer of blood, which by now the shore crabs had distorted with their persistent nibblings. Wesley had brought along his five year old son, Perry, who immediately commented, "Uncle Georgie needs sap." Realizing the mistake - bringing the young child - he got the native boy to preoccupy his son with excavations for the giant horse clams in a nearby intertidal pool. It took some while for Wesley to realize a "p" was missing in the first word scrawled so carefully, and a "w" in the second word. The crabs had trotted their sidewise crawl marks over the other letters too, but they proved easily decodable. Wesley had anticipated the obvious, a statement somewhat similar, though considerably more brief than a last will and testament. Quite possibly this was his brother's confession to a shameful deed kept secret from all the family, or, even more likely, in those final moments he realized who his killer was. However, the tiny three-word sentence didn't permit any of those possibilities. Maybe Georgie reasoned poorly while he scribed? When other Jenzens and other islanders arrived, they agreed with Wesley's resolution to the puzzle.

Their fool kin had written, "Pipe blew up."

tongues of fire lick clean impure bodies

1923-1928

PERRY JENZEN OFTEN HAS dreams where he sees his Uncle Georgie lying dead in the bottom of the rowboat. For no apparent reason, they started when he was nine years old, about four years after the murder. Up until that point, he hadn't thought much about the discovery on the beach despite the fact that his parents, relatives and their friends often discussed the event; speculated on how it happened, why it happened, or where the outlaw might be now. These dreams – more like tattooed memories under the thin skin of his consciousness - did not disturb him as nothing ever happened in these nightly visions. The boy had never been to a picture show though he had a mechanical understanding, as his father had once explained how photographs moved on reels of film. To Perry's way of imagining, the scene was nothing more than a single picture on a stuck reel. He appreciated that the dream was frequent enough to allow the opportunity to study the details of his uncle's death, but also regretted that he could not back up the reel - frame by frame - to see the whole incident materialize. If only there could be animation.

Gradually, this static dream evolved in peculiar ways. For instance, on a given night, he could see close-up the bug-eyed, sidewise crabs crawling on the dried blood, but nothing else; and then another night, he saw only the shattered pipe bowl,

| 29 |

but not the hand holding the broken pipe stem. There were increasingly expansive variations too, but still nothing ever moved. He stared at his uncle's entire forlorn body, the bag of sap bottles with a few scattered on the floorboards, a broken paddle, the rowboat punctured in the stern from pounding on the rocks, his father unscrambling the sentence scribed into the dried blood, and the native boy looking proud because he had made the discovery. Then Perry saw macro-vistas too. The lonely expanse of rocky beach, the calm blue waters of Lewis Channel, the awesome gateway to Desolation Sound and the jagged snowy mountains along the coastline – every piece to a jigsaw puzzle contained in one celluloid frame. These nightly experiences exhibited themselves as if his dream used a magnifying glass and led him around to study the intricacies of the crime scene, presumably those the dream thought most important. Or, maybe the dream used a telescope; the closeness, the remoteness, simply depended on which end the dream encouraged him to look through.

Now the boy welcomed bedtime. His parents no longer had to fight with him to put on his pajamas or to turn off his kerosene lantern. Perry came to believe that some strange but friendly entity directed his dream and that the entity had in mind the unveiling of a secret to which he would be the sole witness and recipient.

One morning he mentioned to his mother that he had strange dreams every night. By strange, he meant the motionless aspect, not the disturbing content. When Madeline Jenzen heard Perry describe the things he saw, she jumped up from the breakfast table and confronted her husband who was on the front porch relieving his bladder.

She said, "Wesley, you were a very stupid man dragging Perry along the day Georgie was found dead on the beach. Your son has nightmares every night about your brother all shot up." Madeline had criticized Wesley before for taking their son along on the search; finally she had a tangible reason for challenging his authority. Wesley said, "Well, that's food for thought."

Perry's father buttoned up and went off to tar the hull of his fishboat, annoyed that his stream had been interrupted and doubly annoyed that Madeline would not let the matter rest.

The boy thought his mother made too much of the incident and decided not to mention his dream life ever again. They were dreams, not nightmares – more like photographs or drawings. If he had been asked to identify the most exciting moment in his life, he would have immediately, without the slightest reservation, said that day on the beach.

He sketched elements of the tragic scene and made moderate efforts to conceal these drawings, but they, or at least some of them, were found in his desk by his teacher, Miss Willow – the boys in the class called her Weeping Willow since one of her eyes always teared, as though half of her lived in a state of constant remorse. She took the artwork to Perry's parents. After a few sips of complimentary tea, she put the pencil drawings on the kitchen table for Wesley and Madeline to inspect. When they had sufficient time to study all six candidates, she said, "They're upsetting aren't they."

Madeline said, "He has been having nightmares."

Wesley said, "I never saw such good drawings. He's got Georgie's rowboat to a tee and look at the detail in that little crab."

Miss Willow, with both eyes tearing this time, commented, "I agree Wesley, that the drawings are exceptional, but he is consumed with reproducing still lifes of that horrible scene."

Perhaps sensing that an argument might break out, Madeline quickly replied, "We both appreciate you bringing this to our attention." She pushed her teacup and saucer toward the centre of the table signaling the visit was over.

Not quite finished, Miss Willow said, "There is something else. Things are out of step in the class because Perry lets the other children see his drawings. Now all thirteen of my pupils have dreams about Georgie's murder. I have had many complaints from the parents. They have not approached you out of respect."

Wesley intervened at this point, "We will thrash the boy and that will stop it."

WELL IT DIDN'T STOP it. The thrashing ignited a far greater hysteria. Soon the school children emulated Perry, unleashing their own creations, which, for a time, they kept secret from the adults, often meeting in the forest after school to look at each other's handiwork. Excepting Perry, this new world Renaissance of creativity could be judged primitive at best. The boys produced nothing better than stick men, usually the Outlaw – that's what they called Frank Waterman – waiting patiently atop Ambush Bluff on a lovely sunny day for the fool to fill the crosshairs of his Winchester rifle, or Georgie rowing his boat as fast as he could, back to front, of course. Bobby Archer showed up one afternoon with a drawing of the Outlaw raising his wicked knife over the head of poor Georgie and Georgie defending himself by covering his eyes thereby leaving his scalp easy pickings. And Jimmy-James Ballentyne, otherwise known as JJ, had the Outlaw making his getaway with a boatload of cash, the pile so high it looked like it might sink his rowboat. And on went the inventions of immature minds. What else was there to do on Cortes Island except explore variations on the general theme by taking wrong turns from the actual event - confusing the issue, yet fertilizing the world of their dreams?

A MOST UNLIKELY DRAWING came from the quiet and shy Wilkes boy, Darwin, who actually made a reasonable representation of the Outlaw exploding his brains with a six-shooter. JJ challenged Darwin on his picture, by saying, "Seen his body laying around anywhere?" That got some nervous laughs. And JJ's sister, Martha said, "Why don't you look under your bed, Dar?" The shy boy sulked away not to return to the secret forest gatherings.

Adam Wilkes, Dar's older brother, witnessed this mean teasing of his younger brother so he retaliated with a charming journalistic piece basically supporting Darwin's pictorial thesis, though it is not certain Adam actually believed what he wrote. Being an aspiring writer with a lush and luminous mind, his head was most likely filled with fancy beyond the normal. Adam read his little story to his curious classmates at the secret meeting place in the forest on a rainy day while the wind rattled the branches of every tree. They listened attentively because he was older, and as well, acknowledged the best writer in the school outshining the preeminent girls. In the last paragraph of his reading, Adam argued thus: "Frank Waterman, an American renegade from the Wild Wild West, was so overwhelmed by guilt from committing the terrible misdeed that he burned his shack, threw his money in the ocean, sunk his rowboat, smashed the sap bottles, and then stood on the cliffs of Mary Point and blew his brains out with his trusty six-gun. He fell into the ocean and sunk quickly to the bottom of the sea, because he had filled his pockets with gold nuggets. Then the crabs ate him up. It is the opinion of this writer that the police authorities should come to Cortes Island and recover the gun or his skeleton and thereby prove that the Outlaw was not only a heinous murderer, but a cowardly committer of suicide too."

Case closed.

Leery of a black and white world, the lucky girls had crayons so they could explore the utility of colour. A lot of red got smeared and smudged; Georgie drowning in blood, Georgie's head floating in a sea of blood, Georgie screaming from a red tongued mouth and the Outlaw's shed consumed in brilliant red and orange flames. For all one knew the girls believed that truth itself might get murdered without that vivid injection of pigment. There were abstract pieces too, where objects didn't look like anything in particular. Sorry attempts to express unadulterated and unambiguous emotion like the lingering fear that the Outlaw might return someday. Marlene Archer, Perry's official sweetheart, and her sister, Maddie, who also carried a crush even more passionate than her sister's, both confessed they had seen the Outlaw hovering over their bed, which they shared. Apparently the Archer girls saw a bullet hole in Frank's head and confessed that he howled like a wolf. Those multiple and identical disclosures touched off a new round of nightmares for the adults to pacify as Frank's imagined ghost made his midnight rounds pulling out all stops to create panic and alarm.

Perry kept the hysteria at a distance. His dream persisted though his interests changed. He increased the volume of his work, but veered off in directions outside the reference points in the dream. He drew a beautiful still life series of the lilac stopper bottles, some of them full of sap, others half empty and others half full – take your pick. He produced a series of scalping blade drawings. They varied considerably except that each one showed the decorative tassel of human hair. He lamented that the Outlaw had not allowed him to see the knife when he had so bravely asked on the evening of the community dance those years ago. He drew the 44 Winchester with its lever open and a casing ejecting into the eye of the viewer. His parents did not see any of this and the rest of his schoolmates only got to see the odd drawing, none of it charged with the emotion that characterized their own undertakings.

To negate the misgivings of his parents, and more importantly, to emulate the wiles of the Outlaw, who he had progressively elevated in his mind to a superior being, the boy launched a diversionary tactic and cleverly concentrated his artistic aptitude on the boat traffic in Lewis Channel. When a new vessel sailed or motored by, he quickly sketched it, managing to get the details highlighted with an accuracy that might have impressed any art teacher; tall exhaust stacks puking coils of acridity, sails flaccid in a calmed sea, spindrift splashing from a sturdy hull when the Northwest screamed down the channel, and vessel bows burying themselves as they snorted into a Southeast, the waves shrouding the wheelhouse. A novel feature included the drafting of an exploded view of one outstanding feature of every vessel and usually these were inserted in a corner or down an edge of the drawing; an anchor with its chain, each link perfectly intersecting the other, a winch and the wire cable passing through double and triple pulleys, or the sweep of a particularly attractive bow. These drawings he left around the house so that his parents would see them. Wesley was very impressed with his son's talent and frequently complimented him on his uncanny ability to reproduce faultless representations. His father melted one day when he saw a wonderful drawing of his own fishboat - the only anomaly - Perry had renamed the vessel from "*Madeline II*" to "*Pride.*" Madeline was not so happy about the name change as it triggered in her mind the biblical reference, Proverb 16-18, "Pride goes before destruction, a haughty spirit before a fall." Nevertheless, she began to believe that her son had moved on from his fixation.

The general hysteria subsided as things like that usually do. No more did parents need to administer stiff shots of paregoric when their children woke in cold sweats in the middle of the night. Miss Willow encouraged her students to renew their focus on the three R's. She steered clear of art class and received parental support for that decision. If they practiced reading, she would say things like, "If you can't read, how are you going to know what your fish slips say?" And if the subject were arithmetic, she would stress, "If you can't add and subtract, and divide and multiply, how will you know if the log scaler cheated you out of a few cubic feet of timber?" Those practical comments, mainly directed at the boys, helped a bit.

Perry continued to enjoy his dream. It telescoped in and telescoped out. Nothing new, but occasionally puffs of inspiration exploded in his brain. He developed a routine. Each night, before going to sleep, he would think about the Outlaw, wonder what actually happened to him, who was he really, why did he have so much money, how could he have fooled the whole island – even the adults, even his father? To these questions he came up with few answers until much later.

WHEN HE WAS FOURTEEN – a premature adult already with an overnight shadow and hands like meat cleavers - if he wasn't at school, if he wasn't having intensive bouts of smooching with Marlene or Maddie Archer, if he wasn't drawing and drafting, if he wasn't fishing with his dad, if he wasn't building his first boat, *Pride*, he would be sorting the mysteries at Long Legs Bay.

Salal, weed alder and a pretty stand of purple foxgloves now grew where the Outlaw's shed had been. Perry pulled on a young alder sapling, dislodging it from the burnt over ground. Embraced in the root ball was a sap bottle. I'll have the biggest collection on the island, he thought. He decided to clear the whole area where the shed had been. He walked down to the shore and retrieved a grub hoe from his rowboat. He pulled the juvenile alders out by hand and then removed the foxgloves with the tool. The tangle of salal had a more firm footing than the alders or foxgloves so he cut the stems off at ground level with his jackknife. If he encountered charred wood, he threw it aside. A roof timber had not burned completely so he wrestled it off the excavation site by flipping it end for end. He noticed nails spaced every foot or so and these were only partly pounded in. The Outlaw must have used the beam for hanging stuff, Perry thought. The weight of the beam had produced a concave impression in the ground so he got down on his knees to work along the depression. He found a fry pan and a coffee pot. By the end of the day, though he had only excavated a third of the area, he had assembled a nice collection of cooking artifacts and a few tools including a chisel blade and a hammer head - rusted and warped - the hardwood handles burned to char. These items were not of much practicality, but Perry decided to keep them nevertheless. He loaded the boat and headed home, but stopped at Mary Point reef and jigged a few lingcod along the edge of the kelp bed to make it look more believable that he had been fishing. He hid his collection of artifacts in a defunct smokehouse when he got back to Seaford.

That night he had a hard time falling asleep because he couldn't make sense of the fact that the Outlaw left without taking his essentials. Why would he do that? Perry had decided a long time ago that Frank Waterman's every move would have been calculating and deliberate. In fact, he had tried to emulate that essential quality into his own way of being in the world. He even invented a little mantra, *think before you act*, and always repeated the phrase before initiating any action - not necessarily a novel belief, but a principle that might give him advantage over the next man. Perry couldn't imagine the Outlaw without a plan and did not believe the guilt laden and silly suicidal theories of the Wilkes brothers.

At daybreak, he told his father that he wanted to make a quick trip to Mary Point. He said, "I saw lots of feed surface yesterday and a couple of smilies jumped."

HIS DAD SAID, "I don't want you down there all day. We need to get *Madeline II* in shape for the season."

As he approached Long Legs Bay, the sun emerged from the clouds and a glint caught his eye – a single flash, but enough to stir Perry's interest. It came from Ambush Bluff, the location everyone assumed the Outlaw used to commit his treachery. He climbed the mossy bluff and searched, not really knowing what he might find. Maybe, a shell casing? he thought.

The shadow of a vulture passed over the ground and Perry glanced up to see it. His eye stopped before it got to the bird. He saw the scalping blade impaled high in the trunk of a pine tree. The only way for the knife to be there would be if the Outlaw threw it, Perry thought. No wonder the police didn't find it during the investigation. They wouldn't have looked up.

Perry had to shimmy the branchless lower trunk of the pine tree. Though lodged there for nine years, the natural elements had not harmed the knife. The blade was tarnished and the handle had sprouted green lichen on the shady side – easily cleaned. He saw notches filed across the top of the blade - eleven. And the blade was still sharp, but the human hair decoration gone. He resolved to produce new drawings of the knife now that he had the real thing. He thought, This will be my gutting knife for the rest of my life.

Now Perry had lots to think about. He discarded the idea of further excavating for the time being. He hid the knife under a floorboard of his rowboat and went back to Seaford to help his father paint *Madeline II*. That activity gave him time to wrestle with his next move. Should he tell his father what he had found? *No,* came back the answer. He would complete his investigation before revealing anything to anyone. Again he had a terrible time falling asleep that night. Why would the Outlaw throw away his most valued possession? Once he fell asleep, an unexpected dream took shape and in the morning he remembered only a fragment. The Outlaw came to him, walking over a road carved into the sea. When Frank got close, he said, "Perry, I wanted you to have the knife."

He played truant from school on a Monday and made his way overland to Long Legs Bay. He took the grub hoe and a shovel. In one corner of the cleared plot, he encountered a large rock that lay just below the surface. He excavated around the rock and eventually managed to roll it out of the hole. Underneath he found a bucket full to the brim with Dominion of Canada dollars. Perry presumed these were the dollars embezzled from his father and all the Cortes families. He felt tempted to rush home and show his father. However, while kneeling there, rubbing the luxurious cash, he remembered witnessing a conversation between Uncle Georgie and his father. Georgie kept insisting, "He flashes an American wad with fifties and hundreds." After three hours of digging, he encountered another boulder. He pushed and pried, but this boulder was much too large for him to move. He dug a trench at one end of the rock and then excavated a tunnel underneath. Perry found three more buckets: Canadian dollars, American dollars, Confederate notes - assorted denominations - gold coins, silver coins, and gold nuggets too. He hid the loot under a rotted log on the way home.

That night the Outlaw made a second visitation. On waking, Perry remembered all the details this time. He found himself at the entrance to a cave blocked by a huge boulder. A wild-eyed, mangy, long-legged wolf stood there - perhaps a sentry. He yapped once, and then retreated into the darkness, squeezing between the rock and the cave wall.

Though the boulder was immense, Perry had no difficulty rolling it out of the way. He followed the wolf and was able to see easily without a light, the impossibility not questioned by the dreamer. The tunnel floor was slippery, covered in centuries of guano accumulations, upon which vast colonies of cockroaches fed. He crunched his way forward spooking great droves of bats hanging from their ceiling roosts. They panicked for the light of day, a river of winged mammalians echolocating his every step, a million near collisions as they streamed by and pulsed screeches of abuse at their intruder. He followed the wolf through the maze of tunnels encountering upside down forests of icicled stalactites and then vast spaces of skyscraping stalagmites and they paddled through warm shallow lakes until they came to a huge cavernous room – a gallery of wall paintings of ancient birds and animals and the hunters who pursued them. At the far corner he saw the wolf slip through a small opening in the wall and noticed a flickering light issuing from inside. Perry crawled through the hole into a brilliant room. The walls were covered in sparkling white crystals, which reminded him of the white chrysanthemum flowers that grew every summer under his bedroom window. In the middle of the room a fire burned though no coal or wood or dried dung fueled the blaze. The wolf sat in the fire and so did his companion, a naked man. The man washed his body with fire and the wolf licked the flames as they dripped off the man. When Perry approached, the wolf stopped licking and the man stopped bathing. Then the Outlaw looked at Perry and said, almost in a fatherly tone, "That was real smart to move them rocks and find my loot."

the first time she was a dream

1945

HIGHLINER OF THE FLEET, last off the grounds, well after a fine crease between sea and sky had melded into a seamless glow, *Pride II* pushed for Bull Harbour down to her scuppers with a full load of fish. Spring, Tyee, King, Quinault, *Oncorhynchus tschawystscha* - call them as you like. Sweet of smell, bright of eye, armored scales afire. Girthed beyond adequacy and far beyond desire. Each belly iced and dressed comfy in their frozen beds.

Conners entered the wheelhouse and stood at the helm beside his captain, Perry Jenzen. The deckhand had finished gutting and icing of the day's catch. Another good day.

"Gutting's done, icing's done."

"Did you pitch the old bait?" asked Perry.

"Everything's done."

"Where's the blade?"

Conners wedged the knife and sheath in the usual place - a safe, friction fit between the brass binnacle cover and window frame. Perry gave the sheath a nudge to make sure it was tight.

He remarked, "The notches are almost worn away."

He had made that comment often, so Conners did not reply. Every fish had to be gutted with his heirloom. Like most fishermen, Jenzen had his repertoire of superstitions: salt over the shoulder before meals - right then left, coffee stirred counter clockwise, no other jam but strawberry jam, lures and bait stored portside, and a twenty-five cent Confederate note carried in his right breast pocket therefore he always required shirts with right breast pockets, which were not necessarily common, so his wife, Marlene, had to report for duty with needle and thread as new shirts required alteration.

They studied the sea, now darker than the shore ahead. The wheelhouse grew dark too, lit only by the compass light.

"First out like always," said Perry.

They would make the usual turn around. Sell the catch, wash down, take on ice, fuel, bait and freshwater. Two hours - dawdling was not an option aboard *Pride II*.

What was left of the rosy western sky vanished at their stern. An easy wind wandered aloft and a scintilla moon climbed above the mountains of Vancouver Island guiding them over the shallow bar that separated the safe haven from the whole of the Pacific Ocean. *Pride II's* wake slapped the rocky shores and her throaty Cat diesel disrupted the quiet of the night. Jenzen flipped on the running lights. He hooded *Pride II's* compass as the glare from the light prevented a clear seeing of the darkness outside.

"What about the sounder?" asked Conners.

"Don't need it."

Pride II had the latest gear – Kaar radiophone, Signal Fathometer, Husun echo sounder – fruits of wartime technology. Perry knew Conners wanted to play with his gewgaws. No, he couldn't play.

When they throttled down inside the harbour, his deckhand said, "The whole fleet's tied tonight." The non-question meant, "Can I go ashore before closing?"

As they settled the account with the cash buyer, Jenzen raised one finger. With the smallest smirky smile, Conners disappeared ashore to the noisy beer parlor adjoining the hotel and general store. Perry stowed the remaining boxes of bait and finished the other chores. While he tightened the bung on the starboard water tank, a deckhand from another troller stopped to elicit vital intelligence.

"Staying the night, Perry?"

"Heading for Traverse." He knew the deckhand wouldn't believe him.

"You looked low when you came in."

"Got a few pieces," said the captain of understatement. The deckhand made for the pub and Perry appreciated that within minutes the fleet'd be debating where *Pride II* would fish tomorrow. His fish plan formulated en route to Bull Harbour had taken on a rock-hard commitment. He had reconfirmed the wisdom in his strategy to do the night run to Traverse Point when the weather channel had blared the promising forecast: barometer steady, high pressure, winds negligible, fog patchy, and tide turn at 0730. He had a feel for the rendezvous. The bite would be on, *Pride II* atop the fish, and more importantly, the fleet in port pissing the dregs of their beer.

CONNERS HADN'T RETURNED. MORE than a little disappointed, Perry headed for the pub. A pall of smoke hung over the packed barroom. Three waiters sweated with full trays of beer. Complimentary bowls of peanuts had been requisitioned as ashtrays and the thirsty customers pyramided their empty glasses awaiting refills. The noise level punished the ears. Perry didn't want to be there and didn't think it necessary or right that he should have to fetch Conners. He negotiated a gauntlet of greetings.

"Last one in, eh?"

"Jeff says you're high boat again."

"There's room at our table."

The place reeked like slime on old fish.

Stanley Gendro commanded the table Conners sat at. Over the din he had just begun the tale of his brother, Les, who had once motored into Siren Channel – officially known as Barkers Passage – to never return. Perry knew the story, all the Siren stories. His father Wesley and Stan had trolled side alongside for years, and Perry, on one occasion, at the tender age of fifteen, deck handed for the old fisherman. When Stan eyed him standing behind Conners, he raised his glass in greeting, "Young Conners here says another Jenzen's on the way - congratulations."

Conners jumped up.

"Thanks Stan, looks like the end of October," said Perry, a little off put, now that his personal life had become part of the public record.

Stan slid a full glass across the table bumping into Conners' empties. Feeling trapped by a mariner's protocol, Perry took Conners' chair. He hoped Stan would be brief.

Who hadn't heard the Siren stories? Siren, Barker, whatever you wanted to call the passage, was around the corner from Bull Harbour, a short cut to Traverse Point and points beyond. Due to actual mishaps, legend, myth, dubious parables and a generous dollop of allegory, as well as farcical fabrications from unimaginative minds, most mariners took the open and longer route skirting the Rocks of Sharon. Even Perry had avoided the so-called sinister passage, though only for real and practical reasons, such as extreme flood tides or screeching and funneling gales. The government chalked up past incidents to conflicting currents and a local penchant for freak weather conditions. They posted warnings in the Pilot's Log – "Current exceeds twelve knots at high flood and advances from both entrances." And the hydrographic chart had written "Dangerous Rapids" across the passage. Bit sections of the channel were still uncharted, hardly posing danger. Apparently, it all had to do with the Japanese current colliding with Vancouver Island - one stream heading northerly for the inside passage and the other slithering and slipping southerly along the shore.

Stanley told his story - head hung, eyes starring into his foamy beer and knobby arthritic hands resting on the table. He announced that today was an anniversary of sorts - exactly ten years since his brother had been taken by the seacow. Perry checked his watch. He'd give the old man a respectful five minutes. The others at the table - drunk, stiff-necked, young and gawky - leaned in closer to hear. Perry looked round the room. Pitiful, he thought, how the government entrusted louts like these to feed a wartime nation. Why not let them fight?

"Just so you understand it's not me stretching the truth, you can check with the local tribes, like the Nuu-chah-nulth, who know of the seacow from very personal experience. And if you do, you'll not just hear of recent misfortunes, but be told that these occurrences have happened off and on for centuries. Two hundred years ago, their legends recount the Russian fur traders and Spanish explorers having mishaps right at our doorstep, and very similar ones to the kind that got my brother." Stan scanned the table to see that he had an attentive audience.

"A part of her magic is that she materializes in many forms. Usually an appealing one near the entrance to the channel – I'd say femininely attractive, if you know what I mean. And once near the exit, that's if she lets you get that far, then the Siren shows her revolting side, still female, of course. The tribes believe that sacrifices can keep her confined to her territory and before each new moon, when her appetite is most voracious, they strap carcasses of fish, seals and even sections of blubbery whale meat to logs and set them adrift to catch an inflow tide. This, mind you, is all done under instruction from the elders, though you never hear much about it. I know it sounds a little extreme – the sacrifices – but without them, we might have had a much longer list of tragedies."

Stanley cradled his beer with both hands and took a swallow, then carefully wiped his lips with each thumb. Conners put his empty glass down and picked up a full one. Taking advantage of the pause, Perry placed a two-dollar bill on the table and said to his deckhand, "We're going." He made an apology to Stan – the customary, *have to catch a tide.* Conners shrugged his shoulders and quickly downed his beer as well as the one Perry had failed to touch. He followed his captain who was already charging into the cold night air.

THEY ENDED ON THE wrong finger of the government dock. Conners had run ahead, perhaps thinking a show of enthusiasm was called for.

Perry yelled, "Wrong," but the deckhand didn't hear him.

When he caught up, the delinquent was on his knees puking over the rail of the dock and would have fallen overboard if Perry hadn't grabbed his collar. They were broadside to *Pride II*, but separated by a twenty-meter rectangle of quiet sea. The rigging of the berthed vessels jingled quietly and the night sky glittered with stars. A new moon hung above *Pride II's* tall mast like the crowning ornament on a Christmas tree. With an assist, Conners got to his feet, but stood mesmerized by the compelling ocean waters. He suddenly broke into an uncontrolled giggle fit and then clicked his heels and saluted. "Cap'n Sir – the seacow's got the *nocta luca* fraternizin' with the stars."

Night-lights were nothing new for either of them. For a moment, they watched stars floating on the surface of the sea and they watched ghost trails of bioluminescence from feed-fish dart beneath. Interesting, even enjoyable, if you had the time.

"Let's get back to *Pride*," said Perry.

CONNERS SAT SLUMPED AT the galley table while Perry filled the kettle for coffee. He noticed a diesel smell and took the lid off and sniffed. Oily beads floated on the water and immediately he knew why.

"Judas! Judas! You bloody put fuel in the port water tank."

The deckhand abruptly came alert. "Only a bit. The mistake was only an instant…not even a cup I bet."

Jenzen decided to look for new crew first opportunity. Find a closer relative. And not a drinker.

Conners took the bulk of the workload to right his wrong, which required three hours of repeat draining, flushing and filling of the fouled tank before his captain was satisfied they could leave. Still, each time Perry tested the water, residual drops of diesel floated on the surface in his cup.

During the clean up process, Perry rejected the idea of sleep. All-nighters were nothing new and given the need for supervision, he could not succumb to the pleasures of the bunk. Besides, anger left him alert and speedy. In the past he had found that if venomous emotions hindered performance, the best antidote was a return to the calming effect of routine.

He occupied his time with assorted duties. He studied the tide tables and charts. He updated entries in the logbook: weather conditions, positions, bait used, weights, type and value of last catch - the accumulated details of a fisherman's life that would serve as a guide for future voyages and future Jenzen generations. Next he indulged in the greater pleasure of his architectural drawings for *Arrogant* – a deep-sea troller, considerably larger than *Pride II*, larger than any other troller on the coast, which he would rig for albacore and the bigger tuna. With the war on, these species fetched a higher price than the premium salmon. He reconsidered his measurements for placement of the small stateroom for himself and the three bunk locations in the bow. Perhaps the small changes could be made though work was already underway. Benson Shipyards had his deposit and the keel had been laid three weeks earlier. They promised the ship to be finished end of August in time for the tuna opening. Crew for *Arrogant* would be family only – cousins, maybe an uncle. Eventually, sons. They already had Bradley and their next child would be a boy as well; he was certain.

By now, the beer parlor had emptied and all fishermen gone to their boats and bunks. Conners sobered up and worked quietly. The only sounds in the night came from the hose filling the water tank and the overflow spluttering down the hull sides and splashing onto the sea. Occasionally Perry went on deck to check on his deckhand's progress. He paced on the dock along side *Pride II*, aware that his presence had a chilling effect on his deckhand.

The dock planking and railings had sprouted a thin crust of hoar frost, which crunched, fractured and sparkled with each of his restless footsteps. The vault of night sky had reached the zenith, unleashing an abundance of twinkling, rushing and stabbing starlight. When Perry looked from sky to sea, he noted that the conditions of reflection and biolumines-cence that earlier mesmerized Conners had now amplified. Constellations, shooting stars and comets swam, darted and swarmed below the depths while all manner of scaled, flippered and finned *pelagia* basked on the lens of the sea. This distor-tion of sky below and sea above, and the predictable inverse – fish where they should be and stars where they should be – sometimes cloaked in eerie magic light and sometimes not, was nothing more than a game nature played for reasons not yet understood by mere mortals. Not phased, nor in the least concerned that his senses could deceive, Perry understood he witnessed only a temporary misalignment of illusion and reality. A kind of beautiful hallucination. Prudence required that one let these moments pass – maybe even enjoy them as they traveled by – if you had time.

UNDERWAY AT 0400 HOURS. They motored slowly out of the bay and over the shallow bar leading to the Pacific Ocean. Perry knew they would have to thoroughly steam clean the pipes and water tank at season's end, but for now, live with the consequences of a partially contaminated water supply. He had decided to keep *Pride II* rather than sell it; lease it to a relative until Bradley was old enough to take the helm. Perry gave the Cat more throttle and flipped on the fathometer and sounder. A patchy morning fog had formed and *Pride II* ran in and out of the varying shades of darkness. Soon they felt a hint of ground swell and set course for the Rocks of Sharon. Occasionally groups of sleepy gulls flew up in front of *Pride II's* bow, not yet ready to seek out their daily feeding pastures. He sent Conners below to his bunk, the man now close to useless.

The radio acted up. Static on all channels. He turned it down.

An hour and a half out, the sun crested between two peaks on Vancouver Island and brightened the scattered islands of fog tumbling over the sea. Anchovies bubbled and boiled beside *Pride II*. He was tempted to throw out the gear right there, but smothered the thought. Stick with the plan. Think before you act. Perry turned up the radio and it had fixed itself. He listened to the new weather forecast: high-pressure, negligible winds confirmed. He spun the dial wondering if he might pick up other trollers, the silence comforting. Every five minutes or so, he repeated his sojourn for local chatter. A freighter broadcast her position but she must have been a few hundred miles out to sea. He wondered if she traveled with an escort or if the reported position were a cipher to outwit the Japanese. He heard music on Channel 10, likely an AM frequency polluting the transmission - no tune, no rhythm – an Eastern musical scale skipping across the Pacific and disturbing the Western ear. He turned to 06 and left it there. He put up his binoculars to see the mouth of Siren Channel to his starboard. Looking to the west, he saw a series of dark dots, the Rocks of Sharon. A pod of Orcas blew far to port.

As the black dorsals sliced the smooth sea, he thought of the summer he had deckhanded for Stan and remembered the fisherman's frequent retelling of the loss of his brother. The Gendro brothers had always fished together and were keen competitors. One day, near the entrance to Siren Channel, as they ran side-along-side, they argued about whether or not to take the shorter route to Traverse Point. Neither of them gave in to their locked positions, so Stan went for the Sharon's and Les for Siren. Stan watched through his binoculars as his brother's fishboat grew smaller and smaller motoring into the calm passage. Then his binoculars fogged and when he had wiped them clear, the boat had disappeared. All he saw was an empty peaceful channel. He refused to go after his brother due to his stubborn nature, so Stan motored the four hours around the Sharon's and at Traverse waited and waited for Les to appear. In the late afternoon he returned by way of the Sharon's to the southern entrance and saw the boat adrift. When he boarded, his brother's face was contorted and blue. He had tied himself to the wheel with a gannion line. At that moment of seeing his dead brother, Stan heard a seacow's beckoning wail come out of the sea, and later, when he had thought over the incident many times, he argued that she earlier clouded his binoculars. Even at the impressionable age of fifteen, Perry suspected the screeches of Siren an embellishment, the same for the foggy binoculars, and all the subsequent refinements that adhered to the story year after year. He accepted that a heart attack explained the death quite nicely - the official and medical explanation. As for the singing Siren and her escort of elephant seals, the harlot upon the beast, her head putrid and pulsing with maggots, the thousand, gnashing backslanted shark teeth, a serrated dorsal erupting from her slimy black back, rapier-like breasts sheathed in shiny metal, the lower extremities feathered or scaled or tentacled in a miscellany of Galapagos creations, and the suggestion that she provocatively and gleefully rubbed her loathsome nether regions on her bull killer Orca were fantasies of the purest bullshit.

Off port, he noticed the Orcas had sounded. Now he ran abeam to Siren Channel. She was a mile and half wide at the entrance and narrowed to a restricted opening at the far end. Perry corrected ninety degrees and lined the clear shot. They entered on a slack tide and would probably be an hour late for the bite at Traverse Point arriving 0830. The sun cleared Vancouver Island and all traces of fog had long disappeared. Gulls glided by *Pride II* and seals surfaced displaying their shiny heads and stiff whiskers. Feedfish sprinkled, spewed and spun as they tried to escape pursuit from diving ducks.

The sea changed colour from a rich algal green to a dull muddy brown, and as *Pride II* pressed further, the colour progressed to an awful orange and finally a dark blood red. First blotches and pools, then streaks, wider streaks, and soon small rivulets, until the entire surface of the sea had turned into a great red lake. Perry reflected that April was not the usual time of year for plankton blooms, and as well, he had never seen a red tide so intense and never seen a section of ocean change so rapidly. The water thickened reminding him of a swampy slough. It looked sticky and the thickness seemed to retard *Pride II's* forward progress. When he looked back through the open wheelhouse door, he saw that the stern wake billowed a fine sanguine spray. He saw minute whirlpools form on the surface of the sea and bloody gossamer whill-a-waws dance without trace of a generating wind. Ahead he noticed that the water was the same algal green as before, and though his ship had a difficult time getting to the transition point, when she did, her speed increased and everything returned to as normal as it ever gets.

It was no secret that the sea could mask and guise so things would magnify or shrink from what size they really were. So often in the fog a little island had become a whole continent. At times an object would catch his eye and he'd estimate the distance at least a nautical mile, but in the next instant go hard to port to miss a log. He had glimpsed seeming lifeless forms floating on the surface of the sea, and, as if given a signal, watch them roll over and turn into huge fluking whales. There were days when the sun became the moon and nights much brighter than day. These inconstancies in no way meant the gods tinkered with what mattered to Perry.

Again the radio blared static and he turned from 06 to other channels but every one crackled, scratched and cawed. He turned the volume down. The problem was intermittent, where even though you manage somehow to find a fix, you never really know how, or if the fix is lasting. He resolved to swap radios when he had a chance, as he had a spare just for such occasions. He called to Conners and got no response. He should have gone down to wake him – two more eyes at this point would definitely be comforting. At that moment, however, drift appeared on both sides of the ship: beach worn logs, uprooted trees, tangled islands of kelp and clotted masses of debris. All washed in a thick, briny, red liquid. Through this bad stretch he needed to be particularly alert, but *Pride II* eased the situation by steering herself. Not quite accepting this shift in authority, he wrestled with the wheel, but she somehow seemed stronger, and the course she traveled a product of her own calculation. To regain a portion of control, he tried to back off on the throttle as the drift was now whizzing by alarmingly fast. But there again, she wanted to gauge the speed of their voyage too. Grudgingly, but proud also, as he had designed and built her, and more importantly, since she handled herself beautifully under pressure, Jenzen conceded *Pride II* did a fine job.

On one of the floating islands of kelp he saw a head with a hair-like attachment of seaweed. Then he saw naked and emaciated bodies lying prostrate over logs, disheveled, with limbs bent and posturing in awkward positions. They projected in his mind either a forgotten or new version of obscenity. Suddenly, a putrid odor penetrated the wheelhouse. Once more he considered waking Conners, as he played with second doubts about his vessel's ability to manage this portion of their voyage. Perhaps together, they could wrestle control back; yet the circumstances, the need to be completely prepared for any contingency, his deckhand's condition and disappointing record of failings, and now these frequent near collisions with the drift, meant he couldn't leave his station. At any rate, it was too easy to seek help prematurely. He reassured himself that outside the wheelhouse, he witnessed nothing more than mere acrobatics – nature games.

He watched fissures open in the sea and whirlpools appear in a long line of zigzagging pairs. *Pride II* chose to motor between them, as though this section were merely an obstacle course cluttered with benign phantoms. His ship was being tested, and as her creator, he too shared in the contest; perhaps he took the brunt of responsibility. They cruised the highway of churning potholes, which grew larger, and swirled faster, and *Pride II* progressed at her confident pace. Perry looked down into swirling vortices, as though he stood on the rim of a volcano, as if he surveyed the whole of an unknown world inside. Now the whirlpools ended in a plethora of disconnected arms, legs, torsos and heads and he saw darkened antechambers hidden in the red watery walls and long flights of spiral staircases leading only to impasses and the impasses sealed with interwoven bones as in the vast catacombs under the ancient ruins of Paris. A pool abruptly counter-rotated and appendages flew into the sky. He imagined they hung there in a bid to emulate the patterns in the stars and he followed the performance, as would an ancient navigator searching the heavens for direction – the reading of an augury to an unknown port. Then another and another whirlpool repeated the performance of their brethren and eruptions of parts and pieces splashed into the red syrupy sea, but none landed on *Pride II*. Remarkably she bobbed and weaved and handled herself with natural grace. Imagine, he thought, the performance that *Arrogant* might give.

He went out on deck thinking he could trust his ship to the helm for a few minutes more. He needed, and wanted, to be closer to the excitement. Leaving the protection of the wheelhouse, exposing his flesh to the temptations of Siren was a step farther than any he had ever taken before. Unshielded, unprotected, looking forward to forty days and forty nights on a liquid desert, Perry welcomed this newest thrill of nature imitating chaos.

They threaded through the narrowest section of Siren Channel. A spray of pink spindrift impregnated the sea-air and sweetly moistened his lips. Derelict barges and freighter hulls appeared stranded on rocky shores, sometimes only remnants of ribbings and keels remained, looking more like skeletal debris from the ages of dinosaurs. He saw smashed Haida war canoes with sweeping prows bearing sketchy carvings of wacky sea and bird creatures and he saw a Russian fur trader beached, her back saddled, two masts piercing the pale blue sky and a canvas sail torn, tattered, fluttering without a wind. He saw Japanese mines bobbing like bloated porcupines and destroyers holed, half sunk, black smoke billowing from funnels and he saw jet fighter planes stranded in trees – now wingless, poor featherless raptors of the modern day - and he heard the screams of drowning sailors and burning pilots.

They were very close to shore. Perry watched a woman running on a fine white sandy beach. Ah, there she is. Siren waved as if she were in distress. He wondered, Could she have expected his arrival?

Effortlessly, she ran along the white strand keeping pace with *Pride II*. Long wavelets of golden hair fanned out over her shoulders and trailed behind. She wore a white muslin nightdress, transparent as evening dew. Beads of pearls hung about her neck and breasts. He was so close he could look into her clear liquid eyes and watch them glaze and see the tears form and fall; he could have touched her. And wanted to. In fact, the wispy wavelets of golden silky hair tickled under his nose and made him sneeze. He almost reached out to reel her in, but knew better.

Now she sang to him and knew his name. "Perry," she lilted, "Perry, my lover, don't leave me." Such a lovely lonely voice flowed from her sweet lips, but then a harsh static from the wheelhouse marred the moment. She was messing with his radio again. Enough of this. He went back inside, hoping to abandon this faux feminine cunning. He did not care that he risked an escalation in her fury. There was nothing really to concern one's self about, really.

He could not turn the radio down. Each attempt resulted in an increase of the harsh static. He wondered how Conners could sleep through the racket. And beneath the static he soon heard that same tune, that skipping radio wave which had decoupled from its eastern source - disturbing, non-rhythmic, high-pitched without lyric.

NOW PERRY REALIZED HE steered *Pride II* again and that he had never lost command of his vessel. He looked forward, port and starboard, and then took a hurried glance astern out the wheelhouse door. She was gone. He returned to the helm. He could see Traverse Point ahead. The radio went quiet and he began to relax. He thought he might as well check channels and see if any of the fleet had rousted themselves. All quiet, except on channel 10, he heard her lovely voice again, "Perry, this is a matter that has always puzzled me. Why are you so eager to die?"

WHEN CONNERS STUMBLED ON deck, Perry worked at the stern and already had the checkers brimming with smilies. The sea had developed a chop. It didn't take the deckhand long to see they were a mile off Traverse Point trolling toward the big sweep of Bellows Bay.

A bit chagrined, not knowing what to expect from his captain, he asked, "How was it off the Sharon's?"

"Never saw them."

"What do you mean?"

"Did the Siren."

"Yeah, bullshit."

"How do you think we got here in time for the bite?"

"Jesus!"

Perry quickly baited hooks with whole herring, eager as always to have all lines working the water.

Soon Conners asked, "Well, what was it like for Christ's sake?"

"The sounder found a few uncharted shoals."

"That's it?"

"Bit a kelp in the prop."

alone with an ocean's wildness, they moved the clock

1950

I RAN UP THE stairs.

"Bradley – sit down Bradley."

I came in for my own glass of water. I wanted to go right back out. Every one was out at Matt's across the street. We were playing go-go-stop, but I was thirsty, and next would be kick-the-can and we would do swing-through-the-trees as long as Matt wanted to do it. It was the best summer and the big kids even wanted to play with us every day. Why did my mum want me to sit down?

My Granny rinsed the glass, which took too much time.

"Sit down Bradley," said my mum again.

I grabbed the water and drank it fast. Granny took the glass out of my hand and pulled out the chair for me to sit. My mum's hands were full of papers and she was reading and humming. She always hums.

"Bradley, this is an application for boarding school."

I did not know what she talked about. She showed a picture with a big brick building and another building beside it, which was not so big, but made of wood. I thought about the three little pigs for just a bit. Some kids played in a field. Football. The grass was cut short. A white cloud floated over the wood building and flowers grew in front of it. It looked okay.

"Do you know what a boarding school is?"

"No." I could hear them yelling go-go-stop, go-go-stop through the open door. Matt did the yelling and if I didn't get back real quick he'd start kick-the-can.

"It's like any other school except you live there with other boys. You get to play lots of sports."

Granny took her glasses off and wiped her eyes with the handkerchief, which she always stuffed up her sleeve, but she stuffs it in her belt if the sleeves are too short. My mum looked at Granny, who was crying. Her tears hit her glasses. On the inside.

My mum pulled my chair closer. Her hair smelled smoky. "The name of the school is Vancouver College. Your grandmother and I think it would be best for you to go to boarding school because you need to have the influence of men in your life."

Granny wanted to say some words but I did first.

"Matt's almost a man."

Now Granny got in there. "He's only eleven."

"Can I play with Matt after school?" Kick-the-can was started. I could hear it banging on the street and Matt called out "Bradley" a bunch of times.

"Bradley," said my mum, "you won't be coming home everyday…only once in awhile…on weekends sometimes."

"Is Matt going?"

"This isn't a public school. This isn't like your grade one." My mum drank from the glass that looked like water. But wasn't.

My mum pulled up the papers and wrote on the lines with her fountain pen and Granny walked over and looked over her shoulder. My mum looked back at Granny and said, "I might need a blotter," so Granny got one from my father's desk that doesn't get used. Granny gave her a new blotter, but my mum didn't use it because she didn't make a mess. So it didn't get mussed up.

My mum said, "It's a Catholic school run by the Christian Brothers of Ireland."

Then Granny got another one in, "You're a Catholic and Matt isn't...so he can't go, can he Marlene?"

My mum said, "Your Granny's right, Brad. But some of the other boys from the *Arrogant* are going too. Their mothers think it's a good idea just like me."

My brother Jim cried in the bedroom. That's all he ever does because he got his collar bones broke when he was born and his head was squished. I still like him a lot. I could hear them yelling the Tarzan call so the swing-through-the-trees had started.

I WALKED UP THE path to the wood building. It wasn't a path. It was a sidewalk of cement and there were gardens of flowers on both the sides. Mum said, "Aren't the gladiolas beautiful?"

My blazer was blue and the pants were short and itchy and made of wool. There's a tie, too. The tie is made from my father's but it's small because Granny sewed it short. Mum carried the bags, which were suitcases, and I carried my new lunch kit, which I wanted badly. A big man wearing a black dress waited on the porch of the wood building.

"Hello Mrs. Jenzen, let me carry those for you," said the man.

"Thank you, Brother O'Malley. This is my son, Bradley."

"Nice to meet you, son."

The big man shook my hand only a little hard and mussed my hair, which my mum redid. Later. I saw a cross of Jesus in the room that we walked into, which was the hallway. We had to walk up many stairs to get to the big bedroom. The stairs creaked, but the man had soft shoes on his feet so they didn't squeak. He had black pants under his dress. A boy came down the stairs going the other way but I didn't get to meet him.

I saw rows and rows of beds.

"Bradley, you get the top bunk. Underneath will be Johnny Ballentyne, who you will meet downstairs. You'll get to meet Will Archer too, whose bed is down there just a little ways. There will be twenty-six boys just like you sleeping in this dormitory. You are the juniors...there are intermediates and seniors in the other dormitories."

The man knows who I know.

My bed was not near the window and I had to climb up a ladder to get to the top. I saw no blankets and no sheets. Just a mattress and a pillow. My mum had the sheets and blankets in the suitcase and she made the bed and put the slip on the pillow. The man showed her how.

The man said, "You'll be expected to make your bed every morning, and if there's an accident, your pajamas and sheets will have to go in the laundry."

My brother wets his bed every night and my mum says she can't take it any more. Granny does the wash in the ringer.

"Brother O'Malley, I'd like to stay and help Bradley unpack."

"It's not necessary, Mrs. Jenzen. We have a locker and two drawers for his things. We like to see the young men do the unpacking themselves. We think it helps them settle in."

We went down the stairs. They had Jesuses on all the places where the stairs turned the other way. The Brother O'Malley talked with my mum. "I did some rearranging so that Bradley and Johnny would be close to one another and Will won't be far away. I understand they are all cousins."

My mum said, "A cousin and a second cousin."

I said good-bye to my mum out on the porch. She gave me two dimes and a nickel. She said, "What does your Granny say?"

"A nickel for a pickle."

My mum said I might be able to buy a treat sometime and not to lose the money.

The man said good-bye to my mum, too. "Mrs. Jenzen, it was such a tragedy for you and the other families when the *Arrogant* went down. Though this is not much consolation, I'm sure all the fathers would approve of your mutual decisions to send your boys to Vancouver College."

She walked down the path. I squeezed my money in my pocket.

THE MAN TOOK MY hand and we went into the hall and down the long hall to the recreation room. His hand had lots of hairs all over the backs of the fingers. A Blessed Mary stood at the end of the hall. The room was dark because the blinds were pulled closed, but I saw a white light inside a wooden box in the corner of the room sitting on a big table and a high hum sound came out of it. The white light had an Indian plastered across it. A chief with feathers. I saw many chairs in the recreation room and many quiet boys sitting in the chairs. They watched the Indian, but it did not move.

"Brother Cavendish, this is the new young man I was telling you about."

"Hello Bradley. Welcome to boarding school, Bradley." The Brother O'Cavendish knew my name.

"Bradley, Brother Cavendish is your moderator and he's in charge of the juniors."

My eyes got better in the dark. The big brother with the soft shoes went out.

Then the Brother O'Cavendish said, "Its almost 4:30, son. Howdy-Doody will start right quick. You sit down with the rest of the boys. We watch the television until six o'clock and then we have our supper."

I could see no seats.

"Have you not watched the television before, son?"

"No."

"Bradley, you say, 'No, Brother.' We are called Brother, here. I'm Brother Cavendish and that was Brother O'Malley who brought you in. You never just say, 'No.' Do you understand now?"

"Yes, Brother O'Cavendish."

"Cavendish, not O'Cavendish."

"Yes, Brother Cavendish."

"Good fellow."

Now he was not so mad.

I found a chair. They watched Howdy-Doody and they watched Captain Marvel. I liked Captain Marvel best. The box could have its knob turned like the radio. I liked the station five because the big boys liked station five. Howdy-Doody had strings coming out of him that you could see and that's how the mouth moved, but it wasn't real.

THE CAFETERIA IS IN the brick building. They had to wait outside in a long line because the food wasn't ready. A crow landed on the grass beside the line of boys. A boy said, "Feed him something." One boy threw his Kleenex but the crow did not want it. Another boy pulled his button from his shirt but the crow did not want it. A boy beside me had a cookie in his pocket and he threw it, but the crow pushed it around and hopped one hop away.

Somebody said, "Give him something shiny."

Nobody had nothing shiny.

Another boy said, "If I had my cigarettes, I'd give him the silver paper…he'd take that for sure."

I took the nickel from my pocket and threw it at the crow. The nickel landed lots of feet away but the big black bird hopped right over there and picked up the shiny nickel and flew away.

The boy who said, "Give him something shiny," said, "I told you so."

The other boy beside me said, "Only dummies throw their money away."

The Kleenex got left on the grass and the thrower picked up the cookie, but I still had two dimes.

THEY SAY THE GRACE before they eat the food. Johnny showed me how to make the sign of a cross, but I already knew that one. They looked at another cross on a wall when they did it. They had to say, *Bless us oh Lord and these thy gifts which we are about to receive.* And then, *Amen.* Then they made the cross, the head, the heart, the left and the right. Then the hands together.

They had to stand in long lines to get the food. Johnny said the Indian Chief was a test pattern. A Chinese man spooned the mashed potatoes. No one did the meat. They just took it. Mrs. Muldoon did the carrots and peas and gravy, which was very brown. Johnny wanted to trade Sunday night dessert for Thursday night. It was Sunday. I did not know what Thursday night was and Johnny did not say. Sunday was peaches so we did not trade. Johnny said Tuesday morning was French toast and syrup and as much butter as you could ever want. I had not eaten French toast before. Just the regular. Johnny's eight. He said I am the youngest. Will was not here yet but he will be here when his mother gets the time to bring him down from the island. The Brother Cavendish stood over top of me and Johnny and then walked down the rows of tables of boys and then stood over top of us some more times. He had the soft shoes too. The knives and forks and spoons made noise when they were put down and the plates rattled much worse.

Johnny said his father sank with the *Arrogant* boat and I said so did mine. I said mine was the Captain. Johnny said his father wrote poems but his mum burned them. And Johnny said they could have got to shore but nobody found them yet. I figured that one too, so maybe I wouldn't have to stay.

They go to Benediction every day at night after the dinner. The kneelers are wood. I count nine of the Brothers, but a priest does the ceremony. The juniors sit in the front and then the intermediates and then the seniors when they don't kneel. Johnny says we pray when we go to bed and when we get up and we pray when we go to mass and we go to mass every day except Saturday. He does not know why not Saturday. Brother O'Malley is the chief of the brothers. Johnny says they pray before every class and that we should pray whenever we have nothing to do. Junior confession is Wednesday at 4:30 so you miss Howdy-Doody. Johnny says you always get Hail Marys for penance. And we must not be bad. Punishment is kneeling for a long time or putting the nose way up in the circle of chalk on the blackboard and standing on the tiptoes until your legs really hurt. Or the ruler on the hands or the strap on the bum. The juniors go to bed first every night.

There is free time after the Benediction but I must go with the Brother Cavendish to unpack my things so that I can settle in better. The drawers get filled but there's nothing for the locker. The locker must have a lock, which my mum forgot. The lunch kit won't be used and must get taken back. Now I get the free time in the recreation room, which I wanted badly, but the television must not go on. I sit and watch them play games of cards and watch them do arm wrestles and one of them hopes the crow will fly back because he has shiny paper. But I still got my dimes.

addled by silence, I fail to recall the who of you

1954 October

AT THE BEGINNING OF the school year his classmates elected him president of his grade five class. A month later one of his teachers suggested he join the Sodality and at the first meeting the students elected him president. Will Archer didn't know what the Sodality was or what he was supposed to do. His moderator, Brother Cavendish, gave him a pamphlet, which stated, "A confraternity or sodality is a voluntary association of the faithful, established and guided by competent ecclesiastical authority for the promotion of special works of Christian charity or piety." Brother Cavendish assured him it would only take awhile before he got the hang of things. A few days later Will found a note in his desk saying, "God is calling you." He didn't know who wrote the note, and though he told no one, wondered if the message came from an angel.

WILL MET WITH BROTHER Cavendish and the other presidents of the Sodality. They were to organize a work bee. The Catholic Charities Service had purchased an old mansion on the edge of Shaughnessy Heights; the home needed extensive repairs and cleanup. Once put into "ship-shape," as Brother Cavendish explained, the building would be operated by the Sisters of Saint Mary and used to house unwed mothers. "Unwed mothers" was a term that Will had never heard before.

Upon thinking about the term's meaning, however, he got himself entirely confused because he leaped to the conclusion that the Virgin Mary was probably an unwed mother, until he remembered Joseph. And then he further complicated his confusion when he realized for the first time that his grand parents were named Mary and Joseph, so maybe the angel was singling him out after all.

During weekdays, for a period of four weeks, carpenters, roofers and plumbers repaired the mansion, and on Saturdays the Sodality members cleaned the mess made by the workers. They also painted rooms and hallways, applied wall paper and stained and waxed the hardwood floors. Outside they raked leaves, cut grass and pruned back the overgrown shrubs. They pushed landscaping rocks into position for the ornamental garden. Each Saturday they built a large fire at the far end of the backyard to burn the waste scraps, sawdust and other debris. The moderators of the Sodality supervised the boys. Will's crew, though the youngest by far and fewest in number, accomplished the most – at least, that's what Will thought. They didn't fool around or wander from job to job or joke about unwed mothers.

On the final Saturday, at the end of the afternoon, Brother Cavendish took Will's crew to the White Spot, a drive-in restaurant, for Chicken-Pickins and milkshakes.

Brother Cavendish said, "Well boys, you ran circles around the older grades."

Johnny Ballentyne said, "I wished we could have kept score."

Brad Jenzen said, "Just think what we could have done if we were older." Brad and John were in the front seat beside Brother Cavendish. The brother reached his arm around Brad and gave him a hug. Will was squished in the back seat with three other boys. Two, long, narrow trays stretched from window to window across the car doors, front and back. All the boys ordered the same – deep-fried Chicken-Pickins and vanilla milkshakes in their aluminum canisters. Brother Cavendish had a bottle of Coke and Chicken-in-the-Straw – Straw meant, French fries, and was a bigger portion than the Pickins.

The boy beside Will said, "If we'd been older, it wouldn't even have been a contest." He slurped on the dregs of his milkshake. Johnny said, "The older kids just wanted to stand around and watch the fire." Everyone agreed. Brother Cavendish even laughed.

Will had looked forward to these work bees. For the first time since he'd been at boarding school the brothers had turned into real people. Instead of dressing in their white collars, black cassocks and a rosary draped from their belts, on Saturdays, they wore baseball caps, T-shirts, running shoes, work gloves and scruffy old pants. He noticed how they sweated and smelled of sweat and wiped their brows and had sweat stains under their armpits. When their hair got mussed, they didn't seem to care. He had the impression that Brother Cavendish didn't shave on those mornings. He even overheard the other moderators call Brother Cavendish, Keith. In the car, Will sat directly behind Brother Cavendish and saw a twig in his hair and a smudge mark on his neck – he assumed from the ashes in the fire. This new way of seeing a Brother came as a surprise, mainly he guessed, as he had never considered there was anything else to see.

Previously, among themselves, all the kids had called him "Cav," but now Will felt it would be slightly disrespectful to abbreviate the name as well as remove "Brother." Back at the boarding school, when they piled out of the car, Brother Cavendish shook everyone's hand and said that they all had much to be proud of. Will thought he was singled out more than the others because he got a hug and the others didn't.

WILL, BRAD AND JOHN browsed Brad's comics in the recreation room and the other boarders played card games and
board games. Some of the seniors played pool on the new pool
table – only the seniors were allowed. Brother Cavendish
checked on the boys every once in awhile, spending only a
few minutes pacing through the room and then returning to
his own room, which was in the hall between the recreation
room and Will's dormitory. On the pretext of going to the
lavatory, Will walked by Brother Cavendish's room sneaking
a quick peek, since the door was open. The moderator wrote at
his desk. Often he left the door open and frequently Will had
noticed other boys standing there asking him some question
or other. He knew too that at other times Brother Cavendish
summoned a boy for an infraction, and if the infraction were
really severe, the door was closed so that no one could hear or
see what went on inside. If the boy came out crying, usually
they never found out why. When Will returned from the lavatory, he saw that Brother Cavendish was still writing at the
desk. It seemed like a good opportunity to knock, but he chick-
ened out.

Will walked back into the recreation room. It was just about
bedtime. He sat down with Brad and Johnny.

He asked Brad, "What do you think of Brother Cavendish?"
Brad wouldn't answer or look up from his comic. He had been
cranky recently.

Johnny answered, "The seniors say 'Cav' eats chocolate
covered ants." Will made a horrible face. What a thought!

For a month he had tried to summon his courage to talk
privately with his moderator. He rehearsed questions and the
questions had to do with his responsibilities as class president
and Sodality president. Of course, the note in his desk took
on an importance too. The fact that he had been picked as
president – twice, plus the appearance of the message, seemed
like too many unusual coincidences. The "Call" from God got

him thinking there was something special he should do, but he didn't know if the special thing was to be done right now, or did it mean he was called for a mission in the future. His mind had ranged over a number of possibilities. Should he become a doctor who helped poor people, or a scientist who discovered an important cure, or should he just do more in the Sodality? In reality, he really wasn't sure what he would talk about with Brother Cavendish, and for that reason, was cautious if the opportunity presented itself.

THE DOOR STOOD OPEN. Brother Cavendish sat on his bed reading from his breviary. Will knocked. He still wasn't sure what he would say or why he was there.

"Come in son," said Brother Cavendish.

He motioned for Will to sit on the hard wooden chair at the desk. The walls of his room were painted the same pale green as the halls and classrooms. The floor was the same linoleum tile – beige. His bed frame was tubular metal, the mattress sagged and the bedspread tucked in tight just as all the boys had been taught. A large cross hung from the wall above the bed. A dark wooden closet stood near the foot of the bed and Will saw a door ajar leading to a small bathroom. The desk, chair, bed and closet left little space for other furniture. Will noticed a missal on the desk and religious books lined against the back wall, one the New Testament. Will had chosen the quiet Saturday afternoon for their talk as most of the boarders were home for the weekend or playing basketball in the gym. Will couldn't go all the way back to Cortes Island just because it was the weekend.

"Did you come for a visit, son?"

Will bit on his lip and rubbed his thumb into the palm of his other hand. "I was wondering about the Sodality."

"What were you wondering?"

"Is there something else I'm supposed to do because I'm president?"

"You're doing a fine job, son; you're doing everything that's expected."

Will was reassured. He said, "Well, thanks." He got up to leave.

"Don't be in such a hurry. We haven't really visited before." Brother Cavendish shut his door.

And then he said, "We'll have more privacy this way."

Will sat back in the chair and worked his thumb into his palm. He thought of the mysterious message in his desk. He said, "I got a note put in my desk."

"I put it there, son." That possibility had not occurred to Will; in fact, the more he thought about the note, and studied the handwriting, he had nearly convinced himself that the message was indeed written by an angel. He even figured out which one: St. Michael The Archangel. Will's birthday was September 29, the same date as his patron saint, St. Michael, who had fought Satan and the fallen angels all the way down into the everlasting fires of hell. Will, mistakenly, had imagined that God Himself gave the Archangel the task of delivering the message, "God is calling you."

Brother Cavendish reached over and pulled on the wooden chair so now they were closer. "God might want you as one of his foot soldiers."

"I thought He meant I was supposed to do something special."

"That's right. You might have a calling. He might want you to be a priest or a brother like me."

Brother Cavendish grasped both of Will's hands and held them tightly while he described the day he had been called. Will's moderator hadn't received a note but was told by a voice in a dream that he was to be a "fisher of men." Will thought of his father who had been a fisherman, but just a fisher of fish.

"There are many ways of being called, Will. Now, God has asked me to fish for you."

Will did not show his disappointment, but wished it had been the angel who sent the note. If St. Michael had sent the note then there was a possibility that he might appear to him in a dream or even for real. Will imagined the huge wings and the blinding light radiating from his chest and a sword bigger than the Excalibur. He could even ask the angel to check on his father in heaven and maybe they could send messages back and forth.

Brother Cavendish told Will that he had fought the voice in the dream until one day he gave himself up to it, and that's when he entered the seminary. Will learned that he, too, would resist until one day he could resist no longer. Brother Cavendish told him that God had arranged for the other boys – though they didn't know it – to elect him as class president and as president of the Sodality.

"God always wants the leaders," he said, gripping Will's hands more firmly than before.

That seemed to make sense since St. Michael was his very own saint and his angel was the leader of all the angels. When their visit was over, his moderator said that Will should come and visit any time he wanted and that together they had much important work to do. He hoped they'd become good friends. He kissed Will on the top of the head when he got up to leave. Will was grateful that the door was closed because he wouldn't have wanted any of the kids to get jealous when they saw that he was the chosen one.

In bed that night, Will wondered if all boarders - the lucky ones who had fathers - ever had neat talks like that.

desolate limbs, trees without leaves, winter now

1954 December

THE DISCOVERY OF THE logbook comes about shortly after the advent of rock 'n' roll. Brad is at home from boarding school for the Christmas holidays and in a bad mood. He and his mother, Marlene, and younger brother, Jim, live in a prosperous neighbourhood of Vancouver. Their home needs maintenance as the damp climate of the West Coast has taken its toll in the nine years since Perry's death. Green mold grows on the north side of the house. The roof leaks. Shakes are missing, others spongy or rotten. Moss grows in the spacings and the valleys between ridges are filled with years of autumnal debris. The paint on the trim of their home bubbles and peels. An exuberant, twisting wisteria threatens to collapse and rip open the veranda porch. The fence, if in good repair, would have made for good neighbours, however, in this case, the fence is in bad repair, and therefore, the corollary is true. Their yard, front and back, is hopelessly overgrown. Perry was not meticulous on home maintenance when he was alive. Christmas decorations? Not a chance.

The family doesn't have a television set so they don't have anything to look forward to in the evening. They have a radio but it's broken. They have a record player but it's broken and the records are broken. The subscription to the News Herald lapsed many years ago so the family has no idea what goes on in the world at large. The car rusts in the garage. This state of deterioration has not come about because they are poor. Perry left them a bundle.

Jim, the diminutive seven-year-old, is in tantrum mode this afternoon. Not unusual. And Marlene is in the well-practiced ignore-Jim mode. Romance novels and continuous cocktails are the key ingredients to her success. Bradley hides in his bedroom. Marlene hasn't thought about dinner yet. It will be macaroni and cheese, but cooked by Brad, who always does the cooking when he is home from boarding school, which has been frequently of late, as he alternates his truancies from school and family. The new invention - automated, mechanically sliced white bread slathered in strawberry jam - will grace the table for dessert.

Suddenly, the house goes quiet. Marlene puts down her romance novel, abandons her drink and runs into the living room. She discovers Jim with Perry's logbook.

"Where did you get that book?"

Marlene is shocked that Jim has it. She doesn't want him to have it. She had conveniently forgotten that the book, and others like it, existed.

"pa gib me."

In his cute little hands, the logbook looks as alien as her memories, though the book had been quite familiar at one time. Jim looks strange too, even comical, thumbing the pages from back to front, rotating the book in an effort to discover if there might be a right side up, struggling to make sense of a senseless thing with his senseless mind. Marlene doesn't laugh. This isn't a laughing matter.

Jim takes a giant step backwards and poses when he sees her; the publicity shot of the prophet with his tablets, one hand clutching the book into his chest, and the other pointing back at himself, "brad sae my wurd."

Marlene has him suspended from the floor, her two stout legs planted firmly into the carpet, and his legs flail in space, while her hands clutch the log, not Jim, the two of them connected through book and blood. His strong fingers clutch the ship's log until it compresses under the force of his grip.

Soon she relents. The determination, the clenched teeth, his squinting eyes and savage grip frighten her. An omnipotent lamb. And then, one more time, in the juxtaposed confrontation, Jim still unaware of triumph, shouts at his mother, "my tori book – brad sae my wurd."

Oh, Marlene thinks, When did Brad get a say?

She lets go. Jim crumples on the floor but does not let go the book. Marlene's eyes burn; her nose runs and welts break out on her wrists. A revisit of asthma and allergies – the damp, moldy thing is infectious. She stumbles over to the hallway and yells upstairs.

"Bradley, what have you done?"

And again, now wheezing and choking, "Bradley…get down here!"

BRADLEY HAD BEEN ENJOYING the peace and quiet before the bomb went off. After he had given Jim the book, he went upstairs to his room and sat on the bed. He stared out the window. As the sky was overcast, he couldn't see the mountains, a view he had grown to appreciate, but he could see Burrard Inlet with the sea chaotic and zigzagging. What fun watching the freighters straining at their moorings and the giant aircraft carrier was a sight to behold. A week earlier, he had overheard the kids at school say everyone would get to go on tours, so now he regretted that he had run away from school for the umpteenth time. Brad had never been on a ship before, but wished he had. Imagine a warship the size of three football fields. Imagine the Coral Sea fitting under the Lions

Gate Bridge and what a great name for a ship. How would it fit in Vancouver Harbour? One kid said they would take down all their antennas, otherwise they might knock the bridge over and another said that if the ship went through at low tide, they'd get stuck on the bottom right under the bridge. He loved thinking about things before they happened, or things that would never happen, and hated thinking about things that had happened.

A wayward branch from the wisteria slapped on his windowpane demanding his attention. Then he heard them start up again – his mother and his brother battling, always battling.

All he had done was come upstairs from the basement with the logbook that he found in his father's stuff. He doesn't know why he picked that particular thing. Eleven-year-olds don't even know what a logbook is. He had no curiosity about it, nor did he open it; he hardly remembers carrying it up from the basement. But he does remember that as soon as he put the book in Jim's hands, the crying stopped. The crying stopped.

"Bradley!" There she was again. He knew that if he didn't go downstairs, and right away, if she had to lumber up the stairs after him, then things could go very wrong very quickly.

"Take it away from him," she demanded.

"But Mum," Brad said so reasonably, "It stopped the crying."

"I don't want him to have it."

"It's just a book, Mum."

Marlene, beginning to panic, turned to Jim. Her asthma was getting the best of her. The boys saw the tears running down her face. She swiped at her nose with her handkerchief and then rubbed the welts on her wrists against her chin. The boys had seen her mad before - many times - but they had never seen her cry.

"I'm not crying. I'm allergic to the book."

To them, it looked like crying.

Believing that her backward son might achieve enlighten-
ment through repetition, she said, "It's not interesting Jim,
it's not interesting." She wiped her tears and repeated, "It's
not interesting."

But he clutched the book further into his chest and then,
like a minnow seeking refuge from a shark attack, he darted
into the corner of the living room and tunneled under his
father's desk. "pa gib me, my tori book, brad sae wurd myn."

Marlene staggered and her gasps for air came in spasmodic
intervals. Tightening in the chest. Swelling in the throat. Brad
took her by the elbow and helped his mother, who went will-
ingly into her bedroom. He helped her stretch out on the bed,
propped an extra pillow under her head and covered her with
the patchwork afghan quilt. He fetched her a glass of water
while Jim cowered under the desk, "my wurd, wurd myn."

Between sobs and furious itchings of the welts, she pleaded
with her eldest son, "Tell Jim it's only compass bearings and
weather conditions – tell him it's not interesting."

IT SEEMS IMPROBABLE THAT Marlene could be wrong concerning the logbook when she said to her youngest son, "It's
not interesting Jim, it's not interesting." At that moment, she
seemed so certain of herself. And one might also agree with her
conviction that faith in repetition would eventually rule the
day, even though, some years later, she would still be mouthing
the same tired sentence in her futile efforts to discourage him
from keeping the book. As we analyze her reasoning - slightly
influenced by the clear liquid - it goes thus: Jim is retarded and
long explanations tend to confuse him, so the briefest clarifica-
tion, like, "It's not interesting," is a superb approach. No one
has yet mentioned that Jim can't read - most seven-year-olds
can't read well - and, more importantly, no one has hinted that
he will ever read. These bits of information support Marlene's

strategy. However, taking the negative in this debate, one could speculate that she might have been more successful in getting Jim to abandon the book if she had simply ignored the situation and hoped that he would lose interest.

That Sunday afternoon when Marlene found Jim in the living room playing with the logbook, she didn't need to open the book and turn its pages or read the words to know what was written. She knew the contents were nothing more than daily records of sea conditions, estimates of catch, distances run, gear used and names of headlands or place. She knew, without taking the opportunity to open the book, precisely, because she had been to sea herself – only for one summer did she fish with Perry - and that was enough to know what kind of information went into a ship's log. What young child, especially if he were mentally challenged, would be interested in a book like that?

Marlene fished the second *Pride* for one summer – she never did get to go out on the *Arrogant* except for the christening launch around Vancouver Harbour. She remembers where the log was kept, in the rack beside the helm, at least, that is where it was supposed to be. She found the book in many locations on board the fishboat; on the galley table soaking up coffee spills, once in the engine room with a gob of grease smeared on the back cover, in Perry's bunk, stuffed in with the charts and drawings, or buried under a pile of racy novels. And she remembers how he was both sloppy and careless about making entries. He missed whole columns and days, and guessed at compass bearings. He boasted – not in so many words - that when it came to the sea, all pelagic knowledge swam in his head. "I can remember every fish I ever caught – where, how deep, the lure, everything."

His carelessness with the log, misplacing it, making entries a week after the fact, getting the pages stuck together with strawberry jam, caused Marlene to take on the responsibility of data entry that summer. Perry was happy that she did. She did it properly and thoroughly. After all, the real purpose was bureaucratic. The government needed to know where the fleet was, which species were being harvested, how many, and so on. As someone official might look at the book, she was intimidated, and her intimidation motivated her to do the job properly.

The logbook that Jim has isn't the one that Marlene maintained all those summers ago. No doubt, hers is down in the basement with the others (except for the last one). She knows that the book is no different than any other, so, case closed; the book isn't interesting.

THE WORD "LOG" IS derived from the Greek word *logos* meaning, "word". A logbook, thus, in so many words, equals many written words. In philosophy, *logos* – the word, often denotes an ultimate principle of truth or reason. In Christian theology, it refers to the Word of God as the origin and foundation of all things. The 6th century BC Greek philosopher Heraclitus was the first to use the term *logos* in a metaphysical sense. He asserted that the world is governed by a firelike *Logos*, a divine force that produces the order and pattern discernible in the flux of nature. He believed that this force is similar to human reason and that his own thought partook of the divine *Logos*. Marlene would have laughed if anyone had made a comparison between Heraclitus and Perry, especially if they inferred that he also "partook of the divine *Logos*." And when the mother and her retarded son fought like wild animals, when her fury and his sparked between the covers of Perry's logbook, she certainly wouldn't have acknowledged that a "firelike" divine force was present. Marlene knows that the logbook Jim thinks is his – a so-called gift from his father – did not come from the lofty places Heraclitus spoke of. She suspects, as she is well read, that there is power in the written word, but this does not imply that the words contained within Jim's logbook have power.

To prove her point, she could open the book at any page, and show us the words (and numbers). Due to allergies, asthmatic flare-ups and hurtful memories, she is unwilling to do this, so we must do it ourselves. These are excerpts from two typical pages. They definitely speak to Marlene's point and no further comment will be necessary.

Example 1:

Aug 1	1400 hours	left Bull Habr	w 1/4 s	36 mi	34	spring
Aug 2	0400 hours	fished Langara	s.	16 mi	248	coho and spring
Aug 3	0500 hours	fished Langara	s.	22 mi	154	spring

Example 2:

July 22	Grub Goose Bay	23.00	Total Fish Sale	968.27
	Fuel	10.84	Total Expenses	48.39
	Laundry	1.55	Marlene's Share	96.80
	Grub Bull Hbr	3.00	My and boat share	822.08

Further comment is necessary. Please note that the expense side of the ledger is minute on a relative basis compared to the income side. Also note that "Total Expenses" are overstated by ten dollars. They should read, 38.39 not 48.39. As well, a rough calculation indicates that Marlene's share is ten percent, however, there is a rounding error and she has been gypped out of three cents.

BRADLEY KNOWS THAT A miracle occurred. A way has been found to pacify his brother who has been crying for all of his life. He believes this is a miracle in the true literal sense, not a fluky serendipity, which caused him to pick up the logbook and place it in his brother's hands. In any case, Brad is determined to let his brother keep the book and damn the consequences.

Marlene is thankful that the book can pacify Jim, but she clings to the hope that his crying jags can be contained some other way. She believes that Jim's cranky nature, along with his slowness, was caused by birth trauma. He came out of the darkness just as Perry cruised into it. Like every child, Jim arrived naked, slippery and wet, the longest baby born at St. Paul's Hospital – twenty-seven inches. Not the heaviest baby, but he did weigh nine pounds and fourteen ounces. After seventy-two hours of difficult labour, Jim arrived with a distorted head (the Tectonic Plates had shifted), two broken collarbones, and the umbilical cord made two secure wraps around his neck. As the Jenzen family professed the Catholic faith, a Caesarian section had not been an option. The doctor did mention however that she must have been overdue "by a mile." The joke fell flat. When the nurse first gave her Jim to hold, two weeks of semi-conscious recovery had expired, and he was crying his head off. The doctor said he was colicky. Marlene knew it was more complicated. She knew that everything happened for a reason though the reason was often unreasonable.

THERE IS NO CONNECTION between Jim's nightmares and Perry's disappearance. The child never knew his father, probably didn't know he had one at the time his nightmares began, and probably doesn't even know what a father is. Marlene remembers how he would wake in a hysterical sweat and then his screams filled the long nights. She did motherly and unmotherly things to console him, to stop him, to comfort him, to silence him. She took him into her lonely bed and gave cuddles and stroked the damp curls and, when that didn't work, she shut him in his room and abandoned him for long periods. She would relent eventually and then give him drinks of juice and bowls of vanilla ice cream but he slapped them away. She cradled him in her arms, smothered him to her bosom and walked through all the dark rooms, back and forth, shushing and humming and rubbing and petting and patting and rocking. She sang her meager repertoire of lullabies, *"Night, night. Night, night. Night, night my boy, night, night. Close your little eyes, dream a little dream, Spy a little boat floating down a little stream..."* and wiped his tears and snotty nose, but he cried and cried and cried so that no other sound might survive. She covered her ears and hummed, but her humming was never as loud as his crying. She threw him on his bed. She covered his mouth with her hand. She threatened him in various original ways. She gave him sedatives and more than the recommended dosages. She even mixed a datura blossom in a fruit juice drink because she had read that daturas have soporific qualities. He could never tell her why he was upset. She acted shamefully. She acted lovingly, while he grieved for everyone. Yes, everyone.

Poor Brad couldn't sleep either when Jim ballooned in tears and bellows and shrieks. He would get up and sit on the couch in the living room and rock back and forth with his hands pressed over his ears, humming a rhythmless tune, seeking refuge in an induced catatonia. During the day, the three of them wandered the house like wretched somnambulists. Until the log showed up, nothing comforted Jim. When Brad said so reasonably, "But Mum, it stopped the crying," such a possibility hadn't crossed Marlene's mind. At that point in the family's saga, she had come to accept that nothing would ever stop the nightmares or the crying or the tantrums. She was resigned to life being like this forever. She knew that time, regardless of how slow or fast it whirled through the universe, could not and would not heal the wounds. Yet she still doesn't want Jim to have the logbook.

IN THE BEGINNING OF the Gospel of John, Jesus Christ becomes the *Logos* made incarnate, John 1:1-3, 14: "In the beginning was the Word, and the Word was with God, and the Word was God...And the Word became flesh and dwelt among us." When Jim posed with the logbook in front of his mother, he reminded us of Moses holding the Word of God, but that is only because many of us remember a certain J. Arthur Rank production called *The Bible*. Charlton Heston played Moses. Our minds are filled with graven images from Hollywood so when we see a connection, like the one between Jim and Moses, we imagine something is there that usually isn't. These are moments of fancy, that should be suppressed in the midst of our exuberance, that distort our true vision of life, that take us down blind alleys. Everything is wrong with the image and comparison. It was Brad, not Jim, who received the word. Only later, did Jim receive the "wurd." Remember Brad went downstairs to find the book; he didn't need to climb a mountain to find the tablets. When he picked up the logbook, it wasn't glowing inside a golden aura. He saw no burning bush in the damp corner of the basement. And when the big brother came upstairs and gave the word to the little brother, he didn't know what he was giving him, unlike Moses, who knew exactly what he gave to his brother, Aaron, and his people, the children of Israel. In the Jenzen fiction there is no parting of the waves, no dancing around the golden calf, no miraculous manna scattered on the desert floor, and no rules for the road of life, yet the lack of these crucial ingredients does not deter Jim.

SO, JIM WAS WRONG about the log being a "tori book." When Marlene accused Brad of putting the idea in Jim's head, he denied the accusation vehemently. All he did was give the kid the book and then he went upstairs. He didn't say, "Here Jim, here's a story book that your father wrote. It's yours Jim. It's exciting. It's thrilling. It's all about adventure and your dad's the best hero of all time." Somehow, who knows how, the idea that the logbook transformed into a story book got into Jim's little head and he never stopped thinking otherwise, but Brad didn't plant the idea, that much is ever so clear.

"YOU GAVE IT TO him, so you read it to him." That's what Marlene said to Brad later on. Things had changed slightly. Brad's attendance at school was sporadic. And Jim was no longer happy just holding the book or sleeping with it under the pillow. He needed it to be read aloud just like a nursery rhyme. It didn't matter what Brad was doing, even if it was a backlog of homework, or matter that his reading skills weren't fully developed, he would have to put everything down and begin the reading. And this might be the same page for the fifty-thousandth time. But first, if it was close to bedtime, he'd tell Jim to brush his teeth and put on his pajamas – they called them "jammies" – and have a pee. Jim would do everything he was told. "reed log brad, reed log," he'd say. And from her recliner chair in the living room, Marlene would yell, "Squeeze the toothpaste from the bottom."

They could never do the readings chronologically. Brad would say, "Let's start in the beginning and every night we'll start up where we left off the night before." But no, it couldn't be that way. Sometimes they'd go for days and all Jim wanted to hear about were the grocery lists scribbled almost anywhere. So Brad would spend half the night flipping pages and scanning for grocery lists. Way off in a margin he'd see "salt" so he'd read "salt." And the next night and the next night, Jim would say, "fyn salt brad," so he did. Brad would make a game of it though, and stretch the whole thing out. When he finally found "salt," it was like they had unearthed a treasure. Jim would jump up and down on the bed and Marlene would slur from the living room, "Be quiet in there." The focus on the salt and the locating of other food references got Brad thinking. He found cases of canned milk and cases of coffee and cartons of cigarettes but little by way of fresh vegetables and fruit. When he expressed his concern to Jim, his little brother would say, "look mor, brad." So, he looked more, the search was on, and soon Brad had his father enjoying the delicacies of a pagan feast. Jim loved those parts in the book.

A similar situation developed with "gear run."

Jim would say "geer run brad." And Brad would read, "Jan 5-herring, Jan 6-herring, Jan 7-herring, Jan 8-herring," and so on. Occasionally, however, his father would use the new fangled green plug and that was extraordinary. You can imagine the suspense building, when finally on January 21 the climax unfolds, and he changes his gear from herring bait to green plugs. Jim would clap and cheer when Brad said "green plugs" and then Marlene would tell them to be quiet.

They made a game of it, of course. Brad would read, casual as hell, up to January 20 and then on January 21, he'd look at Jim and say, "What kind of gear do you think our father ran on the 21st Jim?" Jim would "tend" he didn't know, for about an hour or two, and then finally say, "plugs brad plugs." They'd slug each other on the shoulder a few times and jump around on the bed, laugh for about half an hour more, and then Jim

would go to sleep with a big smile on his face. What an exciting story! If things stretched on like this, Marlene would fall
asleep in her chair, so Brad would have to wake her up and
help her off to bed. If he couldn't wake her up, if her use of
vodka had been excessive on that particular day, then he would
put the afghan over her, prop her legs on the ottoman, turn
out the reading light, take her glasses off and put them on the
side table, dog-ear her novel, and leave her there. Sometimes
he just looked at his mother for a while, before he turned off all
the lights in the house and locked the doors and went to bed.
The man of the house.

THE WORD LEGEND HAS its root in *logos,* too. Legends
often refer to a collection of stories; for instance, the stories of
the lives of the saints. A legend is a total body of such stories,
usually about a central character, who goes on an extended
journey and has many exciting adventures. Think of Homer's
Odyssey. Legends are bigger than life - epic. That's why we say,
"the stuff of legend," "legendary," "a writer of legends," or "to
inscribe a legend."

they took us to the roof where the sun shone

1955

THE CORTES GANG – Bradley, Johnny and Will – spent the weekend together. The name, "Cortes Gang," had been coined by one of the senior boarders. The term stuck and was used by their dormitory moderators as well. Most boarding students at Vancouver College went home for the weekends, but Johnny and Will couldn't go all the way back to Cortes Island – they would only get there in time to turn around and leave - and Bradley, who had lived in Vancouver for as long as he could remember, didn't go home because things were simply "too unsettled" as per recent communications with his mother. Since activities were seldom organized during these Saturdays and Sundays, the Cortes Gang, bound by their common heritage and tragedy, were pretty much left to themselves, except for Will, who needed to consult frequently with Brother Cavendish about his Sodality responsibilities. The Brother claimed that weekends gave them the free time necessary to plan for the following week. Very often, portions of Saturday, and the same could be said for Sunday, were taken up by Johnny and Bradley waiting in the hallway for Will to emerge from the moderator's room. As Bradley had an exhaustive supply of comics, they occupied their waiting time reading favourites. Sometimes Johnny doodled in his scribbler or wrote simple rhyming verses.

On one particular Saturday morning, when each of them read a comic in the series of The Three Musketeers, Brad asked, "Johnny, who do you want to be today?"

"Aramis."

"You always pick Aramis."

"You always pick Porthos."

Brad had not really chosen the character, Porthos. Will and Johnny assigned it mutually. That role for him came about for two reasons. Firstly, Brad was big for his age and Porthos was a giant. Secondly, Brad was a big eater having won the French toast eating contest in the cafeteria three times and Porthos had achieved similar accomplishments in 19th century France. The parallels were undeniable. Even though the three boys were all big for their age and good eaters, it seemed Brad was stuck with his portrayal of Porthos.

He continued, however, to bargain for a character change – at least for one day. Imagining himself as a comic character was an indulgence he enjoyed immensely. Brad said, "I don't always pick Porthos. I just got him. Why don't you be Athos?"

"Athos is too old. I'm sticking with Aramis," said Johnny.

Even though Aramis had a reputation for being a womanizer, Johnny forgave this blemish in his nature because Aramis believed in the sacred concept of friendship and was the musketeer who championed the famous phrase, *all for one and one for all*. Johnny had filled his scribblers with that quote, not only in English, but French as well, *tous pour un, un pour tous*, and whenever the three of them were together, even if they weren't impersonating the three musketeers or their good friend D'Artagnan, he was sure to use the quote in their conversations as might a marine radio operator who stopped every transmission with "over" and terminated them with "over and out."

"Well, you can't be D'Artagnan because Will always gets him."

"I never said I wanted to be D'Artagnan."

Neither of them had ever challenged Will about being D'Artagnan. Will was a leader. D'Artagnan was a leader. Certain facts didn't permit modification.

Tired of waiting for Will, Johnny said, "Let's go shoot baskets until Will is done."

The April day was warm and sunny so they used the outside court, which also served as a tennis court. First they had a foul shot competition and then they played one on one until Will showed up. Johnny pretty much dominated Brad during the wait. As Will approached, Johnny threw him the basketball and said, "Let's go two on one until lunch."

Will said, "It's just about lunch."

They walked to the cafeteria. Lunches on the weekends featured glasses of juice – orange, tomato, apple - jugs of milk, stale leftover pancakes, soup, and beef and mustard sand-wiches. The Cortes Gang sat at a table by themselves and the older and louder Mexican students, who obviously couldn't go home for the weekend, sat at a table by themselves. A few of the Brothers occupied the table nearest the food. It seemed that each location had been chosen by each group in order to achieve maximum distance from their neighbour. Otherwise the cafeteria was empty.

Bradley asked, "What'll we do this afternoon?"

Johnny said, "Let's go downtown."

The gang often took the bus downtown on Saturday after-noons, even though that was an infraction of the rules. Usually they hung out on Granville Street, down three blocks, cross the street, up three blocks, watching people, surveying the theatres for good films, though they never went to one, pausing overly long at the peep-show store and sometimes venturing a quick look through the door just to see what might be inside.

Will said, "I haven't got any bus tickets."

Bradley said, "I've got some."

Will said, "The Cav said I should stick around in case we need to do more Sodality."

The boys drank their juices and finished their sandwiches. The Mexicans left for the pool table. The Brothers went to chapel to read their breviary.

Bradley said, "Let's go to the furnace room and see Mr. D'Arcy."

Mr. D'Arcy, the school janitor, had a small apartment in the furnace room. The gang often visited him on the weekends. It was warm in there and they got to sit around on the old stuffed armchairs and read comics. Mr. D'Arcy had read all the books by Alexandre Dumas and knew everything about the Musketeers.

Will said, "The Cav thinks I shouldn't hang out with Mr. D'Arcy, because of the Sodality."

Johnny said, *"All for one."*

And Bradley said, *"And one for all."*

Will reluctantly said, "Okay."

MR. D'ARCY TOLD THE gang the plot to "The Man in the Iron Mask" from Dumas' "The Vicompte de Bragelonne," the third and last novel in the D'Artagnan Romances. He would have read them the story, but he did not have an English translation. They were at the part where the giant, Porthos, the first of the Musketeers to die, is crushed by a dislodged boulder. Unexpectedly the door to the furnace room flew open and Brother Cavendish entered. He said, "I've been looking everywhere for you Will." Then Brother Cavendish addressed Mr. D'Arcy. "I'll be needing Will for awhile. The other boys should stay here."

Brother Cavendish and Will left the furnace room. He held Will's hand as they walked up three flights of stairs to the top floor of the building. He gripped a brown paper bag in his other hand. He unlocked a door that Will had never noticed before. The door opened to a storage room, but also had a small staircase leading to a hatch. The Cav unfastened the hatch that led to the roof. He stepped onto the roof and then signaled for Will to do the same. Near to the hatch, but shielded by a large chimney, Will saw a three-sided frame sheathed in highly reflective aluminum.

Brother Cavendish said, "Will, I want to show you something."

The Christian Brother proceeded to strip off his clothes, leaving only his shorts on. Then he took a large towel out of the bag that he carried and placed it inside the aluminum frame. He lay down on the towel and said to Will, "What do you think of my sun parlor?"

"It looks good."

"This invention of mine keeps me out of the wind; it's very private and the reflection from the aluminum gives me a tan quickly."

Will looked across the roof and noticed that this was a very private place like his moderator had said. He could see houses in the far distance, but those across the street were hidden by the jack wall perimetering the roof.

The Cav pulled the waist band of his undershorts down and said, "Look, there's no tan line."

Will asked, "Why?"

"Because I sunbathe nude. That's how they do it in heaven when they bask in the rays of God, Will."

The Brother stripped off his undershorts and then sat on the towel. Will tried not to look at his moderator, especially since he had never seen a naked adult before, let alone a Christian Brother of Ireland. Recently, things hadn't been going well in their planning sessions. It seemed they rarely talked about the Sodality any more. Instead, the Cav asked him personal questions like, "How's your health?" or "I notice you have chapped lips; do you want me to rub salve on them?" He had done personal things too, like once he rubbed Will's bare chest for a long time and said, "Jesus did this to Lazarus to wake him up." And the kisses, when he left each planning section, were longer too, and not just on the top of his head, but on his cheek and close to his chapped lips. If ever Will resisted his moderator, he would be reminded that he was the one who had been "Called," but if he continued to resist, then there were other lambs in the Cortes flock. He had said, "Lambs are lambs, Will."

The Cav patted the towel he sat on, and said, "Your skin is so white. Take your clothes off and lay down beside me."

As Will understood unclearly what was about to happen, the child decided to do as instructed - whatever the outcome - mostly because he believed that resisting, or even refusing completely to accept the invitation, might trigger an avalanche of danger for Aramis and Porthos. Will slowly stripped off his clothes.

without memory, until the shell spoke

1956

BRADLEY'S MEMORY IS SUPERB when it comes to his comic book heroes. He remembers every image from every scene on every page – bright colours, cliff-hanging tension and the exact words in the loopy balloons. He's a good reader now. With eyes wide open and comic closed – sitting, standing, or lying in his bunk, it doesn't matter – he sees his heroes stretch their bodies like soft toffee or fly straight through giant mountains or magically open tins of spinach with a tobacco pipe. He has concluded that if the world could be exactly like Plasticman's or Superman's or Popeye the Sailorman's, then he wouldn't have to worry.

However, there is a recurring image in his memory – dark, blurred, wobbly and unidentifiable, which doesn't belong. Not anywhere. Not from his comics and not from his dreams either. More like a hovering presence, the reception weak, fading in and out, and at times the fragment is frenetic and a pest, possibly from his own past, but how would he know? This annoyance pops out of the blue, increasingly when he withdraws into the perfect recall games with his heroes, which these days is mostly all of the time. Just the other morning, as he watched Superman struggle with a green nugget of Kryptonite, the chimera materialized –like a panicked moth attracted to a scalding light – and ruined his reverie. The only recourse is this: whenever the apparition flits in front of his face, the boy bats for all he's worth. Since Brad can never get a good swat with either hand, he wishes the light would do its job and scorch its wings forever.

BRAD LOOKS THROUGH A fence and sees water. Beyond the water stands a large white sign on a rocky point of land, REFUGE COVE, WEST REDONDA ISLAND. He closes the Popeye comic he doesn't need to have open anyway and reads other words on the sign, "General Store - Fuel - Provisions - Post Office - Telephone."

What comic is this?

Fiery light laps up the edges of the sign and fills the land and sky. Flames dance on the water. Everywhere bright light flashes as if the whole world burns. Tears form in the corners of his eyes. In an effort to control this welling sensation – to banish his worries and master his life – he persuades himself to relax. If there really were fire, then there would be smoke. And the smoke would sting; his eyes just water. And the smoke would smell; the air is fresh and salty. The time of day is afternoon; and the sky is clear - see all the blue - so the bright light must be nothing other than a very strong sun. His eyes begin to dry as he shields them with his comic.

Still uncertain about his situation, Brad reassembles the images sailing by and imposes another order of logic to make sure the worries are groundless: water, not land; sunlight, not fire; railing, not fence; Refuge Cove, not his boarding school in Vancouver, and all by himself figures out exactly what is happening. He's on a boat, standing on deck, looking over a railing, and going…somewhere. The moth flutters and he swats until it goes away.

The boat slows and a whistle blasts. He cups his ears. They round another point of land and he sees a protected bay just like the place where Popeye lives. Some buildings are floating or half-sunk, cockeyed, weighted down with clutter. Shabby structures skirt the steep shore, all joined by a network of snaking boardwalks and propped on crooked stilts above the tide line. The green forest comes down to the water's edge. Rocky bluffs are bare, the ledges moss-covered. The moss looks soft. And lush. No roads. How come there's no roads? There's a big island in the middle of the bay and a little one off to the side. The place looks wild and temporary as if it could disappear in a storm until Bradley reasons that the village is so tucked away from the open ocean that not even a hurricane could break it loose.

Feelings of relief overtake him. But now the boy squints over the railing and sees something else. He wants to stay with the jumble on the edge of the wilderness at the edge of the sea, but a new picture won't let him look at what is really happening. He sees his mother on a dock - he guesses Vancouver. She walks away, humming.

He wants to say, Turn and wave, Mother.

She doesn't.

A man stands beside him at the railing; they both watch her grow smaller and smaller. The man says, "Well kid, so you're just about twelve."

Brad nods his head.

Then the man says, "See this bottle."

Brad reads, "LCB – Overproof Rum."

"Don't bother me…not even when I finish."

The scene retreats. Maybe that was a memory? Or a dream? It certainly didn't come from a comic.

The boat approaches the head of Refuge Cove. The general store has the same sign on its roof as the one on the rocky point. Bradley thinks someone has quickly moved it. There was a fire after all, and they wanted to save the sign.

The store stands on legs. Even without understanding this new world, by the look, he knows the store would sink or topple if it didn't have all those legs. The dock is queer, a U shape, but one part juts at an angle so it's not really a U but a U with a bent leg, like a dog's. Old boats, beat up boats, are tied to the dock. The only flat spot anywhere, except for the ocean, is the dock where kids play basketball. They throw the ball at a hoop attached to another sign nailed to a building, which reads, "Freight Shed."

He says to no one, I can play basketball. He was the best player in the juniors and when he became an intermediate he was still the best, except for his friend, Johnny, who was even better than his friend, Will.

Men scramble with lines. Booms swing and winches grind. A load of chain and coils of cable hoist into the air. He sees pictures he has never seen before: drums of fuel, tanks of propane, tracks of machinery, outboard engines, a huge crated engine and boxes and boxes on pallets.

People stand on the store porch drinking coffee, but then get up and run down the ramp.

He says to no one, They're coming to greet me.

Maybe not? The kids stop the basketball game and catch tie-up lines and drag and hook the loops on the tie-up things. Bradley has never seen kids do grown-up stuff.

He sees an Olive Oyl lady smoking a cigarette. He looks down at her over the rail. She has a tiny waist and wears a wide black belt with a big gold buckle. How can the waist be so tiny? He recognizes the same rubber boots, as Olive's, in the same skinny legs and the same bun of shiny black hair. She wears a tight red sweater and pouts with very red lips, like Olive, and flickers her red nail polish on her long fingernails. Beside her towers Brutus drinking a bottle of beer. He has thick lips, hairy arms and hairy face, hair on the backs of his fingers and a big patch of hair coming out of his shirt collar.

Someone helps the LCB man off the freighter and two others lead him up the ramp.

Brutus says through his thick lips, "Carl did a great job of looking after the kid."

People laugh. Brad laughs too, not because he understands a single bit of what is going on, but because he feels an attraction. To something.

Another man with a captain hat says, "Son, you can get off now."

Then his mother says, If you hadn't been a disaster, this wouldn't be happening, but she must live in another comic because when he looks in the direction of her voice, she's not there. The moth is back, hovering and flitting. He swats and misses as he climbs off the boat.

"My sister's got her nerve sending you here." Olive Oyl speaks screechy.

Brutus stares at him with large black eyes and then the winch man on the freighter yells, "Conners, don't you want your oyster sacks?" so he disappears from Bradley's picture.

HOW EXCITING RACING IN her speedboat, but they're leaving Refuge Cove. Aunt Maddie drives the boat like a man. He has no picture of a man driving a boat – his father was a fisherman so he must have driven boats, but he can't get a picture of his father, so how does he know that she drives like a man? Bradley looks over the gunnels. As the water races by, it is faster, so much faster than the freighter, so much faster than looking straight ahead. The wind on his face is good, his hair straightens, there's the taste of salt in the air and water leaks from one eye. Is this how a dog feels when he sticks his head out a car window?

They speed on calm water farther and farther from Refuge Cove through a maze of twisting channels and in their progress each channel narrows until they race between steep walls that block the light from the sky. They arrive at the logging camp at dusk and when they unload, Aunt Maddie says, "Christ, I never saw so many comics."

He unpacks his suitcase in a bunkhouse, a large dark room with a wood space heater in the middle. He stows his comics. Aunt Maddie stands in the doorway smoking one cigarette after another. He takes a secret moment to admire the way she uses the smoldering butt to start each new one. Her face glows warmly in the weak light. From wall to wall a saggy clothesline holds smelly work gear. A dirty sock smell invites a picture of the dormitory at boarding school, but he kicks it away. When they leave the bunkhouse, he trips over a pile of caulk boots, which clutters the porch. Aunt Maddie says, "I don't let them wear their boots inside. They'll tear the linoleum to rat shit."

At supper, twenty loggers wolf down steaks and pork chops soaked in Lea & Perrins and ketchup. They whiten their gravy with salt. They speak with full mouths about chainsaws and stumpage rates. He doesn't know what high leads are, or spar trees, or haulbacks or chokers. Understanding the conversations at the dinner table is impossible. Just noise.

The men don't speak to him and Aunt Maddie and Uncle Jake eat separately in their own cabin because they're the bosses. Molly, the cook, encourages him to have another helping, but he pretends he isn't hungry because the confused lad doesn't know who's paying. When Brad excuses himself from the table, Molly says, "In the morning you can feed the seagulls leftover pancakes from breakfast."

Now he has something to look forward to.

That night he sleeps with six loggers. His eyes water during the night, but the snoring loggers drown out the little noises that he makes. In his dreams, he chases flying fish across the ocean on the back of a giant white seagull. The wing tips graze the tops of each ocean swell and the bird obeys his commands as if he were working the reins of a magnificent horse. He's as good at riding his flying horse as Gene Autry, Roy Rogers and Lash LaRue combined.

THE LOGGERS EAT HEAPS of pancakes smothered in syrup, and scrambled eggs, bacon, left over steak, toast and strawberry jam. They drink huge pots of hot black coffee. No one speaks. Bradley wonders if there's a series of logger comics? When they head off to work, he wants to go with them to the top of the mountain to cut the trees, but reasons that he is too small. He thinks, Maybe I'll be big enough by the end of my visit?

After breakfast he walks from the cookhouse down to the seashore. He carries the bucket of pancakes to feed the seagulls. On an outcrop near the cookhouse, exactly where Molly told him to stand, he throws the pancakes into the air. They are sticky and smell like syrup. The real syrupy ones fall apart when he throws, but the seagulls are so quick that it is impossible for a piece to land on the water – not even the falling apart pieces. And there are millions of the birds. One gulp, two gulps. They screech for more.

He takes the empty bucket back to the cookhouse. Molly, toothless now that the men are up the hill, tells him that it takes eight minutes for food to go in one end and come out the other. What comes out, she calls "white splat."

He tries to imagine the powerful juices in the bellies of the birds, but can't. He wonders if the juices are stronger than sulfuric acid because a school picture flies by about acid burning holes in his clothes. Bradley thinks, If I had a watch, I'd time the seagulls turning pancakes into white splat. It would be a science experiment.

She wants him out from underfoot because she has to clean, do dishes, make bread and pies, get the vegetables peeled and scrubbed, cut more steaks and chops from the loins in the cooler and that isn't the half of it.

"You go play on the beach."

He sees a small beach at the end of a trail where she points.

Then she says something he doesn't understand, "Your Aunt Maddie told me about the matches. I don't want nothing like that here." She holds up a warning finger.

The screen door closes in front of him. Now he's confused. Was the bright light around the sign at Refuge Cove from the sun or not?

He wants to ask Molly where Aunt Maddie is, because, he guesses, she should be looking after him. But when he glances through the screen door, he is afraid. Molly pounds a big lump of dough, her forehead sweats and her lips are collapsed into her mouth in concentration. Already he smells baking in the big oven.

The boy walks past the bunkhouses, the bathhouse and laundry, the machine shop and boat ways. Junk is strewn along the trail to the beach, mostly metal, rusted and broken, but everywhere looks like a good place to play.

"I'm walking in a graveyard of iron monsters." The words come from a Plasticman comic. He sees his liquid hero slip through the scary place, a frame at a time.

Mist rises in the channel and he watches the sun hit the far shore. In a while, the sun comes closer crossing the water to his shore. A moth - maybe it's a butterfly - flits by. He swats and it ambles off. He sits on a log and kicks his runners at the pebbles on the beach. For the first time, he sees his new runners. His jeans are new too, but now they are stained with rust from the iron monsters. He looks at his hands and notices how scarred his fingers are – angry looking. They should hurt but he doesn't feel anything. It's quiet here. The wavelets on the shore sound like…little breaths.

He wonders what to do with himself, for this morning, and every other morning for the rest of his days in the strange place. Perhaps he will get to fish, but doesn't know how to fish, or start an engine, or steer a boat. He'd like to fish because his father liked to fish. He knows very little about this world.

Thinking of yesterday, yes, it was yesterday, he likes the pictures of Refuge Cove and hopes he will get to see them again. He knows how to play basketball better than the kids that were there. The Brutus man looked right at him and didn't seem horrible like the Brothers at school. He looks down the beach to a distant area where men walk on floating logs. They push them through the water with long shiny poles and leap from log to log. I could do that if they'd let me.

Closer, not far along the shore, he notices a small shack. The poor building slants toward the water's edge. He thinks everything will fall out if the door opens. A porch is strapped to the shack, where three little girls dangle their legs over the side, and a bigger boy crouches at the shoreline washing a large bowl – he guesses the boy is the brother of the girls. And he guesses that he washes their breakfast bowls. Bradley remembers that he only had to wash dishes at school when he was very bad.

He whips a Superman comic from the back pocket of his jeans. Neither Aunt Maddie nor Molly told him there were kids at camp. Maybe it's the start of summer holidays?

The brother looks about his age and wears white undershorts only. Barefoot: the boy walks barefoot on the sharp pebbles and it doesn't look like it hurts. He doesn't have pictures of his comic heroes ever walking in bare feet on sharp stones. Lava, but not sharp stones. Bradley resolves to toughen his feet on the beach and pretend it doesn't hurt. But later. He will practice, but not now – tomorrow morning he will forget to put his new runners on as long as Molly doesn't catch him.

He walks down to the shoreline and the brother stands up and looks his way. Brad slips Superman into his hip pocket and picks up a stone and throws it into the water. Plunk. Immediately, the boy bends down and picks up a stone and throws his into the water. His rock skips three times before it sinks. Bradley watches the rings get bigger and bigger until they fade away. The boy takes a few steps toward him and selects another stone. The sisters talk and giggle, but he can't hear what they say. Their brother waves at them and then he throws his rock. Five skippers.

Bradley looks for a good rock, round and smooth and flat: perfect. All he can see are rocks with sharp jagged edges, lumpy things, long crooked excuses for rocks: rocks that would be good for toughening feet but not for skipping. His section of the beach looks mined, probably stripped of all the good skippers by the boy on previous days. He watches the boy bend again and make a selection.

The boy hesitates to make sure Brad is looking. After the throw, he can't count the rings. The sisters clap their hands. They cheer from the porch and Brad's not sure he likes them. Once more, the ocean is smooth like glass. Desperately, he searches for a good rock. He moves toward the boy thinking the pickings will be better at that end of the beach. When the moth flits by, he panics however, and selects prematurely a rock that is smooth and round, but not flat. He knows this rock has an imperfection but believes that if he throws harder than he has ever thrown, and exactly at the right angle, then it will skip until the rings could never ever be counted. He throws, not just the rock, but everything. It skips twice and sinks to the bottom.

More giggling and more clapping.

Now the boy stands beside him, but Bradley refuses to look into his eyes. Instead he searches for a perfect rock. The boy does too.

Bradley can't believe how he misses the rock the boy finds. It is flawless and white – the rest are grey – the only perfect white rock on the whole beach was beside his foot. Right beside his own foot and he didn't see it. He thinks, If I were at boarding school I'd pry the rock from the kid's hand, and throw him to the ground.

The brother throws, the angle is as perfect as the rock, the speed like a bullet, and it bounces like a rubber ball. Brad loses count at fifteen. When the rings fade away, he doesn't know what to do. Then, remembering his hands, he suspects that his fingers might be sore from the scars. The scars must be the only reason why he can't throw properly. He is ready to give this excuse, but the boy speaks first.

"I'm Larry."

All he can think to say is, "I'm Brad and I'm nearly twelve."

"I'm thirteen."

A DAY LATER, BRAD and Larry hang off the dock catching pregnant perch. They squeeze out the babies and watch the hungry rockies come from the bottom to gobble them up. The boys spend many days in a leaky dugout and drift the shoreline with their heads over the rail watching pictures go by. Sometimes they anchor in a shallow spot for a close up look of the world under the boat. Larry knows everything. His grandfather has told him the names of all the creatures in the sea and wonderful stories about their power and magic.

They watch rockweed puffed up like clusters of grapes dance lazily in the gentle currents, and they watch barnacles extend their feathery tongues and lick specks of dust from shafts of liquid sunlight. When Brad doesn't know the name of something, or why it looks so strange, he asks Larry. He sees white anemones open and close like crazy flowers with little fish swimming in and out of the waving tentacles. But he fails to see – until Larry points them out - scallops blending perfectly with the rocky bottom. His friend says, "Just wait and watch." Soon the shells peep open, and around the edges, like gaudy red lips sucking life from the sea, the shocking scarlet sacks of roe give their location away. He sees tiny snails and chitons graze the rock algae leaving crisscross trails and then he sees orange sunstars cruise the bottom, twenty-five legs and an army of tentacles marching and marching through the watery universe. He sees the lesser stars, the purple pisasters, the leathers, the spinies and spiders, hunch and strain, pry oysters apart, only slightly though, and then disgorge their own insides. Larry says, "See, they eat from outside themselves." Brad watches as the gelatinous stomach silently slips between the oyster shells and slowly digests the soft delicious meats. He watches long whips of bull kelp held fast to the bottom, wave their graceful leaves. Brad imagines that Lash LaRue lurks in the underwater forests.

Every Saturday morning he and Aunt Maddie make a trip back through the canyoned walls, through the narrow channels, pushing over the watery highway to Refuge Cove to get fresh supplies for the logging camp. If they are lucky, they go midweek too, and always take the camp tender, *Tom Forge*, which is much bigger than her speedboat, but much slower. Molly makes a grocery list and Uncle Jake always needs parts for broken machinery. Brad learns to secure the boat temporarily. His aunt says, "Watch," and then he mimics her clove hitch. He learns how to secure the boat permanently. She says, "Watch," and he mimics her lock the clove with a double half hitch and tuck the end in a splice for safety.

On the third trip, she allows him to steer, but not touch the throttle or gearbox. On that trip, Conners, the hairy man, races by and waves as they enter the Refuge. He goes way faster than Aunt Maddie could have ever gone in her speedboat and he has a dog with ears that look like wings. On the fifth trip she lets him dock the boat when they arrive back at the camp, but she works the controls. On the sixth trip she makes him steer by compass even though the weather is perfect and visibility fine.

She says, "Don't veer from 210 until Point-No-Point, then you get bearings for the Refuge." He's a natural at keeping the needle on target.

He docks the boat at Refuge Cove and thereafter Brad gets to use the throttle and gearbox. Later, he even gets to do the docking in the height of the summer when the crazy tourists are all over the place. He keeps a stack of comics aboard in case things get dull, which never happens. Charts are more interesting. This whole new world is interesting.

That afternoon, Aunt Maddie gives him half of Molly's list, just tears it in half like it isn't an important document, and then he runs around the store fetching the items for the storekeeper to add up. He makes a race out of shopping though, and beats Aunt Maddie, because she isn't really awake, or doesn't seem to care about winning. He even has time to get things on her half of the list. After packing all the grub boxes, Brad carries the supplies from the store to the *Tom Forge* and stows them in the hold, while she smokes more cigarettes on the store porch. The storekeeper says, "You should be working here, Brad."

Before heading back to camp, coming down from the store after signing off the bill, which she let him do too, Aunt Maddie pats her bun of shiny black hair and checks her red lipstick in her little mirror and lights another cigarette and then checks herself in her mirror again and touches her hair some more and cinches a notch in her wide black belt and then she walks up to Conners. He sits in a large wooden skiff on top of a load of oysters in burlap sacks.

He and two others laugh and drink beer when Aunt Maddie interrupts them, "Jake wants you back on the booming ground...says bygones'll be bygones." She inhales her cigarette. The smoke seems like it will never come out.

Conners leaps off the pile of oysters and crab-walks up to Aunt Maddie. His friends laugh at how funny he looks. Brad laughs too. When Conners stands up straight, Brad only comes up to his elbow.

Conners puts his hairy arm around her tiny waist and lifts her off the dock – like he isn't holding anything – and then he takes a gulp from the beer bottle in his other hand. Aunt Maddie's boot falls off and flops on the dock.

"Tell Jake his bygones are gone, but mine ain't."

Her eyelashes flutter. Their noses nearly touch.

"I told him, but he wanted me to ask anyway," says Aunt Maddie.

Still suspended in the air, as if this is how they always talk, she turns from him to puff on her cigarette, which has red lipstick all over it.

"Tell him I'm poaching oysters and stealing logs and having fun."

He puts her down. She slips her skinny foot back into her boot. Aunt Maddie and Brad walk to the *Tom Forge*, but Conners follows.

"Hey, kid. I got you something."

He gives Brad a lilac coloured bottle filled with a white kind of mud.

Then he says, "I used to fish with your daddy – we was partners on the second *Pride*. He had a huge collection of these bottles."

Aunt Maddie whirls on the big man, "You weren't partners and he don't know nothing about his dad and ain't supposed to." Their eyes lock until Conners finally turns and walks back to his friends. He makes a "koo-koo" sign with his finger. At the skiff, he pats Rusty Dusty roughly and the dog wags its tail.

Brad doesn't even get a chance to say thanks or have a conversation about his gift or anything.

They split a brick of vanilla ice cream on the way back to camp. Unlike Olive Oyl, Aunt Maddie hardly speaks, except for times like the first day when they spoke about comics, or the evening when they talked about caulk boots and linoleum, or then on the dock with Conners, or at that moment, when she halves the brick of ice cream and says, "You pick."

But, on this return trip, near the end of the brick, they almost have a conversation.

"Part of the deal with my sister is that I keep you away from guys like Conners."

Half an hour later, as they approach the logging camp, she says more, "I got a similar deal with Jake with Conners."

As they secure *Tom Forge*, she gives him another picture to play with.

"Brad, don't be so dumb…Jake would never say for Conners to come back."

A FEW DAYS AFTER the ice cream trip, while they hang off the side of the dugout, Brad and Larry watch an octopus feeding near the bottom. It opens like an umbrella and then smothers the ocean floor. The lucky sculpins dart away, but the unlucky ones get vacuumed up. The octopus appears curious for some reason and swells his head and sails like a balloon to the surface. His head pops out of the water – red and leathery, fully round, then oval, then stretched and twisted like Plasticman, rippled and grooved like a brain without a skull, pocked like the face of the moon, smooth and pink like baby skin, and leathery again like a gnarled old man, as if it can come up with any old look one after the other – all this in front of Brad's frozen gaze.

Brad could have touched the head but doesn't. He is too shy to be the first to reach out. Instead, he hopes the creature might touch him with its snaky legs. The animal seems odd with an earless, mouthless, noseless head, and unblinking eyes staring into Brad's own bulging eyes. The eyes of the creature are brown and round, large, dark pools, almost human, but lidless. Brad wants the octopus to speak to him. He imagines that the eyes can speak, because Larry hasn't told him yet that there is a hidden mouth.

Suddenly, the creature deflates and leaves behind a cloud of ink. The water turns black.

Larry says, "I never saw one stick its head out of the water before."

He tells Brad that his people believe octopuses are the smartest creatures in the ocean and his grandpa once told him that they are really shellfish, but gave their shells away so they could be free.

Brad asks, "Is that why they grew so many legs?"

"I think so."

Now Brad feels he should have reached out and touched the animal. He misses an opportunity. He should have rubbed the head gently. It would have led to something.

He says, "The octopus was interested in me...wasn't he Larry?"

SOMETIMES LARRY HAS TO help his dad so Brad has no one to play with. Instead of reading comics, he wants to play with the sisters, especially Elsie, who, like Larry, also plays on the beach in bare feet in white undershorts, but he doesn't know how to approach her. It was easy making friends with her brother – just throw a rock. He has now reached the stage where he can walk on sharp stones and easily pretend it doesn't hurt and has even progressed farther to the sharper intertidal barnacles. Often his manner is casual, but occasionally looking back over his shoulder to see if he is watched, and if so, he makes a special effort to pretend he walks on soft moss. Usually no one is looking.

He hears Molly's voice. "You're not swatting at yourself as much."

She is friendlier than in the beginning and lets him set the tables and put out the "fixings" for the loggers to make their own lunches and he even learns to knead dough. In such circumstances, chiefly when they both sit on the porch and peel spuds and listen to the seagulls squawk, or watch the boats go up and down Lewis Channel, or the clouds drift lazily in the sky, she speaks to him like he's an adult.

He learns about her sore wrists and the family she ran away from and how Uncle Jake is a tough but fair boss. Moreover, he learns something about himself.

She has a way of getting clusters of images to line up and make a story.

She asks, "Why'd you burn the school?"

The question arrives like a steaming locomotive. Not many pictures have appeared lately with so much to keep track of. However, when he focuses, a few fragments organize frame by frame so that he can no longer see the potato he peels, but instead, Brad is in the furnace room of his boarding school. Each picture is fringed in a halo of white light just like the sign at Refuge Cove. It is a long weekend; the other kids have gone home, even Johnny and Will. He wanders in there because the janitor has become a friend, the only person he can have a real conversation with.

Mr. D'Arcy isn't in the easy chair, nor answers from the sleeping loft when Brad calls up. The furnace doesn't roar like usual, but he sees embers glowing through the little window in the door.

Newspapers are piled in a corner.

He opens the door and scrunches the papers and throws them in. Fireballs howl up the chimney. Then he finds matches and lights more scrunched up papers before he throws them into the furnace. Once, he panics though, just as he had panicked when looking for the perfect rock; he panics when the flames leap from the newspaper, and throws the fireball where it shouldn't go - into the coal bin.

The coal bin catches fire quickly, exploding as if it were gas.

As the potato re-appears in his hand, he says to Molly, "It was an accident."

"Is that how you burned your hands?" she asks.

He needs one more picture in order to answer the question. He looks at his angry red hands, the scarred fingers. He reasons that a scrunched up ball of paper, even if on fire, wouldn't have caused those scars and not on both hands. Then an image appears briefly and he has just enough time to say before it disappears again, "I helped when there was screams."

AUNT MADDIE SITS ON a log sunning herself and paints her toenails, the same red as her lipstick. Brad isnt very busy so he sits beside her and watches the procedure. She dips the little brush in the bottle, wipes the excess paint onto the rim and then gives a single swift swipe to a toenail. Her nails are already painted so he wonders why she keeps doing it. After every swipe she lifts her foot close to her face and blows to dry the paint.

She brushes her big toenail and says, "You blow."

Brad gets down on his knees and blows on her flared and outstretched toes.

She says, "Well, we finally made use of you."

After applying many coats, with Brad repeatedly performing the necessary drying operation, she sticks her heels in the sand and says, "Now we got to let them bake in the sun so they get real hard and real shiny."

They sit there quietly staring at her toes. In Lewis Channel, armies of trollers motor north to a new fish opening.

He says, "What's that stuff in the coloured bottle?"

She says, "Your mother doesn't want me to talk about things like that."

Now he wishes he had not asked. He does not want his aunt to get mad at him. They sit quietly waiting for the sun to dry her toenails.

"Its just sap, Brad." She lights up a cigarette and lets him blow out the match, a routine they had worked up.

"It probably doesn't matter if I tell you about the bottles and sap. Everybody knows about it anyway. Long time ago there was an American outlaw who came to Cortes and he swindled half the island. Your family got swindled and mine and everybody. Everybody was fooled into buying the worthless bottles for a dollar and then they collected sap thinking the outlaw would pay them a fortune for each full one. He told them it was a miracle medicine. When your father was about your age, maybe a bit older than you, he was the one who found the outlaw's stash of money and bottles and tools."

Brad asks, "Did he keep the money?"

"Ask your mother."

Brad asks, "What happened to the outlaw?"

"Nobody knows, but they sure got their theories. Not that long ago, Gerry and Freddie Holmes from Cortes found his skeleton and gun, or at least that's what they claim."

Brad has about five thousand more questions, but at that moment Aunt Maddie gets up and heads for her cabin. He rounds up her boots and the nail polish and then follows. On the porch, she takes her boots and the nail polish, and then says, "It's your mother's job to tell you stuff, not me."

LARRY AND BRAD WALK a stretch of beach. The tide is so far out that it looks as if they could wade across the channel to Cortes Island. Brad thinks he now has many reasons to visit the island, since that is where his family comes from and his school friends live there too. Larry bends over and picks up the empty shell of a moon snail. He points to the shallows and says, "There's another one." Brad splashes over and picks it up.

Larry tells him to put the mouth of the moon shell to his ear.

"It sounds like waves on the shore," says Brad.

While he listens, his friend says, "My grandpa says it's a voice from a far away world. And you don't just hear one voice either, because you can go inside that world, and you can walk on the shores, and pick up another moon shell and listen to that one, and walk into that world, and pick up another, and hear another, and it goes on and on."

They listen to the moon shells all afternoon. Brad craves the idea of being in more than one place at the same time. Yet still where you are. The sound is a gentle lapping on the shore and at other times an unending murmur. He even hears a crackly static noise. The moon shell feels good in his hand. He imagines that no human could ever have the strength to crush it, not even one of his comic book heroes. With his finger he traces the spirals from the nipple of the shell to the outer edges and retraces back. So rough near the nipple but smooth toward the edges. He orbits again and again, over and over the grooves, farther and farther, approaches the edges of another time almost and then retreats back to the origin where he started. If he explores the smooth mouth of the shell, he begins to touch the world from the inside and that feels glossy, but safe, better in a way.

He makes a project of collecting the moon shells and plans to have a box full when he returns to the city. For the rest of his days at the logging camp, he keeps one under his pillow with the medicine bottle.

ONE MORNING, FOLLOWING A storm from the day before, Brad feeds the seagulls pancakes. The air feels damp and chilly. He thinks that maybe summer is over. He stands with the wind and rain in his face and sees an orange helicopter clapping up the channel on his shoreline. He watches it go over and disappear around the far point and an hour later hears its echo and then sees it clap back down channel tracing the far shore of Cortes Island.

A few days later, on a trip for supplies, Brad sees two coast guard vessels tied at the Refuge dock. The tourist boats are gone. A crowd of people talk with uniformed men. Rusty Dusty lies on a blanket on the deck of the *Point Race*. His fur is soaked and knotted and a snarl is petrified on his lipless jaws. The eyes are gone. Another dog sniffs the dead dog.

Brad overhears the LCB man say, "Everything goes to that beach after a south-east."

They have found the dog on a rocky beach, but not the hairy man. A tide trail of empty sacks led the searchers to the spot where they also found a broken paddle and a lifejacket.

Brad asks a boy standing beside him, "What happened to the lips?"

The boy answers quietly, "The crabs do it."

"Let's go," says Aunt Maddie and they walk to the store. She gives him the whole list and he does the shopping while she stands on the front porch and smokes her cigarettes one after another.

Inside, the storekeeper tells Brad that no one noticed Conners gone. He left at night in a little skiff rather than his big boat, and the search started too late.

"I bet he was loaded like usual," says the storekeeper.

Brad says, "He should have taken his big boat."

"Son, I meant he was drunk."

Aunt Maddie's eyes water on the way back to camp even though they aren't racing in her speedboat. Her voice squeaks from the bunk in the *Tom Forge*.

"Brad, what me and your mom got in common is we both went for wild ass men."

She pulls a blanket over her head and weeps all the way home.

ON A RAINY NIGHT, under his pillow, he hears a voice in his moon shell and when he lifts it to his ear the voice sounds like his own, but many years ago, when he was little. It speaks and it goes out. When it goes out, he picks up another shell from the box under his bunk. The voice comes back. But he can't make out the words. And it might be a different voice. Through the night he picks the moon shells from the box and listens to the voices.

By his count, there are two more trips to the Refuge and then he will go back to Vancouver and his mother and brother, Jim, and a new school even though the school year has already started.

"...if they will let you in and if the doctors and social workers think you can handle it."

His mother has written these words in a letter and also written that she is feeling more restored now. She reports that Jim doesn't cry if he holds the logbook. Aunt Maddie reads Brad the letter because he doesn't understand all of the big words, but she stumbles over some of them too. They sit on the point where he usually feeds the seagulls. For once the birds leave them alone. While she reads, he leans his hot cheek against her cool arm and leaves it there. Even after she finishes reading the letter, he feels the heat abandon his cheek and warm her arm.

RETURNING SEEMS LIKE AN impossibility. He gathers together his comics in preparation. They're scattered everywhere – the bunkhouse, Molly's kitchen, and the *Tom Forge*. On the *Forge,* he finds an old magazine article folded and tucked in behind the compass. He reads the article, over and over. During his last days at the logging camp, he sneaks aboard the workboat any chance that he gets and eventually commits every word to memory.

He makes his final trip to Refuge Cove. During their voyage, he wants to ask Aunt Maddie many questions about the article, such as: What does **R.I.P.** mean? How can the *Arrogant* speak? and, Can memories be the colour green? but knows that she would never tell him. Even though this is their last time together, they have little to say to one another, except off Poverty Bluffs, she says, "You're starting to wander." He makes every effort to stay on course.

As the freighter sails into the Straight of Georgia, Brad feels himself unbearably stretch like Plasticman. He stands on deck looking over the railing. A northwesterly wind pours from the inlets stirring the sea into brilliant white waves. He turns a moon shell in his hand and traces the spirals with his finger. When he puts the shell up to listen, he hears Popeye singing, "I yams what I yams," and then he hears his own voice, and finally his dead heroes. He hears a torrent of voices cascading, one overtop of the other – Mr. D'Arcy, Conners, and at last, Father speaks.

R. I. P.

Shipmates of the Arrogant

Captain Perry Jenzen crossed the bar with his shipmates, James Ballentyne, Robert Archer, and Darwin Wilkes, all of Cortes Island, B.C., when the "Arrogant" was last spoken off Cape Flattery while heading for the tuna fishing grounds to seaward of the Oregon-Washington coast. There you have the bare, grim facts.

But to those who knew the boys and their loved ones, remain many green memories, covering the splendid qualities of these our shipmates, and knowing them so well we can think in terms of the thoughts of Mrs. Perry Jenzen and the host of loved ones left behind. Would that our thoughts could make such grief easier to bear. Perry was young in years, brilliant in the accomplishments of his chosen calling, a very ancient and honorable, as well as dangerous profession. The building of the Arrogant was the sum total result of years of struggle to achieve this ultimate goal.

"I've lived so much of my life at sea," Perry once told me, "that I might as well have a little comfort while doing just that."

Perry had another thing in mind, the comfort of his shipmates. If he could have written these words, his closing thoughts would be those of comfort to those who mourn his passing and that of his shipmates. He would have referred to the crossing of the bar as a departure on the outbound voyage, and that we shall all meet again. Perry has looked up at the stars and far beyond the horizon so many times. He has set a true course and has arrived at his destination. The temporary gap is so terribly hard to bear, and the bright star of hope is that we shall all be shipmates once again. That hope is our only hope, but Perry would tell you that is all-sufficient.

Respectfully to all, Adam Wilkes

October 23, 1945

Western Fisheries

they drove off the edge of world and landed in a patch of hurled stars

1961

I RAN INTO EARLE'S office. The door stood open. He looked like a thin guy with a thin tie and I was breathing hard. For three seconds colliding particles of rare gases sustained the only vibrations in our universe.

He glanced up from his poem.

What's your name, John Ballentyne, What do you want, To be a poet, Why, Failed math, What else, Passed English, Do you think you can barge into my office without an appointment?

The best thing was not to answer. I had learned that trick at my alma mater.

Out of the blue, suddenly, all at once, no warning, like a B grade film, he crumpled his poem and threw it at the waste bin filled with a host of rejected poems. He didn't really miss. It rolled off the pile and landed on the floor. Earle put his feet on the desk and arms behind his head. I saw sweaty armpits, mismatched socks and gum stuck to the sole of each shoe.

Our conversation gently flowed thereafter.

Do you know what similes are, They start with like, What about metaphors, They're not so easy, If you want to be a poet they better be easy.

Earle lit an Export A and flipped his lighter shut. A clatterous clunk. A thought rumbled across my corduroy brain: Mother Meredith will be supremely disappointed; she smokes the same brand. She will laugh uncontrollably. The thought played over, the needle stuck in the groove. Mother will be... she smokes...mother will be...she laughs...mother will be... she smokes.... and laughs. Uncontrollably.

I had anticipated everything. I had prepared and now it was confirmed. There would be more, more and many more, this was the first of many...tests, and quizzes, trick questions, the interrogation had started, the opening salvo to be followed by lectures on what was permitted and what was not. Already there were suggestions, recommendations, opinions, innuendo, hints that one word might be better than another, and soon there would be vicious critiques, attempts to destroy confidence, shameful displays of ego, pride, the greatest sin of all, arrogance, and we hadn't got the introductions out of the way, the comforting requirements of human discourse, the good etiquette – not the bad – that Mother Meredith had taught so well.

A PROJECTOR CRANKED IN the sorrowful silence: celluloid dream, celluloid heart. Earle kept a wasp in his office beating itself to death against the windowpane and blue-eyed flies buzzed where shafts of sunlight stabbed the stale air. His beard was salted, peppered, tobacco stained: hair – harum-scarum like Albert E. As expected, the ashtrays had never been dumped. And his books. I should have asked, Hey, Earle, what are the shelves for? So many books, mountains of books ranged through his office like upwellings from the fastness of literature's womb. Tomb. Boom. Classified by colour. Red. Green. Indigo. And his poems. Pages scattered along the peaks, ridges, plateaus and river bottoms branded with treads of gummed shoes. Painfully, I realized the interview would not go well. I wondered though, Would I have an office one day and would it look like this? Or would it look like my father's?

Neat. Serious. A place of unending calm where thoughts could grow, mature, evolve...challenge, take on pleasing shapes and colours. I made a mental note to myself, Ask Mother Meredith if Father JJ had an office. That would make her laugh. Or did he just write his poems while having his coffee in the galley of the arrogant ship. That would really make her laugh. Or did he compose during his midnight watch on the arrogant ship. Laughter continues. Or when the whole crew slept at anchor on the arrogant ship. The continuance of gut wrenching laughter is duly noted.

I remember once Mother Meredith said he didn't need much sleep. And another time Mother Meredith said his head was buzzing and boiling. That made her laugh. He never stopped making his magic is how I imagine his creative outbursts, never satisfied with a miniature muse, deluged with bursts of delicious *duende*, clicking his heels as he entered the sea, forgetting fear as they drove off the edge of the world. What a laugh.

The telephone rang. Earle answered, I'm busy. He hung up.

Failing math is not a particularly sound reason for becoming a poet, I passed English, Passing English is not a particularly sound reason for becoming a poet either, Maybe I have better reasons, Did you want to share them, My father was a poet, Now we're getting somewhere.

I wanted to sit down, but his room was chairless. My legs hurt from running to his office.

Can I sit down, Sure, Where, Try the blue pile but be careful of my poem, Can I read it, No.

I gave him the poem languishing on an indigo book and sat on the indigo pile. Earle threw his poem onto the red pile, but it fell into a deep dark crevice. The ash on his cigarette lengthened and bent, revealing a Cyclopean eye.

Mother Meredith had warned me, but I had avoided the truth, questioned the truth, neglected the truth. Rejected the truth. She was prejudicial; she had loved a fisherman poet, but burned his poems. She had laughed while the flames destroyed his genius. And I never accepted her explanations that they – poets – were cruel, she had once hysterically said, and another time she had once hysterically said, that they – poets – were calculating and corrupt. The case of the three C's. She wanted me to believe that poets were scum, that they could shine their bright lights into the darkest regions, and when in worse frames of mind use whips and thorns, mockery and silence, razor-sharp, penetrating, steely jabs, parries, thrusts. Word bombs and rocket propelled sentences. To make you laugh and weep hysterically.

Her view was one view. Mine another.

While I thought of my dead father, while I fought the thought that he might be capable of the three C's, Earle's smoke rings coiled up the shafts of light and escaped through an open window. The wasp was dead, but the blue-eyed flies thrived.

Earle said, There's always the problem of knowing what to do with one's life.

I didn't know if this was the way a poet formulated a question. Without a reference point, the guiding light, the star in the sky, the beacon of something or whatever or what on heaven and earth have we done, how does one know how to respond? So. Like my father, I let silence become an ally. Rather than tell Earle that I was almost certain that I knew unequivocally and almost exactly what I wanted to do.

He said, Who's your best loved poet, My father but his poems were burned, Can you recite any of his work, Like I said they were burned and I never got to read them, All of them, Yes, Maybe a few were shared with a friend, No, Too bad, Yes, Are you sure, Yes I'm sure.

Then Earle said, After your father who's your favourite poet, Rimbaud then Lorca, Have you read Rimbaud in French, No, Too bad.

Now I would have to switch from physics to French.

Can you quote from any of Rimbaud's work?

"Long ago, if my memory serves, life was a feast where every heart was open, where every wine flowed."

Earle parried with a likely thrust.

"One night, I sat Beauty on my knee – And I found her bitter – And I hurt her."

Earle took his feet off the desk and studied his poem. He crossed out two words on the first line.

I asked him, Did Rimbaud make you do that, What, Cross out those two words, No, I thought there might be a connection, Why, Because you did it right after reciting Rimbaud, I wouldn't have a single poem left if there was a connection.

Then he changed the subject as I had become too challenging.

What about a portfolio, Portfolio, Don't you have a collection of poems expressing your deep feelings like truth is beauty and that kind of claptrap, You mean already written, Of course.

People had commented that in my athletic phase I was quick on my feet, possessed of a quarterback mentality, agile, anticipatory, instinctual, blessed with split second timing, capable of handling any situation thrown my way with grace and dignity not to mention speed, accuracy and definitive, meaningful gestures to stabilize and solidify...this wondrous gift.

I'll run back to the dorm and get them, My door's always open.

BY 4 AM. THE following morning, I had produced: *All galaxies increased acceleration and the black spaces between shoved like bully kids.* Now I was rhapsodic, not a word out of place, following in father's footsteps, poetry was easy, the beautiful energy had rushed from the depths of the earth into the soles of my feet and the future for the first time seemed to gather unto itself....

A little tired, exhausted, barely able to lurch, stagger, limp, I raced to the centre of creativity, but had to wait for it to open. So I enrolled in French. I hovered, levitated, floated outside Earle's office all day, but then lethargically foot dragged back to the dorm convinced my portfolio needed augmentation. I skipped classes for the next three weeks, hid in the library during the days, scribbling and scribbling, and worked through the nights in my bedroom, took uppers, took downers, as I tried to finish my poem. Or was it finished? My poor widowed mother could now boast to her friends on Cortes Island about her studious son, about how finally a child had left the rock and lifted himself above the drudgery and mind-numbing, injury-prone industries of a feudal past.

Why had Mother Meredith burned the poems?

There was the question. Why had she destroyed my inheritance? In a vastly convoluted way was she secretly or seditiously or unconsciously encouraging me to be like him, but only a half of him, the dead half, not the half that he thought, and I lately have imagined, might live on and on as an essential chink in the chain of immortality...and everlasting. Infinite. Inspiration.

On October 28, 1961, the day before my nineteenth birthday, the exact same age, or thereabouts, that Rimbaud had embarked on his peregrinations through the world, seventeen years and a few days, here or there, after my father learned that *Arrogant* was an inauspicious name for a fishing vessel, or any other vessel for that matter, I sped to my own *Season in Hell*. The truth was that I had not hurt Beauty. Yet. And although, in truth, beauty had hurt me, I didn't believe my father could or would have ever done such a thing. And unlike

Rimbaud, who, at my age, had his entire body of work behind, I only possessed a few lines from one poem.

Even so, I was buoyed by the ever present thought that a complete poem existed, as did a whole body of work to be released when the fathomless feelings of a disembodied life ruptured into...and channeled its nowhere to be found way... through my...even though...there is...what? Perhaps!

TO MAINTAIN THE ILLUSION that space consumed itself, I walked in circles while waiting for rides. Hope, Calgary, Somewhere, Moose Jaw, Prairie sunrise – pink and precious, a big indigo-blue lake – the same hue as the indigo-blue-multi-eyed flies in Earle's office, Detroit, Niagara Falls – a fine mist saturated the air as newly-weds clutched at their naked bodies, already forgetting their pledge of allegiance to their newly minted spouse and the shocked witnesses of the world. Pick a bridge – Manhattan. I had learned so early in my journey that good days were predicated on distance alone.

The Bimbo sandwiches tasted so good. The Heroes were better. Blacks and whites lived in peace and harmony. I wasn't prepared for streets without leaves. The muggers kept to themselves. Sales for fallout shelters were brisk. Inside the Guggenheim, wooden men from the Amazon wrapped their penises in long tapered tubes of bark. Outside the Guggenheim, in the middle of the street where the taxis liked to play, a naked man stood on a box with signs covering front and back, but he didn't have a one-fingered glove like the wooden men from the Amazon. The signs, painted in red, said, "The End Is At Hand." From my childhood bible study class, I recognized this man, who lived in and outside every age and served a useful function.

"Your end is at hand, asshole," said a taxi driver to the apocalyptic man.

Later, more to keep company with the Doom's Day Man, as the tall buildings shuddered in the wind and grazed the remains of the steel-grey day, I unashamedly and spontaneously, stuttered a new line to a new poem, *Is this a l-l-long island?* The man cloaked in signs said, "It's about 118 miles l-l-long."

My reasoning went further than it should. While wandering the canyoned walls of New York City, occasionally kicking rubbish from the curbs onto the decaying asphalt, I came to envy, because I could not emulate, the man who challenged taxis in the street. Out there, he, who had materialized from the pages of Apocrypha, and spoke tirelessly to the mad mad world, possessed a five-word line that was the totality of his portfolio and the only poem he would ever need to write. Whereas I, burdened with Earle's outrageous demand, was now doomed to excavating an entire body of work before gaining entry to the creative mystery.

THE LIFEBOATS ON THE QE were as big as ships. As we sailed out of the harbour, the lady with the flaming torch continued to turn green, while standing on her little pedestal. I regretted not having climbed up into her torch when I had the chance. At the stern a student said you could climb up into her green flame, but another student said you couldn't because the stairs were blocked off, but the guy who said you could, said nobody guarded the blocked stairs so you could. You just had to jump over the little fence in her shoulder socket. The smart students who were headed for the Sorbonne abandoned me so that I could watch the green lady grow smaller...in my solitude, balancing on the keen edge of desolation, dreaming of a world that could not be...unless.

The torch controversy triggered a spasm of guilt and three spasms of laughter. I could not take time out to write my

Mother Meredith. Didn't she know? I worked day and night on the portfolio; down in the mine shaft, pushing gigantic rocks, tapping on bituminous walls, crawling through wet and dank tunnels, following one vein and another, inhaling noxious gases. An impotent yellow light hissed in the gloom. Canaries refused to wrestle with death where I hoped to strike the high grade.

I admit; I am no Rimbaud. I admit; I am no Lorca. Anthracite, not diamonds, is all I ask...demand!

a choice is made, one half enters, the other naught

1964 April

THEY WERE FAR FROM the sea. He was far from the sea.

A truck rumbled to a stop in a high mountain village in the centre of the Peloponnesus during the spring of 1964. In those days there existed a terrible lack of restriction and many young men wandered freely, believing one could go anywhere and do anything and were obliged to experience everything, including the exotic, before settling into the diktats and tic-tacs of society. Some basked in the freedom without a thought to the purpose of their journey. Others made that purpose a prison and looped their way over covered ground, carving a rut in the roads of the world, perhaps doomed to an eternity of monotony like that great Greek rock 'n roller, Sisyphus.

The driver got out of the cab and signaled to the three bearded hitchhikers riding on top of his freight truck. He signaled again. Two hands crisscrossing. The ride was over.

Michael brushed the dust from his clothes and leaped off the truck. He had spoken only of the where's, when's and how's since leaving Corinth. Where was the truck taking them, when would they get there, how come no one speaks English? He consulted his map frequently, at every switchback in fact, but was never certain of their location at any given moment. During the long ride up the mountain he commented too many times to his friends, "We can't go up forever." Michael had been travelling for three months in Europe and hoped to be home by fall for the World Series. They acquired the American – a dropped out student with aspirations to be a journalist - at the hostel in Athens. Perhaps he thought by hitching with seasoned veterans he might stumble upon an unusual story, or acquire a new slant on a flat stretch of road, or more conceivably, take a shortcut in his unauthorized evolution to myth.

"Arketo," said the driver. The tone registered the insistence that could only mean, "Get off."

Kiwi threw the packsacks down to Michael and jumped easily to the ground. He had finished the second year of his "walk about" and would return to New Zealand in time to enjoy two springs in one year. He had been an animal control officer on the South Island, where he culled the wild deer populations plaguing the sheep ranches. Nothing complicated about this fellow.

"Arketo," called the impatient driver.

John brushed the dust from his clothes but otherwise did not move. He had been thinking of snakes and was not fully prepared to let the thoughts slither away. Lately, he found himself likening birds and animals to the roads he traveled. Straight roads through savannahs made him think of rhinoceros. Whereas, over-grown jungle trails made him think of colourful birds like parrots and macaws. And shifting desert tracks – camels and scorpions. Steep mountain paths - yaks. There was some logic there. When near the sea, or on the roads of the sea, he never thought of fish, which had once seemed a puzzle, though now made more sense when he considered that fish were not just the code sign for the early Christian movement but also his legacy to a blighted ambition. These never-ending switchbacks up the mountain had incited his cerebral fantasies; so much so, that if he had not been attentive, they might have slithered, wriggled, coiled and finally struck. John was well into his third year of tramping through countries and continents and had not yet found a way to break the rhythm in his stride.

Kiwi yelled to John, "Get with it, Mate."

John gripped the tie-up ropes as best he could and eased himself over the side. Feeling had returned to his fingers, though they were often reluctant to do what he wanted - grip. His socks had lost their elastics and hung saggily over his leather boot tops. His clothes looked a size too large and his jeans were patched with a variety of materials in a variety of colours. The stitching had been administered at infrequent intervals so the corrective measures, if they had not already come undone, flapped on the remaining threads. Scabbed and bare knees showed on both legs. He favoured his left leg and his left foot was near numb.

Sensing his difficulty, Kiwi said, "Do you need help?"

John shook his head while he lowered himself off the truck. The snake thoughts were gone now, but three lines from his poem took their place: *Frostbite on Kilimanjaro, Frostbite at the equator, Frostbite and failure.* He hoped he would not lose his foot as Rimbaud had lost his leg.

Kiwi approached the driver, who locked the cab door. He shook the man's hand and said, "Efkhareesto."

"Finis," said the driver, and then walked across the road. Before entering a walled courtyard, he turned to face the travelers. More crisscrossing of hands. He went through the doorway.

The sun shone brightly in a cloudless sky - a windless afternoon in the highest reaches of the Greek peninsula. The air felt warm, not hot. There had once been trees on the mountain, felled centuries ago. The three young men stood in the middle of the road, packsacks leaning against their legs, John's pack by far the smallest with a faded Canadian flag sewn on the side.

Michael asked Kiwi, "Do you know much Greek?"

"Just Efkhareesto...and a few other expressions. It means, Thanks."

"I guess 'Finis' means he won't take us any further," said Michael.

John said, "Talking is mostly with gestures." To demonstrate, he held up both arms and wiggled his fingers awkwardly. The intended mime – whatever it meant - awakened memories of the African mountain, so he put his hands down as though he were embarrassed.

The village was nameless – or so they thought – and hugged the upper portion of the only road tracing the contours of the hillside. Scrub brush grew from cracks in rocks - stunted from lack of water, nutrients and continuous browsing. A network of well tramped trails over hummocks of dried grasses and aged outcrops connected the stone dwellings, which were brightly whitewashed - twenty or so – clustered on a handful of level terrains, each structure fenced by rambling, mortarless, rock walls. The doors, shutters and window frames had been painted in primary blues, reds, and yellows. The bold outlines conveyed the possibility that passions might flourish inside, like joy, rage or even sweet sorrow.

"Bright colours," said Michael. He looked to the others for confirmation, but neither traveler commented.

They hefted their packs and walked the dirt road out the village. Kiwi took a mouth organ from his shirt pocket and played. Michael kicked at the dust. John followed dragging a numb foot – his ball and chain.

Michael said, "What a place to live."

They sat near the end of the village on the edge of the road and leaned against their packs. They watched a solitary hawk glide on updrafts, becoming two when its shadow reeled by cliffs of white stone. They looked down into the valleys, perhaps a distance of a half-mile, their gazes held by flocks of sheep dotting the lush pastures below.

Kiwi said, "Just like home, green, green, and millions of sheep."

John contributed to the conversation, "Ireland's got a green that I never saw before."

"Where are the shepherds?" asked Michael.

John squinted. He could see them now. He pointed for the others. If one moved, it seemed like a rock got up and walked. Quietly, he repeated the phrase several times to deposit it in his memory bank, *A rock got up and walked.*

Michael squinted and said, "Oh yeah."

Michael rummaged in his packsack and brought out a journal. He checked his watch and started an entry. He wrote quickly, one page and another. When he looked up, he asked, "What do they think about all day?" Neither of his friends answered. He went back to writing in his journal.

The travelers looked toward the village when an engine started. Their ride headed back down the mountain. Michael dug into his packsack again and brought out a mitt and baseball. He threw the ball up and caught it.

He turned to Kiwi and said, "Do you want to catch some pitches?" Michael had been a pitcher on his university team in Colorado; he had once hoped to do the sports beat on the Denver Post. Since Athens, they had learned many details of his life.

Kiwi said, "Sorry, mate."

Michael turned to John and asked, "What about you, John? That leather jacket you wear means you were an athlete, right."

After a time, John said, "I think the Spartans lived around here...maybe the gods too."

The sun dropped below the mountaintops and the valleys darkened. The long shadows of the late afternoon washed down one hillside and up another and the travelers watched as the shepherds moved their sure-footed animals to higher ground. As they climbed toward the village, the sheep grew whiter and the flocks grew larger, each group mingling together at the intersections of paths and trails. Safely bunched at last in an immense flock, the shepherds in groups of twos and threes, all filed quietly by the travelers. The beasts scuffed and bumped the dust from the road. Those ruminants packed too tightly popped above the road and trotted for a while on the backs of their brothers and sisters. There were a few black animals and a few brown. Balls of dung hung from the wooly backsides of the unshorn. Michael waved to the shepherds, but got no response. Each shepherd carried a staff with a distinctive crook. A unique signature, thought John. As they moved away, the solitary taps on the red earth road reinforced his thought. John took out his journal, unable to break the habitual pattern, and wrote, *a rock got up and walked.* The sheep and the shepherds disappeared in their own cloud of dust. The falling sun offered a shimmering hue to the drifting haze. John wrote another line, *solitary taps on the red earth road.* He put his journal back in his packsack. It had been a productive day, upwellings and gratuities from the depths. He got his journal out again and wrote, *disappearing in their own dust.* Damn, it had been a *duende* day! He was certain there was the making of a poem in those three fragments.

Once at the village, the shepherds corralled the sheep inside the rock-walled courtyards. They entered their homes and soon a yellow illumination could be seen through the windows. Occasionally, shadowy figures disturbed the pale glow. The fading light sucked the bold colour from the doors, shutters and window frames. The buildings took on a finish of pale alabaster. Stars appeared in the heavens, ones, twos, and then galaxies.

THE MOUNTAINS WERE BACKLIT.

Kiwi said, "We'll get a big moon."

Michael pointed. "Why don't we try that bigger building…it might be something."

The travelers moved toward the bigger building. There were no signs; nothing telling them what might be inside. They saw a weak light shining through a high window to the right of the door, and as they got closer, they heard soft music and bits of laughter. Sheep crowded around the entrance and a mist hovered over the animals. *A mist hovered over the animals.* My God, thought John, another page for my passport home.

They weaved through the quiet flock. They needed to push with their knees and lean with their thighs to get the reluctant beasts to make way. Then John had another dazzling flash of insight: I'll call the collection, *Passport Home.*

John arrived at the door first. He knocked, but got no response. Music continued to play and the sheep pressed heavily around him. He worried the animals might trample his numb foot. He worried that he might suffer pain and not know it. *Unconscious pain is the greater hurt.* He thought this mountainous place was still filled with the creative energy of the ancients. He amended this latest fragment, *The greater hurt is unconscious pain.*

In the poor light he could barely see the latch, and when he grasped the lever, it felt warm and wooden – smooth to the touch like a crook-necked staff, he thought. He had expected a cold, metallic sensation. John lifted up, then down.

Kiwi said, "It's a slide."

John tried again. The latch shifted smoothly and he opened the door. A slit of light blinded the travelers though it was merely a gas lantern pulsing in the middle of the taberna. The music stopped. The laughter stopped. John tried to turn back, but Michael pushed on his backpack and he stumbled into the room.

A man stood behind a bar to the left of the door cleaning a shot glass with a rag. He looked up, saw the hitchhikers, and returned to cleaning the glass. Beside the bar, another man sat in a chair with an accordion resting on his lap – the bellows open. Candles burned on wall sconces around the perimeter of the room and they illuminated poorly the faces of the shepherds standing or sitting at tables. Those men closer to the centre of the room, where the lantern hissed and fizzed, had quit their board games. They pulled on long moustaches, fiddled with drinks, and plunged their dark eyes into the hearts of the strangers.

Michael was the first to speak. He took a step toward the bartender and rubbed his stomach and said, "Eat." He lifted his hand to his mouth, as if it held a glass, and said, "Drink." The bartender rubbed the shot glass with his rag and then held it close to a wall sconce for better inspection.

Michael turned to John and said, "What's going on?"

"Maybe we should go back onto the road," said John. Was that not always the thing to do - the thing to do until his poems could be bundled into a neat package and presented to Earle who had forced him into exile?

A voice came from a back corner of the taberna. The shepherd didn't speak loudly enough for the foreigners to hear the actual word - they may not have understood anyway - but they did hear the menace in the tone. The same Greek spoke again, but louder, "Aleman." Then he kicked an empty chair. The chair tipped over and collided with an occupied chair at another table. Another shepherd kicked the chair. The chair bounced against a wall. Another voice grumbled, "Aleman." That voice got up and walked to the chair and kicked it once more. *Voices got up and kicked a chair.* The bartender now had a bottle of Retsina in his hand and slammed the heel on the counter. He stretched out a mean, guttural growl – "Germania!"

"They think we're German, we're too blond," said Kiwi. The three travelers were fair-haired, but not blond.

"It's the beards," said John.

"Lots of people wear beards," said Michael.

He took another step into the room and slapped his chest with the flat of his hand.

He said, "American." He slapped his chest two more times, "American, American."

He moved to Kiwi and gripped his arm, "New Zealand." Kiwi pulled his arm away. Michael put his hand on John's shoulder, "Canadian." He repeated, "Canadian," and then, "Canada."

The shepherds returned with shouts of, "Aleman" and "Germania."

"Show them your flag, mate," said Kiwi.

John took off his packsack and pointed to the flag. He yelled, "I'm from Cortes Island - Canada." John held the packsack higher for all to see. The three travelers joined in a chorus of "Canada," and soon heard a lone echo from the back of the taberna – "Canada, Vancouver."

John moved in that direction through the crowd of angry Greeks, forgetting for the moment that his foot was numb and may in fact hurt. He saw a man tapping his chest, "Vancouver."

"Vancouver…you've been to Vancouver?" said John.

"Bruter."

"Brother – you have a brother…in Vancouver?"

"Vancouver – Bruter."

John turned to his friends and said, "He's got a brother in Vancouver."

The Greek rubbed his flag and shook both his hands. He pulled John's beard and slapped his back. The Greek with the brother in Vancouver clutched John's sleeve and wouldn't let go. Others in the taberna shouted, "Vancouver." John turned to his friends again, "I think he wants to know if I know his brother."

John and the Greek hugged. "It's a big city. I might not know him."

The Greeks toasted Canada and the travelers toasted Greece. The bartender's young daughter appeared and brought bread and lamb stew for the hungry travelers. She honored John by serving him a larger portion of meat and he guessed he was singled out because he hailed from Vancouver, or close to it, anyway. The music started up again – three musicians playing the mandolin, balalaika and accordion – and the shepherds danced in circles, *shepherds danced in circles.* The more adept ones kicked and twirled in the middle of the room. *Kicked and twirled.* John now realized that these fragments had become his flock and he had become their shepherd. There would be one moment in time when each of his flock would organize themselves into one spectacular pattern. He hoped to be wise enough to recognize that state of perfection.

Mainly through gestures, the crowd urged the travelers to sing or dance – it didn't matter. Kiwi performed a ceremonial Maori war dance. He stuck out his tongue, bulged his eyes, constricted his nostrils, slapped his chest and stomped his feet. During the performance, he accidentally kicked a chair and the chair landed in front of Michael who also kicked it. Soon everyone kicked the chair around the room. When it was John's turn, he told himself that he could kick harder than anyone because his foot would not feel the pain. He did not really kick the chair, he stomped on it with his numb foot, and the chair collapsed separating from its legs. With that grand display of ruthlessness, he became the night's hero. The Greeks could not restrain their congratulations. In such a few moments, he had become a throw back to the ancients - the guile of Odysseus, the strength of Zeus, and one of three who held the pass at Thermopolis. Then Michael sang *Some Enchanted Evening* from the Broadway musical, South Pacific, and received a standing ovation. And John sang, *Oh Canada,* but had to start the national anthem over three times before he could remember all the words. He attributed his poor performance to the Retsina.

When the taberna closed, the bartender invited the travelers to sleep at his home again using signals - clasped hands against the side of his tilted head. On the way out, the Greek with the brother in Vancouver gave John his sheepskin vest. John took off his own jacket, a faded, cracked leather heirloom from his football days, number 34, and gave it to the Greek – a snug fit for John and loose fit for the Greek. Everyone had drunk far too much wine. Only much later the following morning was John able to reconstruct what had happened in the bartender's house during the night.

EVERYONE SEEMED SOLEMN IN the morning. John thought the family quiet, but not unfriendly. For breakfast, the bartender served strong black coffee, bread and large portions of white cheese. They ate before daylight at the family table. The mother and daughter stayed in the little kitchen and prepared the food. None of the travelers had much of an appetite, but they drank the coffee. Michael mentioned that they should get out on the road so they wouldn't miss a ride. After many "Efkhareesto's," and some group photos that Michael insisted on taking, they walked back to the edge of the village to wait for a ride. The morning was cool and drizzly. When the shepherds walked by with their flocks, they exchanged subdued greetings of "Vancouver." Then they descended into the lush valley for a day of grazing and solitude. And thoughts of lost opportunity. The continent of sheep turned into an archipelago as they spread into the valley bottoms and soon the shepherds solidified as rocks on a boulder-strewn hillside.

While they waited, John remembered the line from the afternoon before, a *rock got up and walked*. He mentally amended it, *a rock stood and walked* - his critic had no respect for rest. Even so, John was too tired to open his packsack and correct the entry in his journal. In fact, he was too tired to remember all the other wonderful fragments that had flashed through his mind the previous evening.

A truck rumbled through the village and stopped for the hitchhikers. They climbed aboard and headed down the mountain toward the sea.

Hours later, the cool morning air had the effect of reviving the travelers. John tugged on his sheepskin vest trying to cover his throat and chest. Over the engine noise, he heard Michael complain that the Retsina had tasted like cleaning fluid. Kiwi replied that it would have been disrespectful if they had refused the wine.

Michael said, "In America you don't have to drink that much wine to gain respect."

The word "disrespectful" allowed John to follow the winding road into his memory.

HE REMEMBERS STUMBLING INTO the bartender's home. The mother and daughter had greeted them. John rubbed his stomach to indicate that he enjoyed the stew. They had smiled so he was certain they understood his meaning. The father pointed to a section on the floor of the big room. He clasped his hands and tilted his head. They were to sleep there. That much was clear. However, John couldn't recall just how, but he ended up in a small room. The father remained with Michael and Kiwi, but the mother and the daughter joined him. Due to the low ceiling, he couldn't stand up straight. His neck ached and the sheepskin vest cut into his armpits. Those discomforts made him more aware of the numbness in his foot, which didn't hurt. The packsacks were in the big room and he thought that if he slept in the little room, then he would need his sleeping bag.

He said, "I need my sleeping...," but was interrupted. Suddenly, a blanket had appeared in front of him. The mother unfolded a wool blanket and spread it on the floor. He moved into the corner of the room, as there was no place to lay it out. She motioned for him to look closely, so he squatted, and that felt better getting away from the ceiling, but the squatting increased the numbness in his foot. He thought, I guess there are degrees of numbness. Then he realized, They think my sleeping bag won't be warm enough. She spoke quickly and held the blanket for him to examine. This time he thought, They want me to admire it. He said, "That's beautiful," and with his fingers traced the design that edged the blanket. It felt oily. Then he thought, Of course, the sheep. He reasoned that by feeling and rubbing the blanket, they would understand better from his gestures, rather than his words, that he admired the blanket, as well as the skill that had gone into making it. However, he could not refrain from saying "warm" and "very warm," in an attempt to reinforce the sincerity in his hand and finger mimes. He said "warm" to the mother, and she smiled, but she looked at her daughter who was now kneeling beside him, and she smiled too, so he turned to her and said, "Very warm."

The smile must have meant that the daughter made the blanket. He wished his friends would come and look. They should admire the blanket as a way of thanking everyone for their hospitality. He was trapped though, coiled into the corner, and unable to look through the doorway or wave his friends in.

He saw more blankets. They were folded and piled neatly from floor to ceiling. That's why it's so crowded in here, he thought. The mother took the blanket from him and gave it to the daughter, who folded it carefully. The mother took down another and spread it out. He rubbed this new blanket and traced the design with his finger. This blanket was brown and the design white. When he thought back he could no longer remember the colour or design of the first blanket. She was speaking quickly again and pointing at her daughter and pointing at the rugs. Are they rugs? he thought. Finally, he understood. They wanted him to buy a rug.

He said, "Quantos drachmas...how many drachmas?" The mother waved her finger, as if to scold him. She put her finger to her lips and then to his lips. She firmly pressed her finger against his lips. Nevertheless he still managed to say, "Oh...oh your young daughter made the rugs."

The daughter looked embarrassed. Her fingers rubbed the same blanket that he held. He thought it must have taken a long time to make all those rugs. She must have started when she was very young. He thought again that the others should see the rugs, too. He called out to his friends, "Come and see the rugs."

Kiwi answered, "Do you know what you're looking at?"

"Rugs."

"Something else."

"What?"

The mother spoke quickly again, interrupting their conversation. John heard the father speak to Kiwi. Then the father appeared at the doorway to the tiny room and handed John his packsack. John took the packsack and said, "Efkhareesto," and finally realized that he had been correct and they wanted him to sleep in the rug room.

He heard Kiwi again, "John, they're blankets and its her room."

John said, "Who...whose?"

"Mate, can't you see what's happening? Come out and kip with us."

John struggled to his feet and bumped his head on the ceiling. He looked down on the daughter, who was biting her bottom lip, which he now realized was painted dark red. Lipstick stained her teeth. She gripped the corner of the blanket and her knuckles had turned white. She was not nearly as young as he had thought. Certainly older than him. Lines creased her face, especially radiating from her watery eyes, and more noticeable when she bit her lip. She wore a bright orange sweater, and of all things, it looked acrylic. He noticed breasts under her sweater and childbearing hips under a pink acrylic skirt.

He stepped over the blanket, ducked under the doorway and limped into the big room carrying his packsack.

Sorry…compromiso…pardonez…no posible. Two hands crisscrossing. Not ever possible.

THE AIR WAS WARMER now. They had traveled many miles towards the sea. Now that he understood the events of last night, John began a debate with himself during the descent.

The affirmative said, "You could go back to the village. She would look after you and you would get your own flock of sheep. You could write poems while you tended your flock. You could prove that rocks think and feel and tingle."

The negative challenged this notion and said, "You haven't finished your journey. Many roads await the sound of your footsteps. The whole village would want to move to Cortes Island. Your struggle has only begun."

Then he heard Kiwi and Michael talking. They discussed the Cuban Missile Crisis and Michael asked Kiwi to explain why the protesters in Europe had been against the blockade. The American said that it didn't matter where he went since coming to Europe, posters were plastered everywhere. "CUBA Si! YanKees No!"

Kiwi interrupted Michael and said, "Give it a rest…there's the Aegean…and look at all the sheep."

John brushed the hair from his eyes while looking in the direction Kiwi pointed. It took only a moment to understand what he was getting at. He saw a panoramic line, drawn with the precision of a draftsman, separating the open sky from the great blue sea. A few clouds scudded above, but on the water's surface, the whole Aegean ruffled with luxurious whitecaps – *an immense flock ruminating in their blue pasture.* Without their shepherd.

his words, and then his words, and now my words

1964 May

HE DID THE MOST sensible thing in his life. John went to Israel for R & R and lived on a kibbutz a few miles north of Haifa. The administration gave him light duties in the kitchen as they quickly realized that his foot would need to heal before he could work in the orchards and carp ponds. Miriam, the kibbutz doctor, who spoke seven languages, massaged his foot daily. In his minimalist way, he told her that the frostbite occurred while on a mountaineering adventure. She did not inquire further, but encouraged him by saying, "If you can get the blood circulating freely, then the numbness will lessen and your handicap will be minor."

She spoke to him as she massaged - vast, long monologues, always about Israel, the sites he must see including the Wailing Wall in Jerusalem that she thought of more as a "curiosity" than a holy place, because, "not many of us are religious any longer," and "you must take in the Dead Sea," and the salty shores of the fabled and wicked cities of Sodom and Gomorrah, and "climb to the top of Masada to see where the Sicarii rebels resisted the Romans for seven long years before they en masse committed suicide" and "you must see the beautiful beaches of Aqaba and swim in the warm waters of the Red Sea" and on and on. He must experience the "grand collective spirit of a nation" with sole purpose and focused energy teasing life from the desert, providing manna to all, no longer relying on the "magic" from the Old Testament, and instead creating a new improved society, "a real modern experiment gaining the admiration of the world."

During this uncomplicated time he made some sense of his journal and experimented with the fragment phrases he had collected recently in Greece and elsewhere. He spent many hours assembling the fragments much as one would put together a jigsaw puzzle – a blue piece here, a red piece there, find the interlocker. On occasion he thought that many of his efforts showed signs and shapes of actual real unadulterated poetic potential, of course not yet polished enough for a review by Earle, but, at least, he made progress. He slept well, ate well and worked hard. His cadaverous frame added flesh and muscle in all the appropriate places. His mind was not nearly as crazy; thoughts were relaxed and mundane, at least some of the time.

After three months, they assigned John to the carp ponds and then to the banana plantation, where the crew tested him in various ways. He won the banana contest, consuming thirty-three, whereas his opponent quit at twenty-seven. He thought the bananas tasted like candy. In the transplanting contest, he managed to dig up, root-and-leaf prune and replant in the adjoining field one hundred and eighty-six banana trees over an eight-hour blitz, whereas his opponent managed only one hundred and seventy-five. His foot felt better and his hands and fingers worked perfectly. He recognized that this jousting with the crew served as a form of initiation ritual.

One of Miriam's minor duties was to insure that John integrated into the social fabric of their communal life. She arrived at his room most evenings or intercepted him as he tried to sneak out of the cafeteria after dinner, and she insisted that he go with her to a concert, a lecture, a sports event, or a stroll in the commons, though more often than not, he would have preferred to stay in his room and work on his portfolio.

One day he said to her, "I enjoy solitary moments."

And she said, "We don't encourage that sort of thing here, John. People who crave privacy usually end up with a mental illness of one sort or another."

He could not think of an adequate reply, so let the matter slip. Talking, interacting, after these long years of silence did not come easily. He soon began to think of himself as the perfect inmate with a distant view to parole.

Saturdays were the day of rest. Frequently, Miriam took him on outings to Haifa. Usually they went to see or hear a cultural event – the doctor was big on symphonies. One afternoon she took him to the windowless Holocaust Centre, which honored victims of the death camps. She said, "If you want to understand Israel, you have to understand what the Nazis did to the Jews."

He assumed she would go into the museum, but she preferred to wait outside. Miriam also insisted that he take as much time as he wanted. "Don't rush through the exhibits, I have the biography of Beethoven." She held up the book for him to see.

Inside, the Centre was colourless and dark. Thousands of black and white photographs hung on the walls, many cloaked in a black mantle. The white walls had faded badly. The tattered pages from journals and letters had turned grey or pale yellow. The fragments of clothing, children's dolls, drawings and paintings had abandoned their hue leaving the viewer to imagine what the object looked like in better times. Two-thirds through the exhibits, while John was reading an English translation of the daily journal of an inmate named, Marta, who expressed her horror and shame in accepting a food ration from her father, Miriam appeared beside him.

She said angrily, "You're going too quickly."

They retraced their steps to the entrance and began again, this time with Miriam as guide. She displayed an intimate knowledge of the museum. She remembered statistics, an actuary cum laude, able to spout rote numbers without glancing at charts, an automaton without emotion reciting population totals by country and camp, breakdowns by age, countries of origin, sex, education and occupation. As they moved from the general to the particular, the formal to the personal, back and forth between the black and the white and the grey, Miriam appeared unable to move beyond one particular display – a small collection of primitive, miniature cloth dolls, moth-eaten, sucked on, undernourished, under-dressed, endlessly repaired and hairless, seemingly victims themselves. Miriam's catharsis manifested as a grand mal seizure; her convulsions found their crescendo as in the 9th symphony, eyes rolled in her head and her head banged against the concrete floor. She wailed a single, high-pitched, glass-shattering note, while John tried to restrain and comfort her. Attendants appeared and helped them to the recovery area, a comforting place of stuffed chairs, endless pots of tea, and shaded lighting. Miriam had been there before, a familiar face. John learned upon leaving, when one of the attendants whispered to him, "She never gets beyond the dolls."

Travelling back to the kibbutz on the bus, Miriam recovered sufficiently to apologize for the outburst. "I'm deeply sorry for my behavior."

John replied, "Your behavior doesn't require an apology."

She said, "Maybe so."

He asked, "Why do you go, if it upsets you so much?"

After some thought, she said, "John, going through the Centre is the only way I can recharge my rage."

They sat quietly as the bus followed the shoreline of the Mediterranean heading north. Finally she said, "Those of us, who still live, need rage in order to survive. All of us are like this. Rage is as necessary as food and water."

That evening after dinner he retreated to his room for a session with his journal. He wrote line after line, *rage is as necessary as food and water,* until he filled a page. A page of rage. He closed the book and wondered, Is rage necessary? In general, in Miriam's case, in my case? Have I been hurt enough to require rage for my physical, emotional and spiritual being? Do I qualify in the same sense as Miriam?

He opened his journal again and drew a line down the middle of a page so that he had two sections. On the left side at the top he wrote the heading FICTION and on the right side he wrote FACT. He entered *rage is necessary* on the fiction side. Then he entered *rage is not necessary* on the fact side. Then he inverted the two statements on the next line down and continued inverting the statements all the way down the page as if he might be playing the children's game, "She loves me, she loves me not."

The following evening his host allowed him to go to his room and enjoy time with his mind. He read from Rimbaud. "I am a beast, a savage. But I can be saved."

And he read, "I have left behind souls whose suffering will increase at my going." And he read, "I am an inferior race from all eternity."

Miriam knocked on his door.

"John, I came to apologize for yesterday."

"You already apologized though it was not necessary."

"Even so, might I come in and talk?"

He lived in a Spartan room: small cot, a lamp, a dresser and a wooden chair - functional without a trace of emotion or personality. She sat on the chair and he on his bed. She saw the two books beside him and asked, "What are you reading?"

"A collection of poetry by Arthur Rimbaud and that is my journal." He pointed at the journal.

Miriam said, "I wanted to apologize for something else."

He couldn't imagine what other apology there might be.

"What is the something else?"

"I haven't given you the privacy you deserve. I have used my authority on the kibbutz to manipulate you. It is true that the kibbutz places a social expectation on all of us to always be together, at least, in two's and three's, and even better in larger groups, but I have taken advantage of this peculiarity in our collective life. I have used up your evenings and days off, because, I need to temper my rage, because I can't be alone with myself, because I can't kill my aloneness no matter that I try…and because one of those little dolls was mine, and another belonged to my little sister."

He had suspected something like this, though the realization had not surfaced so that he might actually see it.

He asked, "Is your sister gone?"

"Yes, all my family."

"So is mine."

"I am sorry about that."

"My father and mother. I do have cousins though."

"Did your parents die in an accident?"

"My father died in a boating accident when I was very young and my mother…she died recently from the usual things."

"A broken heart?"

"Either that, or a broken dream."

A broken dream.

He did not want to detract from her story, or imply that his story was as momentous as hers. Because it wasn't. How could one compete? And why would one compete? His story, her story…what value were they?

John added, "If I know one thing, it is that time takes too long to heal our wounds."

"Of course, in a sense, you are right, but that should not dissuade us from snatching the odd moment to temporarily forget our feelings, like I have done with you."

John surprised himself that he had so easily become intimate with her. Her needs dominated their relationship - or so he thought.

They were quiet for a few moments. In his opinion, their conversation had become too intimate too quickly, and if continued, would go farther and farther, much farther than either of them wanted. He did wish, though, to say that his aloneness needed killing, just like hers, but lately he had suspected that aloneness was the given condition; all his existential readings supported that conviction and his wanderings supported that idea too. So, bathe in the solitude. If you are able.

He added *baptized in solitude* to his collection.

Miriam picked up Rimbaud and unmindfully thumbed through the pages.

"I probably needed time to repair in a safe place," John said, "so that in the future I might again be alone with myself. Surprisingly, the distractions of socialization on the kibbutz are not so difficult for me and I feel better knowing that they have given you some relief from your thoughts."

"What you say is almost comical. You think Israel is a safe place?"

"I simply meant that it is safe for me…at this moment. Safer than being out in the world doing silly things, especially when one is so vulnerable."

"Are you thinking of leaving us then?"

"Yes, now that I am stronger."

"Have you considered that you may not be as strong as you need to be? Often the return of strength can be an illusion."

The return of strength can be an illusion.

"This is possible, but I must press on with my obligations: the silliness, as I called it earlier."

"I was hoping you might want to become a permanent resident. I know a few of the younger girls here who might step out of their clothes for you."

"I don't think that would ever be possible."

She asked, "Is there someone at home, who burns her light for you?"

"No."

She may have sensed from his terse reply that this discussion made John uncomfortable, or that he had made up his mind, so there was no point in dissuading him.

Miriam then asked, "Where will you go?"

"I need to return to Kilimanjaro."

"The mountain?"

"Yes."

"Why?"

"I left something up there and need to retrieve it."

"What would that be?"

John picked up his journal. "You see this. I left three others on the mountain. They were my oeuvre. The totality. They represented everything that I had accomplished in my life. I must get them back."

"Why did you leave them there, John?"

"It is a long story and I have never told it before…I have never prepared to answer this question."

Now there was a pleading tone to her voice.

"This isn't a test, John. Would you try, even if you don't tell the story perfectly? I need company tonight. I need to forget about Israel and forget about the past. At least for this evening."

So this is how they would say good-bye. He would give her the gift of his story in order that her mind could rest – a temporary relief from the European nightmare and the newer one that had become Israel.

John had been leaning on his arm. He sat up on the edge of the bed and cupped his hands, elbows on his knees. He leaned forward and began to speak, all the while focusing on the pale, plain, tile floor. Possibly on that blank canvas he could see his story reveal itself image-by-image and word-by-word.

JOHN CHOSE EVERY WORD carefully.

"It was earlier in my travels. Nearly two years had gone by. I had tired of Europe and wanted to experience things that few from the West had seen before. As well, Europe was not giving me enough material for my journal, and as I recall, I wanted to breath the freshest of air, thinking it might be a homeopathic of the highest order. I sought a cleansing.

"There were other motivations too. The book you hold; he is my preferred poet, and when about my age, he journeyed to Africa, where, of all things became a slave trader. He eventually lost his leg to gangrene and soon died there, leaving us with a whimper and not the bang, which might be expected from such a creative mind. The simple explanation, if ever there is one, was that I concluded he had gone to Africa to find something, which apparently he did not discover, yet that thing, whatever it might have been, must still be there. So, in a sense, I planned to take up his search and apply it to my own purpose. Are not all journeys searches?"

John paused, expecting Miriam to answer the question, forgetting for the moment that this was no longer a discussion.

He then said, "The story's turning into a muddle isn't it?"

"Not at all, John. Please go on."

He continued.

"Before we start up the mountain, I need to clarify one other thing. Rimbaud is my chosen poet, but my father, who was a fisherman, was also a poet, and I suspect a very good one, so I have reservations in giving this accolade entirely to the Frenchman. If we had access to his work, my father's, that is, certainly a judgment could be made, but that is not possible as all of his poetry, his entire life's creative achievement, was destroyed in a fire."

He hesitated again and debated if he should explain the details of the fire. Should he explain that Mother Meredith had responded to the tragedy by destroying her husband's poems, that during John's entire childhood, whenever he was home from boarding school, he scoured the house, searched in the drawers, looked under the rugs, thumbed through books, and even peeled back sections of loose wallpaper. Often he interrogated his mother about the possibility that she had missed a fragment of a poem until her rages of laughter silenced him. *Rages are necessary.* John rejected the turn down that road, as that detour would never get him to Kilimanjaro.

"There were other reasons for this journey into Africa, eventually targeting the mountain. While in Paris, I visited the famous English bookstore on the left bank of the Seine, immediately across from Notre Dame Cathedral, *Shakespeare and Company*, which had been a meeting place for members of the Lost Generation, including the great writer, Ernest Hemingway. There I picked up a collection of his short stories and the one I enjoyed most was, *The Snows of Kilimanjaro*. The story opens with the following description of the mountain – I have memorized it: *Kilimanjaro is a snow covered mountain 19,710 feet high, and it is said to be the highest mountain in Africa, its western summit is called by the Masai 'Ngake Ngai' the House of the God. Close to the western summit there is the dried and frozen carcass of a leopard. No one has explained what the leopard was seeking at that altitude.* The thing I found most intriguing about Hemingway's story was that Kilimanjaro, the mountain, only got one mention, though it was the title of the story, and that was near the end, when, Harry, the main character and a writer by trade, who, like

Rimbaud, is dying from a gangrenous infection in his leg, sees the mountain in the distance, and I have memorized this part too, *ahead, all he could see, as wide as all the world, great, high, and unbelievably white in the sun, was the square top of Kilimanjaro. And then he knew that there was where he was going.* I might say too, that the leopard was never mentioned again in the story. Why I touch on all of this is because Hemingway gave me a direction to follow, a target as I said earlier. One could say that Rimbaud gave me Africa, but Hemingway gave me Kilimanjaro."

John paused to collect his thoughts. He noted that Miriam had a hint of a smile on her face, which he took as an indication that the story was going nicely.

"Hemingway's short story was about dying and anger, and on another level, about the death of the writer's art. Here is another quote that addresses the point – I might say that I have memorized many passages in the story, having read it many times over the years. *Now he would never write the things that he had saved to write until he knew enough to write them well. Well, he would not have to fail at trying to write them either. Maybe you could never write them, and that was why you put them off and delayed the starting. Well he would never know, now.*

"The account of Harry's last days, nursed by the woman, Helen, who desperately loved him, was interrupted frequently with short vignettes, and these were presented more like ramblings in Harry's mind, but must have been Hemingway's real drafts that he had saved for that day when and if he reached top form.

"I suppose there are less mindful reasons for climbing Kilimanjaro; just to say you did it, to experience the shivers and tingles when walking on the roof of the world, to stare wide-eyed into the mouth of a volcano, to breathe far above the clouds, to be so close you can touch the sun and on good nights the stars, and to trespass, if only fleetingly, into the home of a God. After reading *The Snows of Kilimanjaro*, and as I got closer to the mountain, I fantasized about finding the leopard. For me, locating that dry and frozen carcass had somehow metamorphosed into the search for my own voice. In my mind the animal had taken on an importance greater than the mountain itself."

John looked up from the floor and asked Miriam, "I know there is little logic in anything I have said so far. Maybe even no interest?"

Miriam answered this time. "I'm sure you thought you were being logical about the why of the thing. Being alone with oneself, tricks us into creating worlds just for ourselves, worlds that prevent access by others."

"So, it's all preposterous?"

"Yes it is, but most of life is preposterous and that's what makes it so interesting."

"And heart breaking."

"That too."

"Well, now you know why I chose Kilimanjaro, but you don't yet know what happened up there."

"We don't hear stories like this in Israel, John."

"My journey into Africa was an adventure in itself, even before the mountain. With some fellow road bums, whom I travelled with for a short time, I slept atop the pyramid, Cheops, outside the capital city of Cairo, a practice run for the main event. And clamored around on the Sphinx too, *slouching towards Bethlehem*, as William Butler Yeats called the *rough beast*. And I was lucky enough to arrive at Abu Simbal on the shores of the Nile to see the deconstruction of the ancient Ramses monument and then the start of the reconstruction of the megalithic rocks above on the cliffs overlooking the great river. It would have been such a calamity if the flooding of the Nile, due to the construction of the Aswan Dam, had proceeded without this intervention. Imagine if today the only visitors to the site were very experienced deep-sea divers. And in Ethiopia, I woke one morning with a deadly adder sleeping on the warmest surface he could find – my chest – until the heat of the sun encouraged him to move on for the day. I saw all the amazing animals grazing on the Great Plains, and imagined, as I walked through long stretches of Kenya, that the spirits of our original ancestors walked with me and marveled at how adept I was, traversing upright and easily, reminding them that bipedalism had always been their life's quest.

"In one sense the mountain is an easy climb, taking only four days to reach the summit. I went alone, though I knew an expedition was ahead of me and another would start in a day or two, following well tramped trails through jungle, onto stunted trees and sparse vegetation, a vast section of grassland, always a ridge to climb and always the expectation of the first glimpse of the lower peak, Mawenzi, and then a heightened impatience to see the highest peak, Kibo. At about 4000 metres I began to experience altitude sickness: weariness, headache, inability to breathe easily, unquenchable thirst and sleepless nights. At 5000 metres, I suspect I was seriously ill, however, I did not recognize that my symptoms were all that grave.

"There is a barren plain that separates the two peaks stretching about ten kilometres. Kibo sits across that expanse waiting for you, wanting to embrace you, seemingly square as Hemingway describes. Her sides are covered in snow like a billowing white skirt, which at times is so bright you can't bear to look at a thing so ineffably chaste. My objective was to make the crossing during the course of a day and then camp overnight before attempting the summit. Even though the rise in elevation was minimal from one side to the other, my altitude sickness increased. The headache grew intense and my legs became leaden. I had to stop often - perhaps every ten paces - and rest. There were large erratic boulders strewn along the pathway leading to the crater and on some of these I would sit. On the bigger ones I would lean up against, or sit on the ground in their shelter. They were peculiar rocks, each unlike the other, unique in shape and colour and texture. For whatever reason, they reminded me of abandoned dreams.

"While sitting beside one of those strange stones, I realized that the only way I could continue would be to lighten my load. First I drank all my water, thinking foolishly of course, that I would find a small stream on the other side of the plain. Then I cleverly thought that I should eat much of my food – only save an emergency ration, one tin of sardines, which I envisioned cracking open on the summit and consuming just as the sun rose wet and steaming from the Indian Ocean. I believe that my mind convinced itself that if I carried my food inside me rather than in my packsack, it would be much lighter. If not lighter, then at least the weight would not be noticeable. Soon nausea set in and it wasn't long before I had vomited the whole mess onto the ground. Lastly, I decided to take only what was necessary for the final assault. I kept my rolled sleeping bag and ground sheet in my pack but all else I emptied on the dusty trail - a few sets of underwear, a pair of socks, a shirt, a measly collection of toiletries, sundries, utensils and books. At the time, I carried the collection of poetry by Rimbaud and the collection of short stories by Hemingway and the three journals, which contained my incomplete and raw portfolio of poetry for submission to a university professor at the school of creative writing back in Vancouver, Canada.

"I reasoned – it seemed like reason to me - that I would pick up these things on the return. Since the most important item was my portfolio, I decided to take the extra precaution of hiding the journals rather than leave them on the side of the trail with the rest of my gear. I stumbled a significant way off the path and discovered an even more unusual rock which was pocked with holes - presumably carved by the wind over millennia, or some other aberration of nature. One hole was large enough to hold the journals. I worried that they needed protection from the elements even though I would pick them up next day, so I stumbled back to my packsack and took out the ground sheet. Then I returned to the *Rock of Holes* – that's what I have called it since – and wrapped my journals in the plastic sheet. The package fit snuggly into the hole. It occurred to me to make a map of the area, however, I rejected the pre-caution as I thought it would be easy to find such a strange rock. So I pushed on, now giddy that I felt so much better and had done such a clever thing. It appeared, to me at least, that my mind had finally achieved top form and soon I would be in receipt of the treasure I had so long searched for.

"It took but minutes for the fatigue to reassert itself and soon I crawled on the path - as did our first ancestors - occa-sionally scooping up a tiny patch of ice or snow to feed my thirst. I persisted though, and by the end of the afternoon – it took about six hours to cover the distance to the base camp of the volcano – choose a spot to rest. I had learned earlier that the preferred way to climb the final 1000 metres was to wait until midnight, as then the snow and ice would no longer be soft and slushy from the heat of the equatorial sun. The moon rose as night fell, so that the transition from light to dark hardly seemed a factor.

"I remember eating my can of sardines and I do remember wondering why I was so cold in my sleeping bag. I remember starting the climb when the moon was brilliant above, and as I climbed, the pain from my headache vanished, and my legs felt light and strong. I began thinking of the leopard, dried and frozen somewhere on that hillside. Just as Hemingway had wondered, I too wondered what it was that fascinated the cat that he had ventured to these unimaginable heights. Why had he persisted in such an alien place until he was no longer able to continue? My thoughts of the leopard turned to obsession, so the objective of reaching the summit was not only dismissed, but also no longer considered. Instead, I remember investigating likely places where the cat might have come to his final rest, giving no regard for whether I went up or down or sideways, a manic search was on. I had no consciousness of my body; it was my mind that roved and scampered over the hillside convinced that it, my mind that is, would discover, not just the leopard, but the mysterious thing he had been seeking.

"I woke from an unconscious state in a small hospital in the town of Moshi on the Tanganyika side of the mountain. Apparently, the group ahead of me, who were coming off the summit just as I was crazily searching out the leopard, had rescued me. They also found my things on the dusty plain where I had left them and that is why I still have Rimbaud and Hemingway too, which is in my packsack now. They did not bring back my journals.

"My recovery from altitude sickness, hypothermia and frostbite was slow and complicated by a strange phenomenon, called the laughing epidemic, which had started in a local boarding school, and then spread through the towns in the area, and lasted, I have been told, for a number of years. I only mention this strange event because the hospital was in the clutches of the disease during my stay there and the spontaneous, uncontrollable outbursts of laughter and giggles by the staff, as well as the patients, left me unable to get a handle on my own reality, or theirs, for that matter. Curiously, I was never infected with bouts of insatiable and incapacitating laughter, being immune for whatever reason."

John looked at Miriam.

She got up from her chair and extended her hand to John. She said, "I can tell from your grip that your hands are better just like your foot."

He opened and closed both hands a number of times, "Yes, they are better."

As she left his room, the doctor turned and said, "What a shame that you were immune and did not introduce the contagion to Israel."

BEFORE LEAVING THE KIBBUTZ, John promised Miriam that he would retrieve his journals, but neither foolishly scale the peak of Kibo, nor go on the insane quest for the leopard. As if to scold him, she said, "Go straight to the *Rock of Holes* and then come down the mountain. No detours."

Miriam also asked for a "slice" of his poetry, a tangible reminder of their relationship. He had never parted with a single word, but could not refuse her petition.

a hurried handshake
the parting unanticipated
would they remember the other
care for the other
was this the consequence of light splitting the atom

a wheel rolls over the universe of dreams

1964 November

HE TRAVELLED FOR AN entire night and most of the following day across the immense Nubian Desert on top of a cargo truck driven by an expatriate Italian. During the night they used the stars for navigation and during the day they followed ruts in the sand road. The nighttime temperatures cooled to ninety-five degrees Fahrenheit, whereas the daytime temperatures soared above one-hundred-thirty. They arrived at a small village somewhere in the northwest of Ethiopia. The others riding with John - Sudanese and Ethiopians - climbed off the truck and sought shelter in a mud brick building where tea and minimal offerings of food could be purchased.

The driver encouraged John to join them. He spoke some English, "Get down. The sun fries the brain."

John shook his head. The disgusted driver made the sign of the cross and entered the building muttering catholic profanities.

John would not have been able to get off the truck anyway. His joints ached and his limbs would not move. Through his clothes he felt the sun searing his flesh. Even so, chilly shivers forced his body into spasm.

Beside the truck a skeletal child stood, *wearing only the dust of the road*. A villager approached the boy and positioned him so that he faced in John's direction. The man tilted the child's face for John *to see the eyes that were not there* and he lifted the child's arm, hand and finger to point accusingly.

The villager retreated into the shadows of another building. The child began his refrain. "Signor, I have no eyes."

The child repeated his statement, never modulating tone, never diverting his sightless gaze from the object of his futile hope, and never lowered his accusing finger. Soon the mere act of repetition – "Signor, I have no eyes" - adhered desperation to itself. No longer was this an immaterial statement of fact that floated upon the anonymous desert air, but a personal indictment against John. The boy staked his whole existence on this one phrase; five foreign words – one Italian and four English – comprised his single tool to a respite from hunger and disease. This, John imagined, was the child's best effort. If the foreigner did not respond, then he would become indistinguishable from the dust on the road. Armies of flies crawled over the boy's head, in and out of his mouth, yet never obstructed his vocalizations. They migrated up into his nostrils, buzzed in his ears, noisily tapped on his eardrums, burrowed into the gaping holes intended to capture light, but these distractions did not discourage the child from his performance of the one line play.

As intended, the simple statement of fact became an allegation. Soon John understood completely that he was responsible and knew that his sole opportunity for atonement was a charitable act. He remembered his emergency rations in his packsack, which consisted of six tins of sardines and a few stale crackers. He thought, I am in the play, the stage directions require that I give the child my food, nothing could be clearer. If I give the child my food, when prompted, then the play will have reached its climax. I think I will give him all my sardines. And the crackers, too. I will not save one tin for myself, not one cracker … and then I'll continue with my journey.

Now there was rage in the child's voice. *A voice of rage.* "Signor, I have no eyes."

John took the abrupt change in emotion as his prompt to present the sardines and crackers, but then quickly realized the other problem that had emerged. He could not move; he could not reach out to his packsack and give of the fish and give of the bread. The child screamed his line again, and John, the disciple caught in the nightmare of being unable to give of his flesh and give of his blood, thought there might be a way out of this impasse. All he need do was create an improvisation for the script. He tried to say, "Child, there is food in my packsack. It is yours, you must come and get it." Too bad, John could not recite his line, even though he remembered it. His tongue had swollen in his mouth.

Distracted for a moment, and with a good deal of alarm, he watched his journal of impending poems crawl from the packsack, and mysteriously suspended, vibrate in the scorching air. He watched his newly manicured portfolio cleave its lines from the pages, and they then fell like a shower of delicious, dark, Belgian, chocolate shavings onto the dust of the road. And he watched each line splinter into phrases and further into solitary words and pile around the child, to the depth of his ankles, to his knees, so quickly his skeletal torso was drenched in the mountain of words assiduously collected over the years of wandering and searching. The flies, unaccustomed to swarming words with wings, panicked in their own black cloud, and that allowed John's brilliance to finish the job of drowning the child, who was now choking on an inedible sustenance and gurgling his final and only line, "Signor, I have no eyes."

Pristine pages. The search for anthracite. The purpose of journey. A hungry child consumed by a creative act.

NOT YET TIME TO trace a chalk line around the body. From his plunge into this new abyss, he mustered yet another resurrection in order to finish his worldly chores.

John recovered from sunstroke after a month of dedicated care by the villagers. Initially they applied damp cloths to his entire body surface and cautiously sprinkled water over his parched lips. As he grew stronger he was able to take fluids – water, a weak herbal broth, and later, a grey gruel. The delirium and fever abated and the paralysis in his joints disappeared to be replaced by tolerable aches and pains. During recovery, he spent much of his time leafing through his journal. Thankfully, the gestation of his portfolio had not been aborted; all the words and phrases were still there. He realized that the sightless child had not drowned in his words, and in fact, had never existed.

AN ENTIRELY PLEASANT PART to the recovery process took place. John's father appeared to him in recurring dreams, something that had never happened before. He drove John around their back yard in a wheelbarrow and John loved those rides. Soon, he and his father, JJ, as he had been known by his fishermen friends, schemed a collaborative effort whereby John would accelerate the gathering process of fragments and phrases and his father would take charge of the assembly process. A team effort. He assumed his father would use a more efficient method than his own jig-saw-piece-by-piece approach. Perhaps, this division of labour had always been in place, though never activated until now; the part of John yearning for a fatherly hand, and the flip side, the gift by John - or was it burden - to finish the life his father failed to complete.

One day a truck arrived in the village and he boarded for the next leg in his journey. As payment for rescuing his life, he gave the village elder three hundred dollars – half of his life savings.

EACH RIDE SOUTH TOOK him closer to Kilimanjaro and further from his confusion. Near the border of Ethiopia and Kenya the truck stopped for minor repairs. John and the collection of black riders got off to stretch their legs and relieve themselves. Scrub brush dominated the semi-arid countryside. Walls of dense thorny vegetation lined the sides of the riverbed, which, now, in the dry season, substituted for the road. John walked a short distance from the truck in order to have privacy while he pissed. Curious, the black men followed. John began his business – a long hot continuous stream into the thicket. A little unusual, the thicket shook precisely where he watered the good earth and then John heard an anguished roar. A large male lion brushed by him and stopped in the middle of the road to swipe with both front paws at his steaming wet head. Then he rumbled off into the brush carrying the wounds of an aspiring poet.

His fellow travellers made more of the incident than John could have imagined. From the safety of the truck they jabbered in Swahili. John recognized their word for lion, *simba*, but nothing more. Even as the truck continued on its way to Nairobi, above the engine noise and diesel exhaust, they spoke rapidly – debating, arguing, haranguing. Frequently they pointed at the man who had pissed on a lion, until it seemed a consensus had been reached. They took turns approaching him, crawling over the cargo in order to touch the man who had discredited simba's power. They touched John on the shoulder, the sleeve, his pant cuff, head, often more than once, it didn't matter where, as long as they touched. Even when the truck stopped to let off passengers and take on others, the newly arrived were informed of the sacred personage aboard and they too made their short pilgrimage hoping to acquire the magic that dwelled inside the strange man. John hardly understood his fame, though he did take the incident as a sign that this time the climb to the *Rock of Holes* would be successful. Rimbaud and Hemingway would lead him and his father to their final triumph.

FOR FISHING VESSELS.

From .... to .... Trip No. ....

COMPASS	DISTANCE BY LOG	GEAR RUN	ESTIMATE OF CATCH	WEATHER
	$80\frac{42}{5}$			
	$\times 8$			417
N 6103	643.36			16
	66.72		2502	
9ª 6103	710.08		417	
	41042		6472	

Cover comforter
Sink pad & soap dish
Get bobby socks

Rod Steele
944 E 61
Phone Fraser 3636

Bill Bayshore
Phone. Fair 11987y

da co ho, da spryng, da sok i eat da hay rin fysh

1994

NOW THAT HER HUSBAND, Will, spent whole weeks in Sechelt looking after his aging mother and her two sisters, Marne Archer found herself with a promotion - the reluctant and *defacto* manager of their Cortes Island shellfish operation. September would end soon and soon there would be no daylight tides to work their twenty-acre beach lease on adjacent Marina Island. The couple hated winter night tides - the cold, the dark, the wind and rain, wolves howling beyond the arc of their lantern light, icy toes and fingers, daunting boat rides and the chronic prospect of calamity. They always tried to get their Luddite labour done during the summer months, seeding of the clams and oysters, the culling of predators like starfish and rock crabs, and the without-end cluster busting of yearling oyster cultch. With these projects completed, they would need only to go twice weekly in the middle of the night - November through February - to harvest their standing order, almost a picnic, as Marne imagined, like a fun filled repeating dream of finding money. This year, however, since they were hopelessly behind in their work due to Will's frequent absence, she insisted on hiring help, a thing they had never done before and always pledged never to do. As Will anticipated being away much of the fall, he agreed to her proposal and suggested she do the hiring.

Marne put an ad on the bulletin board at the Mansons Landing community hall. Next day Bradley and Jim Jenzen appeared on her doorstep. She was aware of Will's cousins, but had never met the brothers. She knew that Will and other sons of the *Arrogant* crew had gone to the same boarding school in Vancouver, had even worked together at a barrel factory during their summer holidays, but her husband had never lavished upon her the details of his earlier life. Convincing him to unveil the deep heart's core was akin to having a conversation with a rock.

Brad said, "We saw the ad for beach workers." The brothers wore cut off jeans, T-shirts and gumboots.

Then Jim volunteered, "pa frum corteez so we cum 2 do resurg." Marne noticed a deep purple birthmark on his forehead, which travelled down his cheek and neck. He was very short, a tiny adult with a lean muscular body and heavily shadowed beard. She thought he might have a disability as well as a speech impediment. Bradley looked a few years older than Jim, in his late forties, tall, strong, heavy set, perhaps the same age as Will. Marne invited them in for tea.

They took their boots off on the porch and she pointed for them to sit at the kitchen table.

She asked, "Where are you living?"

"With Aunt Maddie over at Seaford," Bradley replied.

Marne knew the old and reclusive Maddie Archer, but hadn't seen her in years.

Jim chimed in, "ant maddie gots lotsa lubers."

Not wanting to follow the many roads of island gossip, she said, "Will will be so happy to see you again, Brad."

Brad replied, "We've been at Refuge Cove for quite a few years, ever since our mother died. Finally, we're here."

"I'm sorry to hear about your mother."

"It's what she wanted," said Brad.

"r moms lookin 4 pa cuz we put da ashes in da oshen."

"That was a fine thing to do," said Marne.

Wanting to redirect the conversation, she said, "What kind of tea would you like?"

Jim replied, "gotsa b nae bob t."

Brad intervened, "Our father drank Nabob tea, so Jim is pretty much partial to that brand. Any kind is fine."

Jim said, "Da milc gotsa b car nae shun."

Brad intervened again, "Our father always used evaporated Carnation canned milk on the boat so that's why Jim is keen on it. Any kind of tea or milk is fine."

Marne put the water on to boil and laid out her tea service and spoons. She said, "Will and I usually drink green tea without milk. Is that okay?"

Brad said, "That's fine."

Jim laid his head on the table and pulled on his unruly tuffs of hair. His head quietly banged on the table, rattling the cups and saucers. Brad took a book from his jacket pocket and said to Jim, "Here, read your storybook." Jim sat up in the chair and flipped through the pages. The uneasy tension dissolved.

Brad said, "He'll be fine now."

Relieved that the storybook could have such an instant effect, Marne relaxed. She noticed the book was cloth-bound and presumed a judiciary red in its earlier days, which had now faded to dark maroon – only small blotches revealed an approximation of the original colour. Threads drooped from the edges and the binding had come unglued. If there had ever been printing on the cover, the words had long since vanished with the wear of time. As Jim turned the pages, many of which had come loose, Marne noticed that they were yellowed and brittle. Fragments had broken off.

Bradley may have anticipated Marne's concern because he commented, "We have to repair it nightly."

Before she could formulate a response, he added another thought, "If we can't stop the deterioration, I mean, if it becomes ultimate, then we'll be unable to construct a meaningful future."

That comment alarmed her. Up to this point, she had assumed that only one of the brothers had a disability, but now, Bradley had manifested this impenetrable reference to the storybook. How did one respond to a sentence like that? She hoped she had not walked into someone else's nightmare.

She poured the tea, neglecting the necessity for milk. She would ask three questions: did they have previous experience as beach workers, would they be on the island for long, what were their expectations for wages? From any of the answers, she hoped to formulate a legitimate excuse for not hiring the brothers.

Then Jim said rather triumphantly, "told u." He placed the storybook in front of Marne and pointed to penciled entries on a back page. She saw a grocery list, which read, while Jim repeatedly stabbed with his thumb at two of the items, "2 case Carnation Milk, 4 lge Nabob tea." When Jim gauged that she was suitably impressed, he took back the book and thumbed the pages again, commenting occasionally, "told u."

Now that Marne had an improved view of the book, she realized that it was not a storybook after all, but a journal or log filled with indistinct entries made in pencil. As Jim meandered through the pages, she caught glimpses of printed headings, which indicated columns for daily records of sea conditions, estimates of catch, distances run, gear used, and names of headlands or place.

Perhaps, thinking that she had taken an interest in his book, Jim looked up at her and proudly said, "i gotsa wurd book pa gib 2 me da wurds is myn cuz da book is myn." A convoluted statement but comprehensible to a degree, thought Marne.

It seems Brad also assumed she had an avid interest in the book, as he said, "Jim, show her how you can read."

Excited by the possibility, Jim said, "wat paig?"

Brad said, "Why don't you do grocery."

Jim said, "no like gro ry 2 day."

Brad made another suggestion, "What about gear run?"

Jim asked, "febry?" and his brother said, "Sure, do February."

Jim closed the book and held it above his head in one out-stretched arm and began, "feb 5, hayrin, feb 6, hayrin, feb 7, hayrin, feb 8, hayrin, feb 9 wunder poon…" He continued his recital of February while Bradley informed her that they both had read their father's log so many times it was no longer necessary to actually pretend one was reading. He added that Jim didn't read in the true sense. Marne assumed that once Jim came to the end of February, he would lower his arm and quit the recitation. Instead he looped back to "feb 5" and took another sojourn through the month, never lowering his book or arm, showing no sign of discomfort. She wanted to encourage them to drink their tea so that she could intervene at an appropriate moment with at least one of the questions prepared for the impromptu job interview. She hoped that by looking at Brad with a helpless expression he might take a cue and free them from the awkward moment.

Her look set him in motion, but not in the way intended. "I suspect (began Bradley) that our father resorted to artificial gear if his bait was old, or they had run out, or the fish had quit biting altogether. Lures like plugs or Wonder Spoons were simply a response to a desperate situation. Jim and I have done a number of calculations over the years - comparing fresh bait and artificial lures to volumes of catch and we now have established empirically that nothing ever performs as well as fresh herring bait. Most fishermen agree with our thesis, though this may be an intuitive judgment on their part, not at all grounded in the extensive research we have done. We could supply you with the data and analysis from our files if that is necessary."

Not knowing how else to respond, Marne nodded her head and said, "Jim, why don't you put your arm down and drink some tea." She reckoned he was on his forth orbit through February's "gear run." She had the bizarre thought that here was a mystic entranced with a recently discovered gospel fragment.

"When we were younger (Bradley continued over top of Jim's chant) the frequency of herring entries certainly captured Jim's attention and that is still the case. In the beginning, he would pester me, 'wat hayrin brad,' and as soon as I explained what a herring was, he would ask the same question again. As it seemed he couldn't remember my explanation, or his handicap prevented the processing of it, I was continually put in the unfortunate position of re-explaining until I verged on despair. Fortunately however, one night, while I settled him into bed, and as I recall following on his sixth question, "wat hayrin brad," I stumbled on a new tactic. I guess we were fifteen and twelve at the time.

"You see (Brad continued), I remembered a close up picture of a herring in an old National Geographic and I had a pile of the magazines in my bedroom. I went to my room, tore the page from the magazine and went back to Jim. Mother sat downstairs, content to let us do whatever we wanted as long as she was left undisturbed. I taped the picture to the wall above his pillow. Now, with Jim able to see the fish, I patiently explained, as I had many times before, a herring is a fish, a little fish, salmon are big fish, the big fish eat the little fish, herring are bait, you troll bait on lines and hooks, the salmon get hooked when they eat the herring. And so on. At the time I had a grownup feeling that I was teaching a very elementary course in fishing. Well, by taping the picture to the wall, I reckon we started something. Soon I was obliged to find pictures of all objects in the logbook: spring salmon, coho, pinks, chum, sockeye, bread, canned milk, cigarettes, coffee, salt (Jim intervened, 'dat a gro ry dey put on food,' and then returned to his chant) and tea. I even had to find a picture of a telephone for all the telephone numbers collected at the back of the book, which, incidentally, we have called in an effort to answer questions we had about our father. Initially I protested at his insistence that I take the brunt of visualizing for him - locating images when words worked just fine for me. You see he had me in the same bind as mother. If I pushed too aggressively against his will, then I was in for unrelenting tantrums. Nonetheless, as the weeks passed, the demands for more and more images grew beyond my ability to cope, so I insisted that our mother help. Surprisingly, she cooperated, as long as she didn't have to get near the logbook, which had a musty smell then, and triggered her allergies. Her participation, however, added a new wrinkle – a thing I enjoyed as it took pressure off my desperate searches for corresponding images in our father's logbook. Upsetting at first, she did not always ferret out correct and approved pictures as I had, but gave us labels from tobacco tins and empty cigarette packages – Players and Export A, which we have lately had it confirmed were the brands our father invariably preferred. You see, labels, were not a thing either Jim or I had considered. She provided us with an avalanche of Nabob coffee coupons, once in a while showers of Nabob teas, and many too many sprinklings of strawberry jams that she carefully peeled from empty tins. For a while she was the overwhelming source, the wealth of material, though her contributions, as I have mentioned, did not always conform to the project we had before us. In magazines that interested her, she found harbour photos of places like Vancouver, Victoria and Prince Rupert. She found a picture of Hot Spring Cove and one of Bull Harbour – all place names mentioned in the logbook. As you might imagine the walls in the room soon were covered. During this semi-cooperative phase, I would leave her a list of words collected from the previous night's reading and she would comment, "More home-work for the mommy." Our mother kept scissors on the table beside her chair and hummed as she did her cutouts. If she came across something of interest she would hum louder so we always knew when new material would be available. Then she'd yell to Jim, "gots dek rae shon 4 wal" and Jim would come running, "tanks mum tanks." I should mention at this point that she had started the descent into Jim-talk and in her final years spoke only this way. Increasingly though, there were times, when she over stepped the parameters Jim had prepared for us both; for instance, she sometimes insisted on things that could not possibly have been in the book. If I didn't realize the error, Jim immediately did, though I have never figured out how, and we then had to refuse the image, result-ing in retaliation from our mother, which in some instances exceeded in quality and duration Jim's best tantrum perfor-mances. These would have been things like cartons of maca-roni – a staple in our diet at the time – a picture of a perfume bottle, a flower, and so on."

At that moment, for whatever reason, Jim lowered his arm and quit the repetition of February "gear run." However, he resumed thumbing through the logbook. The termination of the chant seemed to be a signal for Bradley to quit his lengthy dissertation on herring.

Marne appreciated the silence, but found herself reluctant to initiate her prepared questions. She had the impression that Bradley had talked himself into a deep depression and didn't know what might occur if she disturbed his state. As the quiet persisted, she read between the lines, that Bradley had just spoken, and concluded that the psychic wounds from the boating tragedy had never healed; in fact, she imagined, they might have festered into an elaborate surrogate for memory that could only be formulated in a convoluted future. Marne was used to Will's depressions and his perpetuation of grief, but suspected that his struggles paled in comparison to those sitting in front of her.

Jim breached the silence. Addressing Brad, he said, "foun da wurd brad." With his small finger, he stabbed at notes scrawled in the middle of the page. The discovery did not garner immediate reaction from Brad, however, Marne's curiosity caused her to lean over and take a peak. She read the phrases, "cover comforter" and "sink pad & soap dish" and "get bobby socks."

"Very soon (began Bradley, as if Jim had released his pause button), Jim's tiny bedroom was covered in pictures and labels. The walls were painted blue so it was easy to imagine that you were looking into the ocean. One afternoon when Jim and I didn't have much else to do, we came up with a plan to rearrange all of our images. I decided to create a feature wall, whereas the other three walls would, for the time being, simply collect the flotsam and jetsam – those items that didn't fit yet, or those items, which were too few to tell a story. I should mention that over time we reorganized those walls too. Anyway, I painted a white line across the blue expanse and asked Jim to pretend that the line was the surface of the sea. To gain a heightened sense of realism, I fluffed up the paint to give the impression of wavelets. Next I took a picture of a troller, named *Leslie M* - as up to that point, we had never been able to locate a photograph of either of the *Prides*, nor the final vessel, *Arrogant* - and pasted it so that the sea's surface was level with the ship's Plimsoll line. I painted over the lower portion of the hull with more white and blue, so that the ship drew an appropriate draft. With the well-judged placement of tacks in the wall, I stretched fish line found in our basement at a forty-five degree angle from the boat to the depths. I added branch lines. At the ends of the lines I nailed rusty old hooks and then glued pictures of herring beside the hooks so that eventually fifteen lines were baited and operational. At each herring, I placed a spring salmon ready to strike the bait and was particular about using spring salmon because they commanded the premium price during the war years. I should mention that all this construction didn't take place in that one afternoon as we lacked the necessary number of pictures of salmon and herring, but over the course of a few weeks we were able to get the wall completed. I had gauged the scene so that the bait and the predator were swimming at Jim's bed-level and when he lay in bed and listened to my nighttime readings of the logbook, he could turn to the wall and look at the fish. As you might imagine, one thing lead to another, since neither of us have ever felt a sense of completion. We pasted a flock of seagulls flying about the boat, no doubt feeding on the offal thrown overboard, while our father cleaned his catch in the stern. I put up a sperm whale (Jim pointed at the words "sperm whale" for Marne) surfacing alongside the troller and not so far away we installed a giant squid threatening with eight long tentacles.

We rechristened the boat, *Pride 11*, and after about a year Jim insisted that I change it to *Arrogant*. I complied even though I suspected that he never got any of the pretending straight – that is, understanding that *Arrogant* was really the *Leslie M*, and not realizing that the log was not from *Arrogant* but *Pride II* and as well confusing the essential fact that *Pride II* was a troller whereas *Arrogant* a re-rigged tuna clipper. At any rate, we had a dolphin leaping into the air and a Mr. Wind with long hair and beard stuck up in the corner near the ceiling, who was trying to blow up a gale (Jim quickly interrupted, "not naem gyrl"). His little room had been so drab up to that point, but soon became a place where you wanted to be. We came to think of his bedroom as a gallery, and over the years the installations changed as we learned more and more from reading the logbook. As long as I took charge of Jim's room, cleaning, changing the sheets, making the bed, throwing out the dirty laundry for her to wash, our mother let us do anything we wanted. As you can now understand, Jim's demand for a particular type of realism forced us to enter into a lifetime of study and not just of the logbook either, but all facets of our father's life. The wall became the catalyst to move us farther, to explore and reassemble, to discover the minutia that collectively might take us closer to the father we never knew."

Brad hung his head again and went silent. Jim closed the book and gave it back to Brad. Both brothers stood up. Brad said, "Thanks for the tea." While they put their boots on, Marne asked, hoping for an answer from either brother, "What about the bobby socks?" Jim volunteered, "don't u no y we cum 2 da ilan, we gots 2 no bout dem sox."

when we get there, I'll leave you, but only for a little while

1997

WILL AND MARNE ARCHER live seventy miles north of Sechelt, seemingly a short distance from Cortes Island. On the eve of his journey south, Will reviewed their workload with Marne: spread the vexars otherwise the seed will grow into the mesh, pick seven more bags of smalls, dig another 50 pounds of manilas and get Burt to help deliver our order. There were a thousand other things, but he felt guilty enough asking her to do the minimum. As an afterthought, he said, "Gawd, you have to hire help, even if its Brad and Jim again."

Will said he'd be gone for no more than three days as the telephone calls from his mother and aunts had been only moderately hysterical. Judging by recent trips, Marne thought it more likely to assume a week.

He drove to the ferry line-up at 5:45 a.m. next morning. The ferry left for Quadra Island at 7:50. He counted the cars. He would get on, probably the second last car. On Quadra, he missed the 9:00 to Campbell River by six cars. He arrived in Campbell River at 10:23 and raced for the 11:15 out of Comox but missed it by a few minutes. He ate his sandwiches. He slept until the next sailing at 3:15 p.m. and arrived in Powell River on the mainland in time to miss the 5:25 out of Saltery Bay. He noted as they pulled into Powell River that Cortes Island was still visible to the north, that he had been travelling for approximately twelve hours, yet was only twenty miles from home - as sensible birds fly, that is. He caught the 7:30 to Earls Cove and drove the remaining distance in an hour to Sechelt getting to the compound at 9:45. Sixteen hours.

His mother slept in her chair in front of a blaring television. He turned it off. He removed the half full glass of rye from her hand and dumped it in the sink. He helped her to the bedroom and helped her undress. He covered her with the electric blanket and old quilt. He turned the blanket to medium and she was asleep again. She hadn't really awakened.

He walked across the yard and checked on Aunt Emily, known as Aunt M. She was asleep in her bed, the light on, an open book flopped on the covers and her cat purred at her shins. He hated the cat. He put the book on the night table and turned out the light. Then he crossed the yard in the other direction and checked on Aunt Maggie. She watched a crime show with the sound turned off and filled in crossword puzzles. He said, "I'm tired," and she said, "I bet you are." He would see them all in the morning.

WILL NO LONGER REMEMBERED the number of times he had made these trips to Sechelt. Perhaps in the seventies there were four trips a year, then eight in the eighties, and monthly visits in the early nineties. Now, as the new millennium approached, turn-around visits occurred more frequently. He wished his mother had never decided to move from Cortes Island to Sechelt to be with her sisters.

Inevitably, a trip to Sechelt was precipitated by a telephone call. Or calls. He pressed one on his speed dial and counted the rings. After fifteen or so, the phone was picked up, but no one spoke. He then said, "Hi Mom," and she replied, "I'm fine." Usually he said, "Mom, I haven't even had a chance to ask how you are." If she simply reiterated the "I'm fine" statement, then he knew she wasn't. If she chose a longer diversionary response, like, "I'm fine, what about you?" then he knew things were close to critical. If she skipped "I'm fine" and skipped "I'm fine, what about you?" and opened with, "How's your back?" he knew it was time to catch four ferries. To verify both the degree and nature of alarm, he then pressed two on his speed dial. When he inquired to Aunt M's health, she usually bypassed her own ailments with a comment like, "I'm fine Will, it's your mother who's not." If she went straight to the heart of the matter and said, "Will, it's Margaret," then that pretty well clinched the need for a visit. Aunt M would never directly ask him to come to Sechelt. Next he pressed three on his speed dial and Aunt Maggie straight away gave a litany of her complaints and complications, the listing of medications and dosages, side effects and the state of the medical system. If she resorted to the "I'm fine" trick, he could be certain a three-way calamity brewed.

A FAMILY TREE – Margaret, Maggie, Emily (Aunt M) – the living branches.

Will's mother is Margaret Archer, nee Kreelman, a widow who never remarried, eighty-six years of age, and the eldest of three living sisters. Her late husband, Bob, his father, was lost at sea fifty-two years ago. He doesn't remember the man, since he was three at the time the *Arrogant* and crew disappeared. His mother has never been forthcoming about his father. He has minimal contact with his father's side of the family, though a few of his remaining relatives live on Cortes Island. He waves to them as they drive by each other on the island roads, but then everyone waves to everyone.

The three living sisters purchased adjoining small Sechelt lots in the early 1970's and gradually moved on mobile homes retiring in turns: Aunt Maggie, Aunt M, then his mother,

Margaret. They call the properties the "compound" as they are bounded by a high cedar fence, which Will built. Initially, life inside the compound went on with little regard for the world outside; in particular, his mother and Aunt M kept busy nurturing their pioneer spirits. Each morning they pulled tight their bootstraps and walked quickly, or ran with ramrod postures, forgetting that retirement did not necessitate a hell-bent-for-leather gallop through the day. Aunt Maggie was not as infected with overdrive as were her two sisters. Will remembers hearing Aunt M discuss Maggie's failures with his mother.

M said, "Maggie should be in a Chekov play. She goes into instant depression for no reason and then wastes precious days with her gloomy thoughts. "

"We all have gloomy thoughts," said his mother.

"Of course we do Margaret, but we don't let them destroy our lives."

"Whose play would we be in?"

"I'll think about that while I weed the garden."

"I belong in *Riders to the Sea*."

"You're right about that."

Aunts M and Maggie have doublewides whereas his mother has a single. M was a World Health nurse, establishing schools of nursing throughout her career in Iran, India, Nepal, Tanganyika – now Tanzania, Burma - now Miramar - and Ceylon - now Sri Lanka. She lives on a comfortable pension. M is eighty-two, the youngest sister, and a career spinster, as she refers to herself. Aunt Maggie is the one with the musical ear, eighty-four, and a widow of fifteen years. She has a facility with money and lives comfortably on the small estate provided by her late husband. His mother's assets have withered and she exists solely on her Canada Old Age Security pension, Canada Pension Plan and Guaranteed Income Supplement. As the years trickle away, Will is obliged to help her financially, as indexing – the government's attempt to keep pace with inflation – invariably lags.

A FAMILY TREE – Monica, Megan, Karl, Archie, and the unnamed - the dead branches.

There were two older aunts. Aunt Megan, regarded by the living sisters as a tramp, died ten years ago. His mother often referred to her as the "whore" and often observed that her soul was blacker than the inside of a cow. Whenever Maggie heard this insult to her dead sister, she replied, "Margaret, how can you say such a thing?" Then M, more concerned with veracity than reputation, commented, "Well, its true." Finally Maggie conceded, "Yes, but one shouldn't say it."

Aunt Monica, the first-born, died sixteen years ago. She died in Michigan in a convent for the retired Sisters of the Order of Saint Mary and had taken her vows sixty-seven years earlier following the jilting from a lover. The living sisters agreed that in those days someone in the family had to become a nun and Monica's decision got them off the hook. Whenever Will thinks of Sister Monica, he is reminded of African elephants wandering off to die in a secret valley.

There was a brother, Archie, whom the sisters claim was illegitimate. Margaret called him a "bastard." Maggie called him "the black sheep." M said that both these statements were entirely accurate. Uncle Archie was a mean sort, who died one night at the age of forty-two gagging on his own vomit following the consumption of large quantities of rum. Will was eleven at the time. He was a participant in this history and home for holidays from boarding school. His mother had taken her brother under her wing and for a few months Archie lived with them, sleeping on a spare cot in Will's small bedroom. He remembers that his uncle's nightcaps most always included a bottle of rum before he fell into agitated sleep. Will slept through that particular night of his uncle's death unaware of whatever noise one makes in the final circumstances – choking, coughing? On waking he smelled the vomit on the floor and saw Uncle Archie with his hand cupping his mouth.

Aunt Megan had the inside scoop on Uncle Archie and claimed the putative father was not "Pop," but the boarder upstairs in their old home in Manitoba. "The top room," she said, and implied that she had been spying. Apparently, Aunt Megan boasted proudly, on occasions when she was feeling mean herself, that she had informed Archie of his paternity at age six, and the knowledge of this small indiscretion accounted for the failure of the man, husband, father and brother. M, perhaps in a lame attempt to rescue Archie's reputation, once commented, "Childhood tragedies stalk us through the years."

Karl, another brother, died of diphtheria at age nine. Six other children were stillborn or lived only a short period of hours or days. M called the totality, a "Baker's Dozen." All the children were separated by approximately two years, their birthdays falling in September or October. As a child, Will recalls Aunt Maggie once saying, "Mother got so used to having brats, she would be out stooking in the fields next day." He had to look up stooking in the dictionary. It seems she became so resigned to the notion of bringing children into the world that, once the labour pains reached the recognizable crescendo, she would simply say, "Let's get it over with." With little fuss the deed was done. Again as a child, he remembers her using that same expression for all the mundane demands in her world. Before each meal, attendance at church, the laundry, or a trip to the grocery store, she would say, "Let's get it over with." Once his grandparents had moved to the West Coast, he had stayed with them intermittently, as his mother tried to recon-struct a shambled life.

Thus we have a typical immigrant family - builders of the great Canadian nation.

HIS ARRIVAL IN SECHELT this time had been instigated by three fairly lucid telephone conversations: Speed dial one; (slurred words) "How's your back?" Speed dial two; "Your mother weeded the rose garden rather severely." As M put it, Margaret gnawed at the base of each rose bush with her dull secateurs and managed to hack each plant to a stub. She couldn't prevent the massacre. Speed dial three; "Margaret's in trouble. Thoughts fly out of her head at an alarming rate," said Maggie.

Though not entirely recovered from his sixteen-hour ferry trip, Will rose at six a.m. and made coffee and toast. While he waited for his mother to wake, he washed the dishes and dunged out the refrigerator. Milk and juices were stale dated. When he poured the milk into the sink it came in lumps. In the crisper he found celery, lettuce, tomatoes, cucumbers, green onions, and cabbage carefully cut and wrapped in paper towels. They were slimy, moldy, and rotten or dehydrated. He discovered the fresh produce in the garbage can under the sink and concluded that she got herself confused. Later, he learned from M that she had scolded Margaret for the state of her fridge. "Margaret, you grow penicillin better than Banting." His mother responded to M's wrath by spending an afternoon addressing the state of her refrigerator as best she could.

He threw out a jar of moldy strawberry jam and another of mango chutney impregnated with chips and chunks of white sealing wax. He found a distorted saucepan on the porch. M told him, "I forgot to tell you about thermal meltdown." And later, Maggie confirmed that indeed there had been a fire. Will vacuumed the mobile trailer. He cleaned the toilet and bathtub and did the laundry.

M came in at nine, and without greeting him, went into his mother's bedroom and shook her awake. "Get up. You can't stay in bed for the rest of your life." He learned from his aunt that his mother had to be forced to rise even though Margaret had always been a worker. M scolded Will for letting his mother sleep in. He ate breakfast with his mother once M left.

His mother said, "I had a stupid dream last night. Nothing but walking."

Will said, "Didn't anything else happen?"

"No, nothing."

"Was there anyone else in the dream?"

"I was by myself."

"What made the dream stupid?"

"I was grown up, but I walked like a baby."

"That's pretty strange, Mum."

"Like a baby, I couldn't count my steps either."

"Did the dream upset you?"

"The walking part was just stupid, but not counting upset me."

"You've always been a number person."

"Exactly."

During his four-day stay in Sechelt, he played crib with his mother who still managed a reasonable game. The stakes were a quarter a game and in the end he was only ahead by a dollar. He said, "Like usual, you're ahead by a dollar, Mum."

She spit at him and said, "You cheated."

He bought new rose bushes at a local nursery and then replanted the bed. He pruned the trees and shrubs and cut the grass in the three yards. He cut to the ground the Montana clematis, which shrouded M's gazebo. He repaired the pull chains on M's lamps; she had ripped them from their switches. He repaired the sliding doors to the clothes closets; M had ripped them off their runners. He cooked the meals except for breakfasts, and they always ate as a group at Aunt M's for lunches and dinners.

He met with a health nurse and they made arrangements for a care worker to come each morning and help his mother get up, wash, dress, take her medication and eat breakfast.

In the afternoon, she would come again to insure that more medications had been taken, and she would also help prepare supper. He learned, a few weeks later, that M discontinued this service as she thought it too expensive, though, due to his mother's income level, the service was free. When questioned about the wisdom in the decision, M said, "I've administered whole schools of nursing; Margaret only needs to ask for help."

He arranged for a Lifeline to be hooked to his mother's telephone. She only needed to push the red button on the side of the phone each morning. This alerted the call centre that everything was fine. If the call button wasn't pressed by 10 o'clock, then a continuous beep went off. If the button wasn't pressed after fifteen minutes, then an attendant was dispatched. As it turned out, M pushed the button each morning. "I got tired of the beep, beep, beep...it didn't seem to bother Margaret."

The nurse gave a technological gadget to his mother to wear around her neck. She was to push it in the event of an emergency. He discontinued that service when he discovered the loss of the alarm a month later. Both sisters suspected Margaret threw it in the garbage, though they had neglected to inform him. Will took his mother to see the doctor. Together, they agreed it was time to look for a facility. The doctor guessed she might have Alzheimer's, but that diagnosis could only be confirmed by cranial autopsy. "And we don't want to do that," said Dr. Conroy. The doctor decided to put her on a new medication. "It can't hurt," he said. Will visited a number of care services in the area and found the Westmount Inn, an assisted living centre. He put his mother's name on the waiting list and paid a $200 deposit - forty-sixth in line. Maggie scolded him for not getting her higher on the list, "You could have been more assertive."

Cocktail hour at M's provided the enjoyable part of his visits to the compound. He poured the drinks. Scotch for M. Brandy for Maggie. Rye for his mother. He drank scotch while he made dinner. He tried to limit them to two drinks each, but found they needed a third, since, apparently, he mixed weak drinks. The conversations drifted into recollections of the past. He enjoyed hearing about the "olden days" and found that his mother was surprisingly with it, when they spoke of her childhood. He learned, for instance, that Pop, his grandfather, was a poor provider, and only the indomitable will of his grandmother, her constant berating and badgering, got him off his behind. It seems Pop much preferred to play his fiddle or solitary games of chess. As children, they had smoked cigarettes in the parlor where he played chess, and never once in all those years did he notice the smell, nor the three of them blowing smoke in his face, or the butts in the ashtray beside the chessboard. His mother recalled gleefully, "We swiped the cigs."

When Will asked, "Didn't you ever get caught by grandma or your older sisters?" His mother said, "Never."

That same evening they launched into the wicked sister routine and revealed the peccadilloes of Aunt Megan, the whore. His mother said, "She shoved her breasts up the nose of every man that ever walked." M agreed that Megan had large breasts. His mother said, "We all do." Maggie added, "Oh, Margaret, how can you say such a thing with Will listening."

Then Maggie described how Aunt Megan always felt the face of every man, feigning that with her poor eyesight, "feeling" was the only way to know what a man looked like.

M added, "And those fingers lingered."

And his mother added, "And those fingers didn't just touch the face."

They persisted with the Megan routine through dinner. Will had prepared baked red snapper, peas, squash, mashed potatoes and salad. Maggie and his mother recalled how, when only eight and ten years of age, Megan took them to a hotel, and they were told to wait outside a room while Megan did whatever she did with a soldier.

M said, "I never heard this story."

His mother said, "Room 22."

M asked, "Why did she take you with her?"

Maggie didn't know, but his mother did, "She was babysitting us, remember?" As a teenager, Will recalled Aunt Megan greeting him with her lively fingers and touching a bit too amicably – no doubt, trying to get to know him better.

Before returning to Cortes, he told his mother that she needed more care, thus the arrangements for a care worker, the Lifeline, and the inclusion of her name on the waiting list at the Westmount Inn. She said that her sisters could help if ever she had a problem. He assured her that both M and Maggie had their own difficulties, and that while they may want to help, neither could be relied upon. He suspected his explanation was unappreciated.

He caught the ferry from Gibsons to Horseshoe Bay and there boarded the ferry to Nanaimo on Vancouver Island, drove the island highway to Campbell River and made connections to Quadra and the last ferry onto Cortes at 7 p.m. The Circle Tour complete as advertised by the B.C. Ferry Corporation; in total, eight ferries. No matter how one sliced it, a day shot each way. He arrived home at eight to learn from Marne that she had employed Brad and Jim Jenzen again. They fought for approximately two hours even though he had given her the "green light" on hiring the brothers. She learned from Will that Bradley burned down a large section of their boarding school and was indirectly responsible for the death of the janitor. She learned that Jim was born with two broken collarbones and a crushed skull, perhaps on the eve of the sinking of the *Arrogant*. This information implied that their resumes did not get top marks, though it seemed they were still good workers.

By way of defense, Marne said, "How am I supposed to know any of this? You never tell me a thing."

Will countered by saying, "I don't tell you a thing because I don't know a thing."

"You just told me a thing or two."

"I only know a thing or two because I was there for the fire and Brad and I were friends and he told me about his brother. I meant I don't know anything about a vast chunk of the past because there has been this damned conspiracy of silence."

Their argument took place around the kitchen table while they drank their green tea. Following a few moments of quiet, Will said, "They always talk about the past. That's the only enjoyable part of being away. But they never talk about what I really want to hear."

"Maybe one of them will answer some of your questions...I mean before it's too late."

"I doubt it."

Marne shifted their talk back to business, "Brad and Jim are strange."

Will said, "You need younger people."

Marne gave Will a list of the jobs that were accomplished during the last three tides. She said she paid them twelve dollars per hour even though they agreed to work for ten. Will read over the list.

In due course, he said, "Brad was always pretty adept physically...even though he was fucked up in every other way. We worked together in a barrel factory one summer and he could out work me and John."

Marne said, "Brad's good, but little Jim's better."

That night they fell asleep in each other's arms. When Will began to snore, she rolled over onto her side of the bed and put in her earplugs. Her last thought before sleep was that the brothers knew lots about the past, perhaps point zero one percent relevant.

FOR SOME TIME WILL had been thinking that their health fluctuated with the seasons. Their ups and downs created a wave pattern cresting in the spring, troughing in the summer, but not spectacularly so, another rise in the fall, but never as high as in the spring, and finally a long slow descent throughout the depths of winter. When he analyzed further, the seasonal pattern remained consistent, and if he plotted all their yo-yoing, the yining and yanging, on a graph, and looked at decades rather than years, the general direction over time trended on a downward slope.

In the most recent telephone conversation he learned from M first and Maggie second that his mother had gone berserk. She backed up the toilet three times in one day. Maggie suspected a reaction to another new medication. From M's perspective, given her background as a Sgt. Major nurse, she felt that Margaret was simply being difficult.

IN EARLY NOVEMBER, HE gave instructions to Marne and set off on another circle tour. He used the Cortes ferry ride to dispel his mind of the many chores that begged attention. He used the Quadra ferry ride to briefly dream - only a fifteen-minute crossing – about the things he had always wanted to do. Work less. As he missed the Comox ferry - he always did - he chose to sleep. Once en route to Powell River though, he found a quiet seat beside a window with a view south to the Strait of Georgia. Soon a tunnel bound his vision so that he could see nothing but empty ocean. He could have been anywhere on any sea, a conscious speck on a vast watery universe. Over the many trips to Sechelt, he had found that his effectiveness with the three aged women was best enhanced by this psychic preparedness. If he lost himself in the vista of the sea, if he induced a stupor before the sea, where nothing ever happened, where the sea was uninterrupted with boats, drift or points of land, then this mimic of meditation – he could not say how – gave him strength to face what lay ahead. On the final ferry from Saltery Bay to Earl's Cove, he spent some moments thinking about the Jenzen brothers. He agreed with Marne that they were good workers, but he didn't agree with her that they knew anything meaningful about the past. Their behavior around the logbook broached on the absurd. A few weeks earlier the brothers had engaged him in a convoluted theory that their father had anticipated everything and used the log as code to communicate with his sons. And now they spent their days, searching for lilac coloured bottles filled with sap from fir trees. They felt as though they were on the verge of a huge discovery. Seeing Marne drawn into their psychosis upset him most.

During the final stretch to Sechelt, he concentrated on his driving skills, allowing the crazies to pass, slowing at the many curves, arriving at 9:40 to find the same scene – mother in chair with half full glass of rye, M asleep in bed and cat on shins, Maggie with crosswords and silent TV. Perhaps there were minor differences from previous trips, but he was too exhausted to notice or care.

His days in Sechelt started out much like others: the lawns, a vast weeding program, turning compost piles, mulching fallow beds, deadheading perennials, another full frontal assault on the Montana clematis, cooking, crib games, updates from the care worker, shopping, culling the fridge, and errands. He noticed, when there, that the fear and panic in the voices of his two aunts lessened. Their complaints about his mother were not as vehement and they relaxed into their chosen routines. He saw that he had a lifetime position as maintenance manager if only applied for.

His mother spent her hours in the bathroom or the bedroom and he coaxed her out with excuses of one sort or another.

"Do you want to play crib?"

"Where are the garbage bags?"

"Put your jacket on and show me where to transplant the azalea."

The first night he cooked Wally and Bill's Bean Casserole, a recipe he learned during his bachelor days, which included any kind of tin of bean, as many as one had on hand, strips of fried bacon, a pound of fried ground round, chunks of canned pineapple, melted cheddar cheese, and tremendous quantities of sweetener including ketchup, brown sugar and maple syrup. While he prepared the casserole dish, M decided to make oatmeal and chocolate chip cookies. While mixing the recipe, she couldn't remember if she had added flour so threw in two cups. "Extra flour won't hurt," she said.

While the cookies baked, she found the two large cubes of butter she had earlier set out to soften. The doubled-up flour and butterless cookies turn out weird.

During cocktail hour and dinner, the conversation centred on euthanasia. His mother joined in the discussions less frequently, but when she did, she still, more or less, had a comment worth considering. The euthanasia chat came about when the three of them had watched a TV documentary concerning the legalization of the practice in Holland. The program apparently had followed the last six months of an aging terminal patient and his devoted wife, the state's intervention, the requirement of safeguards, legal documentation, and the personal point of view of the attending physician, who could only do two or three of these cases a year to allow time for positive moments when babies were delivered or cures effected.

M said, "It would never be the kind of thing you'd want to specialize in." Maggie recounted the final scene in the couple's apartment with the doctor, terminal husband and wife. "There was a religious tone – candles, music and farewell bouquets. Even though neither of the couple professed to any particular faith, it was the most beautiful service I ever witnessed," said Maggie.

"Yes, it was," said his mother.

"The Eskimos used to do it on ice flows," said Maggie.

"Kill the old ones off first," said his mother.

"There were so many times all I wanted to do was give a patient an injection," said M.

"Why didn't you?" asked his mother.

"I didn't, but I wished I had, and I suspect, in fact I know, doctors did it more than you'd expect."

The conversation reached a point where everyone needed to reflect. Will dished out the rice pudding. He gave his mother an extra dollop of maple syrup. They ate quietly. M had recently purchased a modern cuckoo clock. Each quarter hour a small bird chirped. Each hour a larger bird cawed or screeched. When a warbler chirped, the three sisters turned to the clock and then went back to their pudding.

Will noticed that his mother paused for a long while with a full spoon of pudding suspended near her open mouth. Occasionally, she pursed her lips like a fish out of water. He imagined her brain now a mass of shorts and tangles. They all watched her, anticipating the moment when she would take her spoon of dessert, but she put it down and said, "Angels of death."

M immediately made the connection and replied, "No, they're just ordinary doctors."

He poured out brandy for everyone. Maggie and his mother moved to the living room. His mother pulled the afghan over her lap and kneaded like a cat. Maggie worked on a word puzzle in the newspaper. A baseball game played on the TV with the sound off, but no one paid attention, as it wasn't the Toronto Blue Jays. Will and M cleared the table and put away the leftovers, labeling and dating each container before putting them into the fridge. They washed the dishes. M told him about a Dr. Pfizer, who had been a good friend. She described how he had administered his own lethal injection.

She said, "When they found him, he sat upright at the base of a tree and his forehead was bound to the tree with a scarf so that he couldn't fall forward."

When Will asked why, M said, "He knew he would heave and wanted to insure that he drowned on his own vomit."

Will asked why he did it and M didn't know. As they worked on the pots and pans, she said, "When I was in India, I learned all about the Hindu lord of death, Yama-bunta."

Will inquired, "What was special about him?"

"He presided over his court in hell and made sure that there were always lots of recruits."

From the living room, he overheard Maggie ask, "Margaret, what was the worst swear word you used as a child?"

Will poked his head around the corner so that he could hear better what his mother would come up with. She stopped kneading the blanket and looked at the ceiling. After a long wait, he decided she wouldn't answer and went back to the dishes. Maggie resumed her puzzle. Soon he heard his mother's reply, "Bugger."

Maggie said, "Me, too."

M walked into the living room and said, "Margaret, do you know what buggery is?"

"What?" asked his mother.

"Its unnatural sex, its sodomy, doing it with an animal," said M.

Moments later Maggie said, "Just think of all the people we called buggers, even the priests and brothers."

"Some of them deserved it," said his mother.

Indeed, thought Will.

He excused himself and went to the bathroom. He closed the door. And locked it. He turned the light off, as he didn't want to see himself in the mirror. The darkness gave immediate comfort.

On the second day, he thought over the euthanasia conversation and wondered if there was a remote possibility that they had worked out a secret pact. He wondered if M had the necessary equipment and would she be the one to administer the injection or pills because of her nursing background. Would the task fall to her as the youngest? That evening, near the end of the cocktail hour, he asked, "Would any of you ever consider euthanasia?"

M quickly answered, "Of course not."

They watched a baseball game. His mother played with Kleenex tissues, tearing them into tiny pieces and rolling them into wads. In the ninth inning, with bases loaded, a tie score, Toronto at bat, two out, his mother said, "I once knew someone who put their dog down, but the dog didn't die."

M yelled, "Quiet, Margaret."

Will took his mother back to the singlewide and got her ready for bed. After he had tucked her in, kissed her on the forehead, and turned out the light, he walked into the living room and phoned Marne. He gave her the scoop on conditions at the compound and recounted the euthanasia discussion. She said she always suspected they would be capable of such thoughts, but not the deed. He heard his mother get up, go to the bathroom, and return to bed. He caught up on the shellfish operation and then Marne told him that a shopping list in the back of the logbook was really a poem.

She said, "They found an entry in the logbook that said, 'cover comforter, sink pad & soap dish, get bobby socks.' They think it's haiku poetry and now they spend a big chunk of their time at the library researching haiku."

Will viewed this bizarre comment as bait to start another argument, but quickly ended the conversation with, "Got to go. Talk to you later."

His mother was naked, on her hands and knees, crawling along the narrow hallway. She batted at something, as if there were cobwebs obstructing her passage.

He helped her off the floor and put her back in bed. Her false teeth lay on the night table. He realized it was easier for him to see her naked than without teeth.

She said, "I'll be fine now."

He covered her, turned out the light, and went into the bedroom next to hers to prepare for sleep. Through the thin walls he heard her throw off her covers.

"What's the matter?" he asked.

"I'm hot."

He went into her bedroom and turned on the light. He pulled the sheet over her and turned out the light.

She said, "I'll be fine, now."

He went back to bed and left the light on in the hall. He heard a thump and watched his mother crawl by his open door batting at something. He helped her back to bed.

"It's bunnies," she said.

He asked if the bunnies upset her and she said, "No, they're just bunnies."

"How many are there?"

"Thirty-three."

This scene repeated itself throughout the night. Each time he put her back to bed she said, "I'll be fine, now."

As her wakefulness increased, he in turn experienced mounting exhaustion as well as a sense of craziness. He considered waking the aunts, but then realized that might make things worse. He considered calling Marne for advice, but she needed her sleep. He thought of calling 911, but each time he came close to making the call, he thought, I'll give it one more go. He wondered if this kind of thing had happened before. At five in the morning, perhaps she had crawled by his door thirty times. He dressed his mother and loaded her into his pickup and drove to the Sechelt Hospital emergency department. During the drive she pet the bunnies in the truck.

He asked, "What colour are they?"

"Lion colour."

His mother spent three days in a hospital emergency bed. The doctors thought the latest medication might have caused the reaction, so they discontinued it. Fortunately, the government had enacted a new priority system for waiting lists for assisted living centres in the province. With the intervention of the doctor, Will managed to move his mother close to the top for the Westmount Inn. Maggie was pleased. M said that it might be good for Margaret, but she would never go to such a place.

He drove his mother home on the morning of his fifth day and she seemed fine. During those days in Sechelt, when not visiting her in the hospital, he caught up on jobs around the compound. Each night he and Marne had long conversations on the telephone. He was able to tell her that he had worked hard all of his life, too hard, because he felt like he was obliged to fill up two lives: his own, but also, the lost years for his father. Marne wondered why they had to have these talks on a telephone. Why did distance allow them to be intimate?

She told him about Brad and Jim's experiments in drowning research – self imposed drowning trials. This was done when they lived at Refuge Cove and earlier as children. Brad had explained that though he didn't realize the purpose at the time, these adventures were attempts to communicate with or locate their father. Will confessed to Marne that he had thought about drowning when he was a child, a lot, but had never gone crazy on the idea like them. Marne told Will that she had befriended Brad and Jim for many reasons, but primarily because they had become an avenue to understanding Will.

After a week, he left for Cortes. Eight ferries, the circle tour completed one more time.

IN LATE JANUARY SNOW blanketed the coast of British Columbia. Will received a phone call from Aunt M, who said, "She's dying."

Maggie was on life support. He set off for Sechelt in his pickup truck. To guarantee traction on the highways and hills, he loaded the box with wet firewood. On all the ferries, in the waiting lines at the terminals, while driving the wet and slushy roads, he reviewed what had taken place during the last few months. There had been three trips since the bunny episode. Much had deteriorated. The food situation worsened, stove elements left on over night, more melted pots, days when his mother refused to get out of bed claiming to have a cold or the flu, more clogged toilets, hours of sitting, shredding and counting toilet tissues, squirrels replaced bunnies, and the care workers grudgingly performed their duties. M had worked herself into a fury thinking Margaret did all of this to make her own life more difficult. His conversations with Maggie during that period had become brief.

Maggie died on January 29, three days after his arrival in Sechelt. She appeared at peace and lucid, though loaded with cancer, and managed to make good-byes to those she cared about. When Will's turn to say farewell came, they looked at each other for quite some time before either spoke.

And then she said, "I wish you had been my son."

He didn't have a response prepared, but eventually said, "I am. Keep thinking I am."

He addressed the mundane tasks such as arranging for cremation - there would be no service - notifying agencies, placing obituaries, and so on. He recalled her facility at the piano. She could play any tune by ear and had composed her own pieces – jazz and bee-bop. She had organized her own band – all girls - in the early 1940's, and they had traveled throughout British Columbia and Alberta playing in churches, at community dances, and service organizations. Thinking on her death, inevitably he came to ponder his own, and understood that as his time approached, he too would eventually resort to the stock reply, "I'm fine." His mother seemed unaware that her sister had departed, whereas M cried out her sorrow.

One night Marne called and their conversation lasted a little over three hours. He gave her the run down on life at the compound and she gave him the run down on Cortes, including the Brad-Jim saga and the state of the shellfish operation. Then she said, "You received a letter from John Ballentyne. And a small packet of his poems."

It had been decades since he'd heard from his friend. Will assumed that he had died somewhere, someplace, somehow. Will said to his wife, "Open the letter and read it."

"I've already opened it and read it."

"Since I got the letter from him, then I assume he's okay."

"I think he might be. It's not just addressed to you, though. I think it's addressed to Brad as well…I haven't shown it to Brad yet."

"What do you mean…why aren't you sure it's addressed to us?"

"It starts out, tous pour un, D'Artagnan, un pour tous, Porthos."

Will laughed, "Our Three Musketeer names at Vancouver College. John was always Aramis."

"Should I read it?"

"Of course."

She began.

"May the yin from the earth and the yang from the sky connect inside us.

"I assume that our lives have not followed the plot line in the Dumas novels. Brad has not been crushed by a rock, though that has been my demise in a metaphorical sense, and Will has not died in some useless war, which seem to ravage the world these days.

"My assumptions, I hope, are correct.

"For my part, like Aramis, I ended up in a monastery. He, for a short time, and I for a very long time in India, where I now am a faithful devotee of the Buddha. Here, I am able to calm my mind, a condition that would have been impossible in the Western world. Don't you think it odd that I have ended as a part of a monastic order given our experiences with the Christian Brothers?

"Oh, how they endorsed the spiritual life.

"My path has been convoluted. I spent years on a quest that has not been entirely fulfilled, and for that reason and others, has prevented me from returning to our island, and a life that the rest of the world might consider conventional. You may remember my bursting desire to become a poet, to follow in the footsteps of my father. I include in this letter a few poems, not so much for you to see what I have accomplished, for it never was so much, but an indication of the things that occupied my mind during the long nights and years and decades since we last played together and fantasized and suffered.

"I hope and believe that we three continue to embrace the sacred concept of friendship. My loyalty to you today is even stronger than it was in the days when the "Cav" made his attempts to steal our souls, crack our hearts and separate our common heritage and tragedy. That he got to one of us more than the other made for the growth of guilt in the other. Though one suffered more than the other, and though one sacrificed more than the other, the other is not without pain. Rest assured that the greater hurt is always the unconscious pain.

"We have never spoken of these things and probably never will. Perhaps, we were mute for reasons that were similar, but not for the same reasons as our mothers. How odd that rage and love yield a response of silence. From them and us.

"Be assured: that which remains unsaid still carries the weight and burden of the spoken. Perhaps more so. My letter is simply meant to say that I am content. And that I have survived. May that be the case for both of you.

"Our fathers are dead. My father, JJ. And your fathers, Bob and Perry.

"But, this is important too. What of our mothers? Is there compassion for them? My mother, Meredith. And your mothers, Margaret and Marlene. Must we search for them also? And understand their toils.

"Let them all rest, whether it be in the sad sea, under the good earth or the high crystalline air.

"When I say, one for all, you say, … … …"

Marne heard Will crying near the end of the letter. After awhile he said, "I've never really cried before."

"I know."

"We'll have to give the letter to Brad."

"I know."

"And the poems."

"Do you want me to read them?"

"Not now. I just want for us to talk. I want you to know that my exterior conceals turmoil."

"I've always known that, Will."

Over the course of the next few hours, Will told her everything about the sacrifices and his long frightful nights with the "Cav."

WILL MOVED HIS MOTHER to the Westmount Inn in mid-February. No one told her what was going to happen, but when he sat her down one morning for coffee and toast, and said, "Mom, I think it's time to move to the Inn."

She said, "Fine."

The Westmount Inn had been a large motor motel until it became an assisted living centre. It didn't have the institutional smell or look, yet. The rooms were furnished attractively, but he moved in some of his mother's possessions to make it homier. There was a cafeteria where they ate their meals, and a games room, an enclosed rose garden, and a pool and sauna, which no one ever used. They had a resident grey cat that managed to visit all seventy-nine guests on a regular basis. He disposed of some of her possessions in the singlewide during a weekend garage sale, and then sent the rest to the dump and some items to the Saint Vincent de Paul Society. Personal items such as letters, documents, photos; he took home, but didn't have the energy to dig into the past, yet. At the Inn she had her own telephone. When he called, whether in Sechelt or on Cortes, it still took fifteen or more rings to get an answer. She claimed to be on the toilet.

They discussed food frequently, and he became acquainted with the morning, noon and dinner menu, which did not vary from week to week. She gained forty pounds in the first two months. She went through such quantities of toilet paper that soon the management stocked cases in her room and he received the bills - $175 per month on average. Because she plugged the toilet on a regular basis, they supplied her with a port-a-potty. Mostly she spent her days shredding toilet tissue into bits, as would a mouse intent on building a nest. She discarded her productions in a large plastic bucket. She counted each discard as she dropped it and always remembered to start up from the total the day before. The nursing staff and doctor thought it a fetish that probably shouldn't be disturbed - as long as Will could afford it. He rented out her single wide so that he could afford it, and stayed with M whenever he visited Sechelt.

Will thought she was happier than ever before. Without being able to verify this, as his mother seemed impervious to direct questioning, he noticed that she always laboured over a problem, whether that might be the lyrics to a song she had learned in early childhood, a listing of the seven deadly sins, repeating sloth, avarice, greed, but stumbling there, and never coming up with the fourth sin or the other three. She worked on a limerick reciting three lines over and over, unable to produce a satisfactory ending to her poem: "There once was a lady from Khartoum, Who was prone to feelings of gloom, Until her lover said, Honey, ..." The fact that she could never resolve these puzzles did not concern her. Occasionally, she stared into space and mouthed a prospective solution such as the sin of pride, which would get rejected even though it was a correct guess, and for the limerick, "I'll give you my money," which seemed like a good possibility, but this answer was rejected too. On the contrary, he thought that these moments of unfulfillment might be the root of the happiness. The actual process of exercising the synapses gave her joy. If he offered to help her thought process, she seemed not to hear him. He came to imagine her brain a pulsing entity of psychic energy, sufficient unto itself, though it dragged around a frail body, which had outlived its need and purpose. He saw the discards of toilet tissue as the infinte number of possibilities that she considered, and when rolled into a wad and counted into the bucket, a new possibility would always materialize in another tissue.

M concurred that Margaret seemed "positively joyful," as she put it, but over time she was stricken with guilt and grief about losing her friend, neighbour and sister, to the extent that one week she hatched a plan to bring his mother back to her home. M was certain they could get along just fine together; the Inn was too expensive anyway. Will forced her to recall how only months earlier she had been losing her own mind because of his mother. Then M took to delivering daily loads of baking and mountains of chocolate bars, potato chips, cheezies and zoodles, as well as mickeys of rye, which she bought in convenient six packs. Unable to make a connection, she complained about his mother's overeating and suspected that she drank during the day.

IN LATE MARCH, M'S cat died. Will recalled his aunt's comment about Charlie, "You never need a lawn ornament if you own a cat." On April 14, Aunt M died in her sleep. He performed the administrative duties death demanded. He found the three syringes with three vials of clear liquid hidden in a shoebox. Underneath the equipment he also found a small pamphlet, a how-to-manual on suicide, *51 Ways to Kill Yourself*. He read the manual in ferry line-ups on the return trip home and confirmed that one needed to be brave.

As he shaved one morning, he pondered on the multiplicity of his aunts, his prevailing mother, and his long lost father. In the mirror, he saw the likeness between himself and his mother, which had intensified with the passing years; the lips, the nose, he even saw the same wrinkles in the same places forming across his forehead and radiating from his eyes. In particular, the eyes looked at him, and increasingly, they looked like her eyes; she stared through him, and beyond him, their glances not ever connecting over their lifetime, not ever sharing whatever eyes could see. To say the least, the resemblance to his mother came as a surprise while he lathered his face. The likeness upset him too, not that he had a particular attachment to his own appearance, but this similarity negated the other likeness - the portrait of his father, which refused to take shape.

As the years melted away, he visited his mother less often. He spoke over the phone less, but the conversations when they did occur were much longer, helping to drain the reservoir of guilt he had accumulated. She lived in a confused past and her stories mixed generations, people, events and places. Though it seemed too late to breech these years of quiet uncertainty, Will, nevertheless, received a garbled glimpse of the coveted knowledge. Eventually all the stories had to do with his fisherman father.

"Do you remember when we...."

RECEIPT

"ARROGANT" WIDOWS' FUND

Date..

Received from...

....

The sum of $................to be held in trust in the "Arrogant"
Widows' Fund.

RECEIVED WITH THANKS.

Per..

NOTE: Please make cheques payable to:

"ARROGANT WIDOWS' FUND IN TRUST"

c/o Western Fisheries Magazine

818 Richards Street

Vancouver, B. C.

All contributions will be acknowledged through the columns of Western Fisheries
Magazine.

arrogance takes you to feral regions, then you languish

2000

UNWILLING TO THROW THE bed covers off just yet, Mr. Douglas Jones pursued the review of a telephone conversation from the day previous. His wife, Mercy, had passed away a few years earlier and he seldom received phone calls.

The voice – friendly, matter-of-fact, feminine, a scant informal – had queried, "Is this Douglas Jones? I thought no one was home."

A trifle off-guard, he needed to clear his throat a number of times before answering, "This is Mr. Douglas Jones."

"Yes, Doug, I'm calling from Sprint Canada. I was wondering if you were aware of our new long distance calling program?"

In so many words, Douglas, a gentleman resenting all manner of solicitation, had allowed the Sprint Lady to explain her program, as she sounded competent and well researched. Although the woman understood that he rarely, if ever, made long distance calls, that singularity did not parch her enthusiasm to pitch the sale. The suddenness of her intrusion was captivating. She seemed content to let him direct the course of their interview. Nothing pushy here, he thought. Perhaps, Jones detected in the voice an integrity lacking in the modern day shammers.

To protract further the pleasant voice, he had actually enticed her by manufacturing a teeny fib.

"By coincidence," he had said, "it may be that I am required to do considerable long distance calling in the near future, so I'm rather pleased you have called today."

He asked the Sprint Lady to explain and then re-explain the program, not so much because he didn't understand the fine print of the thing; simply, and crudely put, this was a matter of having her strut her stuff. After she recounted the jurisdictional minutia of where the program applied and where it did not, he complimented her, generously mentioning that she had a most pleasant voice, well suited to her tasks. Instead of letting the conversation over stay, for Jones was also a man who had elevated privacy to the status of highest merit, he took his leave by requesting a call on the following after-noon at 3 p.m. By then, he would have checked the competition - though he did not mention this to her. She promised to call at the precise time. Their conversation had lasted a shade beyond eleven minutes by his reckoning.

As light gathered at his bedroom window, he further cross-examined the previous day's event, searching the discourse for points where he may have fabricated a false enthusiasm, or something worse, acted with shameless familiarity. He recalled moments of troubling silences during their conversa-tion, which had cropped up from time to time, and reassured himself that these intermissions were the normal silences enjoyed by persons at ease in one another's companionship – much as silence had become the norm in his bond with Mercy. Thus, Douglas, rightly or wrongly, concluded there existed no grounds for self-reproach. On balance, he calculated a seventy-percent chance he might go with Sprint.

A new item would go on today's "to do" list – anticipate call, Sprint Lady. He routinely underscored priority items.

By chance, Douglas and Mercy had met many decades before, whilst riding on their same Victoria bus route. She was a recent widow then, married only months, when her fisherman husband, Darwin, was lost in a tragic boating accident. Apparently, the fellow had the misfortune, or, more accurately, he lacked good judgment, in refusing to listen to former crewmembers, who thought the vessel unstable. The name of the boat raised a red flag for Douglas as soon as he heard it – *Arrogant*. Might just as well be a flashing neon sign, in his opinion.

WITH THE EXAMINATION OF conscience complete, Douglas flipped the covers from the bed, as might a spirited young man, and at that very moment, a worn passage from his childhood accompanied his fervor. "Rise and shine, the weather's fine, the sun will burn your eyes out."

This was father –incongruous in extremis – waking him to a new day in a distant youth. That scrap of wistfulness had lain dormant for decades. Latterly, reminiscences, materializing sometimes as actual memories, and at other times as seemingly real voices, and often without rhyme or reason, could capture in their trawl the vast expanses of his days and nights.

Activity is the best antidote, he thought.

Still prone in bed: five pelvic tilts held tens seconds per, soles of feet pressed as hands in prayer – two whole minutes - and finally, knees pulled to opposite shoulders, three repeats. Douglas bounced from his bed and greedily rubbed his hands as though the day might concede a genuine delicacy. He dispatched the liquid from his night bottle and flushed. He gave the container a thorough rinse leaving it to soak in a mild solution of vinegar. His doctor had told him recently that frequent, nocturnal micturition was nothing more than a sign of aging, as it were, came with the territory. The mild stomach aches of late were possibly due to lactose intolerance, therefore, he should switch to a non-dairy product like almond or rice milk. And after much probing, an inflamed prostate had been ruled out. They had bantered as he left the examination room, especially when he introduced his other concern, which was uncontrolled flatulence. Young Doctor Wilson said, "I'm afraid your symptoms are hardly worth recording. You look ten years younger than you should and your blood pressure is that of a nineteen-year-old. Better not take such care, otherwise I might be out of a job."

He had enjoyed the jousting. Imagine 120 systolic over 80 diastolic. A full and thick head of hair. Spring leaves on old limbs.

Ablutions in the smaller bathroom. Mercy always had exclusive rights to their ensuite bathroom, but that inequity had never been an issue. A quick sponge bath. Vigorous dental regime. He shaved applying liberal doses of Old Spice and carefully snipped two nostril hairs with her cosmetic scissors – liberated, one might say, sans guilt, from her multi-mirrored sanctuary.

Breakfast. Thwart the flu - 2000 mg Vitamin C. Mock Alzheimer's - 800 mg Vitamin E. Banish Osteo - 900 mg Glucosamine with Chondroitin. A dash of all-purpose calcium and magnesium. Then wheat-free millet cereal, a banana, and tea. He would switch to a non-dairy milk once his present container was finished, which he estimated to be three days hence.

"Promise to preserve your health, Doug." There was Mercy's voice again. In her lingering moments, she had extracted promises and these assurances had attracted to them the aura of mantra.

Yes, yes, he had promises to keep.

Douglas included CBC radio in his morning ritual. "Thank you Judy Madrin, its Friday November the fourth...I'm Lisa Cordasco, your host on the Island...." He would catch the world news at seven. A trifle tardy today – the Sprint lady had put him off schedule. Judy and Lisa, all of them, had become real friends in a real sort of way.

VOYAGE OF THE ARROGANT

He worked out the Friday "to do" list. On this particular morning, he imagined his pen positively quivered with the prospect of exercise. 1. Cereal – price compare. 2. Non-dairy products – price compare. 3. Bananas - if on sale. 4. LCB deposit. 5. Anticipate call – Sprint Lady – 3 p.m. 6. Prepare adequately for call during idle moments.

"...and summing up the news on the half hour, the compensation package for female federal employees has been fixed at..." There was an issue that riled. All Canada engulfed in guilt: apologies for gender, compensation to the Native Peoples, to the interred Japanese – how endless it had all become. Douglas poured a third cup from the pot, gingered more from the news than the tea.

He had to catch his bus at 9:29 and still had time for the five-block walk to the bus stop.

DOUGLAS STEPPED FROM HIS home into a dazzling morning bathed in light. A chill in the air invigorated. Steam wafted from the sunlit rooftops. He noticed a mauve, late-blooming rhododendron as he turned the corner. At the island in the middle of the intersection, he observed that the park's crew had removed the fall asters, ground hugging begonias, and the orange and scarlet cannas. Structural bones remained however. Four, zone-teasing, paddled-leafed banana trees, probably *Musa sikkimensis*, he thought. They looked naked, absurd; he reckoned the crew would be along to store them in a greenhouse for winter. Mercy and he had disagreed, not vehemently, of course, about the exotics; she wanting to take frivolous chances with a zone nine or ten, whilst he went the way of accepted horticultural practice. Out of consideration, he let the many opportunities for gloating pass in silence when her plants turned to mush come first thaw.

Garry Oak leaves covered the sidewalks – yellows, oranges, rusts. A wisp of breeze danced them up and they tumbled like a happy gang of kids chasing a ball in the park. Playful himself, he kicked as they flitted by. Mercy had loved the autumnal colours, and in one of her philosophical moods, or moments, or whatever one called them, she had commented that "fall beauty and sadness co-conspire to confuse emotion." No doubt, something to do with her amorous fisherman plus something to do with the advent of fall, but beyond those suppositions he had never got to the bottom of this statement or others like them. On a practical note, he remembered that they had used shredded oak leaves as winter mulch under their own rhodos when they lived in the bigger house.

A clear and brilliant recollection burst as he crunched on a chestnut husk. Perhaps it was the sound that transported him to another time and country, where a tiny child had watched his grandfather strip the prickly husk. He must have been bug-eyed when his granddad revealed the shiny, smooth, brown nut in his huge hand. With a little pocketknife, his granddad carved a deep depression, drilled a tiny hole in the side and inserted a twig. Douglas recalled holding the make-believe pipe, puffing proudly as his grandfather had sucked on his own real pipe. Possibly he was the same age now as his grandfather then?

He was of mixed minds regarding these onslaughts of backwardization. On the one hand, he luxuriated in the past in order to preserve those golden moments that they might never tarnish. In a manner of speaking, he imagined the very act of remembering served a similar purpose to burnishing. Over the years, he had come to liken his memories to an art collection in a prestigious gallery – each work professionally catalogued, the recollection lighted indirectly yet with suit-able intensity, and the overall environment maintained with proper humidity and temperature controls. One could say that long ago, the inferior pieces had been relegated to the scrap heap. On the other hand, though immediate gratification from permitted memory was entirely delightful, he invariably experienced despondency during the aftermath. Care was required when balancing contrary emotions. In such circumstances, he had discovered that these viewings must be infrequent and cursory; otherwise, there could be heavy weather ahead.

Enough with chestnuts – he would not add them to the collection.

He sat inside the kiosk and waited for 26 DOCKYARD. Something was different. The bench was new. The seat and backrest were made of that compressed and recycled plastic he had heard about. They did that quickly, he thought. He questioned the use of the fastenings, obviously not stainless.

He thought on his upcoming interview at 3 p.m.

The bus arrived on schedule, and he flashed his senior's card. The driver recognized him and they both gave a cheery hello. A very large man with a brilliant red face sat in the handicapped section gasping for air. Someone new. Douglas walked along the aisle and recognized the short, heavyset, Downs Syndrome lady. As usual, she had her little note clutched in her hand and mumbled, "Three. Get off at Vernon." She repeated the third point on her list many times before folding it carefully. Then she opened her purse, took out her wallet and stuffed the reminder inside a slot. When her wallet was secure in her purse again, she began another of her mumbles, "Remember the note in the wallet. The wallet's in the purse." Then she extracted the note and repeated *ad nauseum* point number three. Once, Douglas had rung the buzzer at Vernon, as she seemed confused that day. He never had found out where she went upon disembarkation, but imagined her mumbling point four - whatever that was - as she plodded on the next step in her day. He was surprised she could read.

Further along the aisle, the Asian woman sat wearing a scarf - Zeller orange - and she carried an umbrella, which seemed strange given the weather conditions. The young construction worker occupied the back seat; same blue jeans, ripped at knees, same jean jacket, ripped at elbows, same encrusted leather boots, laces untied, and the same lunch kit, dented and bashed. There he sat, oblivious, listening to his headset. Hardly a busload, thought Douglas.

He took his usual seat close to the rear door. He saw a poppy – pin and all – lying on the floor. He picked it up and fastened it to his lapel, and no one caught him. He recalled the opening stanza to *In Flanders Fields* by John McCrae: "In Flanders fields the poppies blow, between the crosses, row on row, that mark our place; and in the sky the larks, still bravely singing fly scarce heard amid the guns below."

Going east, traffic was heavy. He decided to count pickups. Twenty-six were the most he had ever counted between Quadra and Dockyard. On occasions he did convertibles, but there weren't many this time of year. Another workman got on, strapped into his headset also. The Downs Syndrome girl got off and he was up to six already. He hoped he hadn't missed any. Four passengers got on and he recognized two of them.

He read the bus advertisements. LUPUS, "Lungs are for Life," and a self-help ad for abused women. Above him, a Poetry in Transit poster read, *The Sweet Taste of Lightning*, by Sheri-D Wilson. He lost interest at, "wasn't wearing under wire bra." He had never cared much for modern poetry and questioned the role the transit company played in bringing culture to the masses. "I leant upon a coppice gate when Frost was spectre-grey, and Winter's dregs made desolate the weakening eye of day." At least one could understand what the poet intended. Eight. A middle-aged woman got on and when she passed in the aisle, he noticed the title of her book, *The Cameraman*, by Bill Gaston, whomever he might be.

The Asian lady got off. What's with the umbrella? People wore gloves. He made a mental note to wear them tomorrow. He'd put "gloves" on his Saturday "to do" list when he got home. He checked his timepiece, 9:43. No need to panic as there were hours before his next interview with the Sprint Lady. Then Mercy's nagging second promise materialized, "Promise to keep busy, Doug."

He felt like shouting, "Can't you see that's exactly what I'm doing."

Eleven pickups. His strategy for the second interview with the Sprint Lady manufactured quite nicely. He would reverse the tables. Instead of allowing her the luxury of sitting back and listening to him, he would ask pointed questions, intelligent questions that required lengthy responses. As he read the situation, subtly take the offensive while appearing quite of the opposite persuasion. He would have paper and pen ready, and diligently take notes to preserve an accurate record of their exchanges. Later, in the leisure of his own time, he would squeeze from their conversation the juices that saturated every line. Above all, he determined that regardless of the pressure she applied, he would give no commitments today. She would have to work harder if she wanted to land such a big fish.

Whilst in the kiosk, Douglas had abandoned the notion of checking the competition. Much soul searching had been done through the wee breakfast hours regarding the wisdom in performing such an activity. In fact, many beats of doubt kept rising just as do gnats from over ripe fruit. Would she be offended upon discovering a whiff of betrayal? Would a sly huckster from the other side somehow lure him from a perfectly respectable offer? The behind-the-scenes maneuvering was simply not Douglas' cup of, never had been, and never would be, therefore, in so many words, he would stay the course and allow their meetings to develop simply and naturally, without prejudice from alien sources. His decision made in the kiosk allowed him to concentrate on the tasks at hand. Sixteen.

The large man with the laboured breathing remained aboard. Douglas did a head count - fourteen riders. He saw a postman walking down the street sorting mail with fingerless gloves. A boy with a skateboard got on. He should have been in school. Some homes still had decorations out. Halloween orange: a distasteful colour. A young woman with flaming red hair embarked at Foster. A streak of white ran along the top of her head – almost like a birthmark. He was sure she wouldn't have dyed it that way. She disembarked at Grafton. Why not walk the block? The Pacific Reef Club looked fancy. He guessed all the big brass from the naval base went there and ordered Manhattans or Martinis. Double cherry. Yes, Major. Double olive. Certainly, Admiral.

HMC DOCKYARD EXCHANGE. He had counted only sixteen pickups. A solemn ride. The driver scrolled through to 26 UVIC and turned the motor off. The driver said to the heavy-set gentleman, "This is the end of line" and he replied, "I'm staying on."

The driver got out to have a cigarette.

The ocean was calm. Only a light ripple on an untroubled sea. A freighter zigzagged for the horizon. Mercy's first and brief romance had disappeared out there somewhere. It definitely would be a nice day. He noticed a bird's nest in a tree by the fence. He supposed he only noticed the nest now, as the tree had defoliated in a recent heavy wind. He read the last line of the transit poem, "all appliances spoke in magnetic tongues."

An attractive woman in uniform walked by. He imagined the Sprint Lady would be similarly striking. The guards at the checkpoint waved through the traffic going into the base. Not once had he seen them check a vehicle for I.D. The large man's breathing rattled. The driver got on and read his novel. Douglas would open his upcoming interview with some bland comment on the weather. See where that went.

"Born on the same day, born at the same minute...." Mercy had fabricated this song and there was her voice. She sang beautifully. Though she was born in Canada, and he in England, even accounting for time zones, they realized whilst reviewing birth and baptismal certificates both had slipped into the world within minutes of the other. His memories pressed on. When Mercy was in a particularly playful mood, she would add a third line, "Born at the same second." Douglas had enjoyed the outlandish exaggeration, and though he took little stock in stellar influences and horoscopic predictions, it became generally understood between them, even if never fully articulated, that they had been destined to couple, the fisherman fellow only a foolish interlude. Together they would march the same road through life, and at the end, take their leave within minutes of the other, more or less, arm in arm, skipping the light fantastic into the unknown. So to speak.

10:02. Underway again. The golf course looked busier than yesterday. A young, attractive woman sat in front of him and wore a poppy. He thought it admirable that younger people, especially women, would honor the war dead. Everyone getting on the bus had passes. Mostly students. Half of them listening to tapes. Oblivious. Two women talked frenetically two seats up. He couldn't make out a word. Over the years, he had become very expert though, and very inconspicuous at gathering up people's lives, while pretending not to listen, but today the luck of the draw had him out of range. 10:21. The bus almost full. A few seats available in the back but no one would be able to sit alongside the heavyset man though the seat next to him was free. Seven students boarded at Blanchard and half were Asian. "Ming was tying her shoe laces like she was...," but that was all he could hear. So much laughing, blending of conversations, he couldn't make out head or tail. The mood of the trip had changed quickly since the younger ones got on.

He disembarked at Quadra. 10:31. The heavy breathing gentleman and Douglas made brief eye contact as he walked by the window. He needed to duck into Thrifty's, but was halted in the middle of the parking lot by the visitation of new voices and new music. The occasion was their time in New Orleans – not his first choice for a holiday destination - when by chance they found themselves walking amidst a Negro funeral dirge. They hung back and followed respectfully on the sidewalk rather than in the middle of the street like the mourners. He and Mercy never before had seen the exaggerated, slow dragging, foot-slide to the cemetery, the hearse buried in a mountain of flowers and the mournful wails on the trombones. At the cemetery, they viewed from a distance ever sensitive that they might be intruders. But that death march, that requiem of the highest order, had transformed on the return. The atmosphere sizzled. Everyone danced and shimmied – totally freed themselves from grief and regret. Broken hearts, along with bouquets, were left graveside, as the deceased would have wished. Oh, what a wonderful time – what a wonderful moment that had been when he and his wife fell right into the spirit of the thing.

They felt welcomed and marched gaily with the cortege for blocks and blocks. She shimmied just like the Negroes. A highlight of their trip really. He had held back though, thinking his reserve an eloquence of sorts.

As inconspicuous as possible, he practiced the foot-slide into Thrifty's.

The millet rice cereal was $7.59 for the bulk pack. It had been on special for $5.49 three weeks earlier and he had stocked up. Making a quick circuit of the store, he surveyed the other specials and noted that almond milk was cheaper than rice milk. He purchased three bananas, as they were $.49 per pound versus the usual $.69. He went next door to Starbucks that had a washroom, which he used occasionally. On leaving the coffee shop though, an officious, ballooning, staff woman accosted him. She reminded him that the facilities were for use by patrons only. Douglas refrained from executing a derogatory comment – perhaps it would have addressed the prices of their inadequate coffees - and instead issued a starchy irony. "So sorry, madam." 11:34.

The liquor store. They were a good bunch. They called him, "One a Day Man," and he didn't mind the informality. First, the bottle deposit. Fred opened the window and said, "Here's your dime, One-a-Day."

Someone in the stock room broke out laughing, but Douglas didn't quite hear what that was about. He gave Fred his empty beer bottle. They spent a few moments passing the time. Fred thought they might even get frost before too long and Douglas was inclined to agree. The laughing in the stock room went on and on. As Fred was preoccupied with an inventory discrepancy, Douglas went into the store proper and directly to the singles rack. He chose his honey cream. He had his $1.65 ready and the ten cents for the deposit. He had always thought it curious that he must recycle that dime. Once, he had formulated a witticism concerning the matter with Fred. Douglas had suggested that in order to increase efficiency, he would absolve the Liquor Control Board of the obligation to charge the ten cents while he guaranteed each and every bottle returned. They both had a good laugh over that one. Fred, getting into the swing, had said he would pass the idea on to management. Douglas was able to keep the joke going for weeks. Each day he would inquire about the possibility of a policy change and each day Fred would have some new retort such as, "The proposal has now migrated to board level," or, "I believe the report has gone over to the legal department." The joke seemed funny at the time and had the possibility of infinite extension. He wanted to pass the time with Jim behind the till, but the cashier hurried him along, perhaps because of the impatient person behind him. Midday.

Three hours until his interview. Somehow he had never been able to accept that another had commandeered Mercy's affection. During the years they were together, it seemed she never let go of that relationship – a thing they never discussed. From time to time, but rarely, he had felt as though she had not been completely there for him as he had been for her. One might say he sensed she evoked a second best attitude in their marriage. Douglas had never inquired to the intimacies they had shared and always assumed she would have kept these privacies locked into her heart anyway. My god, the fellow was only a fisherman, so why not let them have their short shot at joy together. The charitable donations for the "*Arrogant*" widows, which came later, were a bit of a bonus, he had to admit.

He walked towards Reynolds Secondary School. Suddenly, across the street, a young man in his early twenties talked on one of those new cellular telephones. He paced back and forth, agitated as all get-out, screaming into the phone, "F... you." He flicked the flap shut and threw it onto the road. Immediately, a car ran over the phone and flattened it beyond repair. The young man yelled another vulgarity, at the innocent driver this time, and gave chase on foot. Then he ran back to his own car, which was a souped-up kind of hot-roddish affair, and exploded from his parking space – possibly giving pursuit to the other car. Most disturbing, the young students from the secondary school mingled on the street for lunch break and witnessed the entire juvenile episode. Never mind.

Near the fence running the length of the ball field, a girl's team practiced their soccer skills. He had watched them many times and was amazed that they could play the game so well. He could see their marked improvement one practice to the next. Douglas leaned upon the fence, enjoying the remaining warmth from the weak November sun and reckoned that by watching the girls at play, he would thereby rid the cellular fellow from his mind. He sincerely hoped the Sprint Lady would never be so unlucky as to engage that crude fellow in a bid to join Sprint. Soon, the delightful diligence of the girls accomplished his goal.

One could say that Mercy had wrapped poor Douglas in knots. On the one hand, there were those unrealistic pledges. "Keep healthy. Keep busy." And on the other hand, Douglas experienced guilt from not partaking in the foot slide to the grave. And latterly, he had allowed a certain questionable fantasy to form; namely, that she capered through the ethers in search of her first and only true love. He further compounded the fantasy with the notion that her desertion was punishment for him failing to die within seconds of her passing. As a dog gnaws a bone, he allowed these deep dark thoughts to become actual betrayal, and this infidelity on her part made him contemplate an extraction of revenge, though he never had allowed himself to acknowledge what tangible form this might take.

The soccer ball rolled toward him at the fence. One of the youngest – or at least one of the smallest girls, quite pretty and an excellent player too - ran up to retrieve the ball. She seemed hesitant. The ball lay up against the mesh wire, so Douglas – on instinct – kicked through the fence and the ball rolled over to the girl. She snatched it up and shot him the most vicious look. What was that about? If this attacking glance were not enough, before running off to her school chums, she squealed accusingly, "You watch us all the time."

Her look felt like a drill penetrating a board. 12:33.

He snorted home. He squashed the chestnuts into the sidewalk and kicked the remaining piles of leaves out onto the street. At the intersection with the planted meridian, he bustled by the park crew now extracting the banana trees – shot right by them. He overheard, "Yes, we have no bananas today."

What a feeble attempt to simulate humour, thought Douglas. He shot right by them.

To be precise, Mercy did not now caper through the ethers. More likely, she drifted with the currents. Contrary to her many final requests, which included a send off akin to the one they had witnessed in New Orleans, he had her cremated. No fuss, no friends and much more economical. For a few years, he had kept her in a blue, raku-fired clay pot in the ensuite along side her cosmetics, but one morning, he put her in a shopping bag and together they caught DOCKYARD 26. For the first and only time he disembarked at the exchange, along with his packet. Once UVIC 26 left, he made his way to the water's edge.

Douglas had picked his time carefully, choosing an outgoing tide that would send her on a sub-surface mission, which he had imagined was her real wish anyway. One could guess that guilt induced this private ceremony, a contrived atonement for his infidelity regarding her dying wishes. As he stood on the outcrop though, and watched the coarse granules speed off on the swift current, a new bout of jealously persuaded him to only pour half of her out. Once aboard UVIC 26 again, with his half in tow, he snickered over a flurry of bizarre thoughts: if by chance she should be lucky and find her fisherman friend, he might not be quite so pleased about the reunion, as she would be a shadow of her former self. So to speak. And then he played with her perspective too, and imagined that she might not be so pleased about the reunion either. Necessarily, her amour would have changed, perhaps half or more of him nibbled away by hungry and persistent fish, forever drifting on underwater currents, a bag of bones petrified into an awkward and futile attempt to reach the surface of a vast and empty sea. The half empty, or half full, raku blue urn went back into the ensuite alongside the cosmetics, Mercy in need of them more than ever. Close on his home, and realizing that he had neglected preparation for the upcoming interview, Douglas now noticed a rare sight - a whole lawn carpeted in pink cyclamens. Immediately, he thought of tropical butterflies bathing in the sunshine. And, as if the lawn had rekindled old memories, he saw the two of them admiring their own cyclamens under a favourite magnolia on a chilly December morning. Even though this memory was delightful, he knew he should retreat, but he would not. His thoughts crowded with accusations, and grew out of proportion, just as they had on the morning he cast half of her to the sea.

He heard a warning whisper, "Doug, take care, cyclamens come along when least expected."

It seemed that dallying by the cyclamens offended her - implying that she, not he, would control when, where, with whom, and for how long, he could savor a pleasure. What was so off-limits about pink cyclamens anyhow? 2.54 p.m. My Lord, how had the time moved so quickly.

He noticed a rusted jalopy parked outside his home. He decided that, if the vehicle hadn't left following his interview with the Sprint Lady, he would report it to the police. Then he noticed that two men stood on his porch, and by their dress, he immediately associated them with the decrepit car. The thought occurred: Had the competition decided to make a house call and subvert the Sprint Lady? But he quickly rejected that possibility as no reputable firm would send outcasts like that, or supply them with such a ridiculous vehicle. They were an unruly sort, shaggy long hair, unshaven, wearing worn and holed dungarees. One of them was a miniature facsimile of a real person.

As he climbed his stairs, the larger fellow said, "Excuse me, but are you Mr. Jones?"

"Yes, but I am frightfully tight on schedule."

He brushed by them and then fumbled with his key.

The larger fellow said, "We believe that Mrs. Jones was previously married to Darwin Wilkes, who was a deckhand on our father's ship, the *Arrogant*, and were wondering if they ever had children?"

Douglas heard the telephone ring, but could not manage to get the key into the lock. Then the miniature person tugged on his sleeve so that he was completely unable to place the key properly into the hole. The little fellow said, while he obscured Douglas' visibility with an antediluvian book, "we doin a vesti gae shun 4 r pa."

The telephone terminated after its sixth ring. Douglas Jones clutched his stomach and initiated a continuous dry heave response. He passed away in the Royal Columbian Hospital at 7.26 p.m.

a door opens into another world, divisions of colour
and sound, unseen/unheard by the rest

2002

WHILE I'M WAITING FOR the doctor, or somebody like maybe a nurse, to put my name in another slot and change the flashing neon blue to a better colour with those new-fangled felt pens, I might just as well retell everything, but with the added in details so that the rightness of it gets corrected once and for all. The whole conundrum got underway with this doctor at the walk-in clinic, who, when I first noticed him, was studying my file intently and tapping his pen against the metal clip holder. It made a racket - the tapping that is - while I sat there in what seemed like the vapors of a steam bath though it was only an ordinary interview room.

Just to keep the record straight, in the olden days I used to go to the steam baths on Hastings Street on a regular basis. We'd get pretty grimy at work and I guess steam was the only way to clean up enough so our wives could accept us. Maude - she's my wife - always joked and said things like: "Steam does wonders, Coop." The worst times happened in the summers when I foremaned the Catholic high school boys assigned to the de-charring of the whiskey barrels. Everybody agreed de-charring was the rottenest job in the factory, but our Catholic bosses had no pity on that score. Apparently, they believed manhood arrived from the bottom up.

So anyway, there I was squirming in the chair and wiping on my brow and thinking the doctor didn't need to tap the pen so loud. For sure, he sensed my discomfort and finally said, "Mr. Cooper, there's something wrong with your story."

That total abrupt break in the silence surprised me more than you'd imagine.

As you've probably figured by now, I don't know how to react because I can't remember telling him anything at all, let alone a whole story.

Then he went back to the file, not expecting me to rebut his statement for all I know. He made notes here and there, sometimes in the margins, or between lines in his tiny writing, while I broke out in more sweats and shivers and wished I hadn't given into the worries of Maude. Instead, I should've stayed put in my favourite recliner chair. Basically just toughed it out closer to home plate 'til I got better, if you know what I mean.

He kept ravaging away on the file until he found the chest X-ray, which they shot when I first went there a month ago, and then he went back and forth, back and forth, from his notes to the X-ray photo, turning God knows what in his mind. I'd say the file was about an inch thick at that point. More than once, my hand slipped off the armrest, despite my gripping it like a vice - since I'm perspiring profusely - and my concentration, which was usually alert beyond the ordinary, wandered from the subject at hand. I noticed that whenever he took another peak at the X-ray, I strained my eyes too, to see what he saw, but the lighting was poor and they didn't like you looking. That reminds me, the doctor last week, a lady and young and not very friendly or pretty either, said there was scar tissue, and a shadow too, when she looked, but this man doctor just kept saying zero. Then I wondered if things had collapsed further and was full of suspicions that I gave him the wrong information without knowing, and that's why he was so screwed up on the story. With the heat in the room skyrocketing like we're in the tropics, and even my socks were soaking, a person didn't know whether it was a monsoon, a steam bath or regular old sweat.

By the look of this doctor – a bit paunchy, tuffs of fur sprouting from his ears and purple livery spots on the backs of his hands – he was the oldest I've had so far. What I decided I liked is that he actually tried to understand, unlike the others, who cut you off in mid-stream as you answered their unanswerable questions.

Last week's lady doctor was the worst. She asked, "On a scale from one to ten how do you rate the pain in your chest?"

It wasn't precisely a pain then, and certainly isn't now, and it wasn't in my chest either, but lower, more like a severe discomfort, and near the lungs, so I tried to explain that discomfort and pain were two separate feelings altogether. Both her eyebrows shot up, her eyes glazed up, I could even see her nostrils flare, and then she interrupted my explanation with, "Just give me a number."

So I yanked one out of the hat and said, "Five."

That number could be where the mistakes initiated, or before then, who knows, and the total build up of examples like that one, because there's more, which I won't go into for brevity sake, have led to conclusions that aren't even close to approaching the truth.

I started appreciating how he struggled with my file and then really appreciated him when he asked, "Take your time and tell me how you feel."

The way he put the question was relaxing – at last someone wanted more than a animal grunt.

I kept wiping my forehead with my soggy handkerchief and coughed up phlegm, which was a black colour so it must have been from the burnt-out barrels. I told him I finished my antibiotic medications, but was still weak, though not as weak as when I had pneumonia the times before. And I said I wouldn't have come except Maude insisted.

He said, "Go on," like he had all the time in the world, which I was really happy about, because in reality it was me - not him - with the time, having clocked seven years, two months and some days on the retirement scale.

Very carefully I explained there were two pains – I decided to call them pains. The first was inside my chest, possibly inside my lungs, or, between my chest cavity and lungs, but I wasn't sure, but he'd know, and it felt like a volcano on the edge of extinction, and each time the volcano breathed, the oxygen rekindled the coals clinging to the sides, so it just felt like burning embers.

To convince him, because his one eyebrow gave the question mark look, I said, "Like the burnt barrels."

Just so you've got it straight, barrel-making was my former profession and we always fired the insides of whiskey barrels – they were oak – and then the tannic acid could come out of the wood to give the flavor and colour. Whiskey tastes different these days since they age it in stainless – the inexpensive stuff, that is. It took talent to char them even and perfect, especially if you had ten burners going at once. The Cortes Island kids – the Catholic ones I mentioned before – took to it like water off a duck's back. They were the best at de-charring them too, which I'll tell you more about that later.

"Barrels?" he asked, instead of frowning it.

I'm too exhausted to re-explain so I skipped to the second pain, which was more like a gripping pressure that began in the centre of the chest, but spread out over the rib cage and eventually trickled up the throat. More like a boulder lodged in the chest, and you had to push it somewhere, but didn't know where. Or a better explanation was a body clamp turning tighter and tighter in one of those second rate torture films from the fifties. I expected him to write some of this down, but he didn't, as I expected he had a better than average memory.

He took my blood pressure and when he pumped it up too tight, I nearly yelled. When he got his readings, I asked how it was and he said, "Like a lopsided basketball score."

I managed to answer, "I don't know much about that sport."

Next in sequence – by the way, right now, I'm wishing they would hurry up and write my name in a new slot - he listened to my lungs with his scope, the metal was icy and startling, and when he took my temperature he said I had a fever. They have the throw away thermometers nowadays, which seems like a waste. He thumped me low on the back – like a cheap shot kidney punch - and then wrote more notes in the file with his gold pen, which looked like 22 carats or better. The room got shadowy and swayed and bucked and plunged like we were on a raft in a stormy sea and the clamp around my chest squeezed a rock out of my throat, seemed more like a whole avalanche, and I thought this isn't what pneumonia is supposed to be like.

"Keep a positive outlook." That's what I said to myself – really I'm only parroting Maude.

Then he decided to give me his conclusion, but sounded further away than right beside me, like he talked through a loud mega-hailer turned way down low.

"Mr. Cooper, the symptoms you describe are not entirely consistent with pneumonia; in fact, they seem more consistent with a heart malfunction. I don't want to alarm you, but I think the safest thing is to have you immediately admitted to Emergency for monitoring."

I guess I didn't quite get the gist as I was still back there thinking about oak barrels and embers and explaining to the boys the best way to do the various jobs, so I asked in all seriousness, "How long will it take to get an appointment?"

DR. ROLAND - I just remembered his name – called a taxi and everybody helped even though I could have done it myself as the hospital was only a few blocks away. Driving over, the taxi driver talked about the weather – what other subject is there in Victoria - but I kept thinking over my former barrel-making occupation and how in my industry technology came along early. "Patented 1889" was stamped on all the machines. I guess they made it so good they never had to change. The crucial point is, if a customer ordered a barrel, something totally out of the ordinary like a long taper, or engraving required, special lacquers, gold plaques, stainless hoops, unusual woods, for instance, yew, or once I worked with mahogany, they hauled me off the assembly line. Then you could think and take your time. It wasn't here nor there for the other few guys that were as skilled in the trade as me, but for me, those were the times it was good to be human - when you got singled out for your artistic talent and gift. I guess I guided the boys on that subject telling them to discover their talent early on and then stick with it for the rest of your life. Whether the advice stuck I don't know.

The interesting point you learn at Emergency is that if you say you have chest pains they roll out the red carpet. The place was full but they shunted me to the head of the line. Even the lean limbed woman in the booth who had to fill out the admittance form said she'd get the information later when I was feeling better, which reminds me, I still haven't done that, so I haven't been here long, or she went off shift and I'll catch her later. Another worry was the taxi-driver and whether or not he got paid. I'll get Maude to fix it.

I'm glad I'm where I am even if it's for the wrong reasons.

There are times when I force relaxation and close my eyes. I find if you concentrate then you can see mud flats and there are a bunch of pure white flamingos off in the distance wading on those long skinny legs. It's beautiful watching them step so lightly, as if they don't want to get their feet wet. Like ballet almost. Embarrassing as it is, I imagine myself doing an imitative dance of the pure white birds, but in slower motion. I'm entirely familiar with estuaries and river mouths being a sports fisherman and bird hunter too, but when I was young. Seems the boys knew all about fishing as their dads were fishermen.

Somehow I undress while my mind is enjoying the white birds and the burnt barrels mixing together. They put me in a nightie, which I hate, because the back end is open to every breeze from the four directions and I hope the male orderly did the helping because I'm not too proud of my backside, being overweight with the buff aspects softened up and shrunk. Muscle mass can't be replaced after a certain age, I read once, no matter what you do.

Oak barrels were the best to work, but we made them from fir too. Oak barrels for whiskey and wine. Fir barrels for salted fish and dried fruit. And casks for nails and staples and kegs for chain and log dogs. The sizes went from five up to eighty gallons. Making casks and kegs was kids play. I got the Cortes boys to do it once and they cranked them out like you wouldn't believe. The bosses said I had a rapport with them so that got me a few marks in the good book. The oak comes all the way from Georgia. The fir comes from here. You can put 298 whiskey barrels in a rail boxcar. I've done it many times. Throwing them up to the fourth level was the hardest. The first three levels were upright and the fourth on its belly. If you put all 298 on their belly, you get less in, only 286, because you can't get the cradling effect to work in your favour. Couldn't figure that out. I never got my master cooper ticket because the guilds had folded before I even started in the business, but they said I was good enough to get it. A standing joke was my name was Cooper and I was a cooper besides – that's what you call barrel-makers. They'd say, "There goes Cooper, the cooper," like my name and my job were identical. They'd say, "Coop, the coop," or "See ya, Coop." Even the boys called me, "Coop." It's a sure bet my ancestors were coopers, otherwise how would I have got the talent. Or the name.

A nurse or two put me in cubicle number two and I look directly at control central. There's a long counter desk for paperwork, a nurse station, and behind that a big chalkboard with the names that I told you about before. I see an official clock straight in front and then another on the far wall with a yellow face and happy smile. It's 4:32 on both of them so we're synchronized. I'm assuming it's p.m., not a.m., and that I just got here. The guys at work were clock-watchers too, but not me. Sometimes we'd get the whiskey barrels for reconditioning into wine barrels, before the grapes came up from California. There were always dregs in the bottom and the bosses let us drink the dregs after shift, but on special occasions only - Friday afternoons. You'd have to strain the dregs. We'd do it through clean towels if we had them. Maude didn't like me coming home with whiskey on my breath. Of course, some guys abused the privilege and you'd find them in the can getting smashed all day and every day. Our motto was, "We Roll Barrels Around The World." And we did too. I worked there for forty-seven years until it closed – the last cooperage in North America. Me and the Chinaman were the longest employed. We called him Wing and he did sweep up, but he could take any position in the assembly line if need be. Unfortunately, the writing was on the wall for my profession even before I started in the business – akin to being beaten before birth. I tried to explain that to the boys and encouraged them to get a good education that might be useful in the modern day. I never got a gold watch, but didn't expect it either. I swept up in the plastics factory next door for a year and a half before retiring completely. Then we moved to Victoria where Maude's sister's at, or was at. She died.

One of the nurses wants to crank my bed down flat, but I tell her to leave me cranked up. I say I'm comfortable up, which I'm not, but I want to see what's going on regardless of the pain. To the left of my cubicle there's a wall painted hospital green with no posters, and then on the right, a dullish white curtain that's wrinkled like it had never been ironed, which I assume on the other side is either cubicle one or three, because I'm two. The wall behind my bed, that I can't see at all, is covered in monitor technology hooked all six ways to Sunday. I got a quick glance when they wheeled me in. The guy behind the curtain, in either one or three, makes annoying drowning sounds. I guess, and this is sad, all the dads of the boys drowned in a boating accident.

Now a nurse tries to close a curtain between me and control central.

"This will give you more privacy," she says.

I give a reflex yell, "Leave it alone," and she whips the curtain back where it belongs. I suppose I frightened her. She looks like she's of the old guard school with her arms bent akimbo on her big hips. Pretty soon I'm ashamed about that emotional breakdown and try to apologize, but she's already marched off for another battle on another ward.

Watching everything going on and the people walking by doing their jobs is the most fascinating part of this experience. The place is busy, but organized, and that gives you a good feeling overtop of the choking and burning sensations. What I find amusing is how alert I am even with the situation getting worse. I decide that when everything gets sorted out, then I'll find out who that nurse is and give her some flowers to let her know how the stress of the moment made me do what I did. I've burst out at Maude a few times, but never at strangers.

If Maude were here, she'd be able to straighten the confusions to date. It's been her side of the roster in our marriage. Once I signed an agreement for a lemon car, but she got them to withdraw. And another time she dug into matters and proved that I had extra pension earnings coming. She has the rare ability to cut through the tape. It's like somebody gave her the talent to push rocks uphill without breaking a sweat. Maude always says women glow but don't sweat. Otherwise, me and her fit each other down to the ground.

Now I'll explain the monitoring technology because I'm remembering it pretty good and it's probably important. The first thing they do is put a pressure cuff around my arm, which automatically constricts every three minutes or thereabouts. They can look at the readings on the wall whenever they want. They have a rubber finger socket that fits on my little finger with a red light bulb on the end, which measures the oxygen in my blood stream, which I never knew we had it there, and the wire from it goes to the wall. I get an oxygen mask I don't want to wear, but they make me, and it smells like newly milled plastic, which I know all about because of that plastics factory. By the way, the only place at that job that requires precision work is the die-cast department. Guys from the old country worked there, mostly Germans. It could have been me if I had gone into the right industry in the first place. That was the thing I always harped on with the boys, "Get into the right industry from the start."

The red finger light keeps capturing my attention and I keep wiggling it. I think of Rudolph, the red-nosed reindeer, and then I get this whole flood of memories from when I was a child, Christmases, and so on, which is nice. Maude and I never were able to have kids, and that turned out to be a loneliness that we have lived with. She would have made a wonderful mother.

Two nurses wheel a mobile X-ray machine and they crank me straight up and down in the bed and tell me to take a deep breath and hold it so they can get a good picture. I hear them say the picture isn't any good. Sometimes I hear alarms going off and beeps and buzzers but I can never tell if it's me going off or the drowning guy beside me. Behind the X-ray lady is the EEG or EEC lady with her machine. She hooks me up with her wiry probes and the machine prints out this sheet of paper for about an hour. She wheels off and the blood ladies take over, but not before that long report goes in my file on the desk counter. There's a reason for telling these details that you'll find out later.

The first blood lady says, "This won't hurt."

It doesn't, and she jabs me in the stomach with an injection of what she calls, "blood thinner." Apparently it's better to have thin blood if you're having a heart attack, which I know I'm not. And then she comes up with these nitro pills that dissolve under your tongue immediately, and are soapy and slippery. So I think dynamite caps. Then she adds more paper to the file and my story piles up.

The next lady hooks up an IV drip bag and says, "It has saline right now, because you're dehydrated."

She has one heck of a time finding a vein in my arm. For some reason, she has to pick the spot where I got the chemical burn in that plastics plant. When I got that burn it almost ate a hole right through. She jabs away and there's blood getting spread around and she's upset because AIDS is a problem with the younger set. So I have to calm her down by saying that I have exceptional pain tolerance and it doesn't hurt, which it doesn't, surprisingly, even though she's making a mess. I do have quite a pain tolerance level, because when I had the chemical burn it only felt like an itch.

Which I tell her, and she says, "Don't scratch if it itches," which is funny, and she was trying to be funny, but when I try to laugh back I only hear gurgle sounds coming from my mouth just like the guy next door. They're definitely nice people here; you can't take that away from them. More paper keeps going into the file and we're now starting to get a two-inch thickness.

After her, another blood lady arrives with a tool kit full of test tubes. She's looking for released enzymes, whatever they are. I begin to realize that when I'm the looker then nobody will look at me, and if I don't look, they all look. So I look and look.

The drowning guy beside me is so loud it's like me and him are in the same bed. Odd, but his gurgling brings back a memory. One of the boys - I just remembered his name - it was Bradley, he and his little brother used to do drowning trials in the bathtub when they were younger. Apparently they got pretty good at it, and after a certain point – way beyond the pain - it eventually became a nice experience. Brad said the body shutsdown but the mind just keeps rolling along. I'm hoping the guy beside me is not too uncomfortable.

I can make a barrel from a block of wood with my saw and adze and drawshave and not many people can do that. Just hand tools. Making a stave is a wonderful thing, but ideas change. Steaming and bending. Fitting them together. Tapering. Narrow, wide, narrow, wide. Check for splits. Pick the best and widest for the bunghole. Give a knock and listen for the lovely pure tone. It really bugs me when I see them chopped in half and used as planters.

A woman sits in a chair and holds my hand. I see tears rolling down her cheeks and shattering on the back of my wrist, and, as it turns out it's Maude, but for an instant, I think she's some other woman and that I'm having an affair. Nothing like that ever happened with us, even if occasions presented themselves. In the poor light, Maude looks younger so maybe that's the cause for the confusion. I need to say it right now. I often secretly wondered if she regretted not finding another guy and then the kid thing might have happened for her. Neither of us ever admitted our doubts about the other, but the lack of family became a dark cloud as the years trickled by.

The clocks strike 4:28. I am peed off, because time is going backwards on both clocks so I say to Maude, "Am I sick, honey?"

She nods her head giving the "Yes" gesture.

Then she says, "Poor, Coop."

I keep feeling explosions, like fireflies igniting, and I hear the sudden flapping of a spooked flock of wings, so it could be the pure white flamingo birds. The tinkling of the crystal chimes in the gentle breeze returns. A very lovely sound when it's all by itself. Did I mention that before?

It was not always the case that I got the custom jobs. Sometimes Wing would be off, because he drank too, so I'd get to do sweep up. And when the whiskey barrels got changed to wine barrels, someone had to carve all the burnt insides off with the long handled shave saw, so you ended breathing in black soot all day. In the summer we had thousands to do, since wine season was coming, so that's why I got to be the foreman for the boys.

Eventually, rebranding the heads of the fish and fruit barrels, that sat in inventory forever, became my exclusive job. The company had box car loads of them because the customers never claimed them, or the company went out of business, or they couldn't pay their account. In those days you used a branding tool to burn in special advertisements like MDF for McCauley's Dry Fruit, CC for Christian's Cherries, HH for Henry's Herring, AF for Arrogant Fish, or ABC Fish Products, though I never found out what the ABC stood for. Anyway, the reason for me getting the job long term – a kind of reward in a way since it got you off the assembly line - was that instead of sanding off the burned in letters, which again was a dusty process, and took a lot of time, one day I got the idea to pound the top hoops off the barrel and then slip the barrel head off and flip it over and tap it back together – the head that was branded that is. Like starting with a clean slate. The *Arrogant* brand gave me the idea. There were so many of them collecting dust for about a century. The bosses were upset to start with, but when they timed me, they realized I had saved a lot of cost in labour. That was another way they credited me for original thinking. The next summer when the boys showed up I told them about my little promotion. They probably thought I was boasting. That's when they told me the *Arrogant* was the name of the fishboat that went down with all their dads aboard. For a souvenir, I rounded up three damaged heads of the *Arrogant* from the scrap burn pile and gave them to the boys. Did they ever get excited. Maybe I was fatherly on that occasion.

I MUST BE FEELING better, since I notice my surroundings. The pains are gone and the guy beside me in one or three is quiet or gone. A steady file of people go by - janitor people, kitchen staff pushing tray-carts of food, a woman, who looks a bit like Maude, walking slowly away, and she's crying so she must belong to the drowning guy next door. I'm just watching like the only audience and they're coming on and off stage doing their parts. Two doctors chat at the counter. A blood lady takes a piece of paper out of a slot and puts one in and goes away. The X-ray lady grabs a file and zigzags off pushing her machine. Like bees going out for pollen on a sunny day. A group of the nurses talk behind the counter and they have a packet of pictures they're passing back and forth. They're going gaga so it's baby pictures for sure.

Everyone here without exception drinks coffees or pops or juices, and those with straws, when they get to the bottom of their drink suck up air, and rattle and stir the ice. Anyway, that slushing and gurgling of the dregs in the drinks is exactly the same sound as the guy next door, who, like I said, has gone.

Something else. The big chalkboard behind control central, which I know I already mentioned, there's a narrow shelf on top of the board lined with soft fuzzy animals, which I didn't mention. Giraffes and monkeys, dogs, and a doll or two and a cute cat and a lizard. I get to wondering why they are there and then see one space left so decide to get Maude to buy one to round up the collection. A scruffy old bear would be best.

The chalkboard is one of those white shiny plastic ones and covers the whole wall, as I already told you when I first began this screwed up story. Because they use felt pens instead of chalk, the marks erase quite easily. I see Cooper in the number two slot, which makes sense, written in that bright neon flashing blue, but the other names, which don't flash, are in black or red, green occasionally, and names get moved around and change colour, but not mine. There's always someone going up to the board and erasing a name or moving a name or changing the name's colour, but it's not one person who's in charge of that. Seems anyone can. Then this doctor comes along and erases "er" so I figure Maude encouraged them to be informal and use my nickname. But then, it's like the doctor has second thoughts, and goes and erases "Coop," which, by the way, had started flashing really fast, so I now figure I'm going to get moved to a new slot, or get the new colour like I expected, or both, but he wanders away carrying my file. I don't know why, but I feel a very calm sensation of peacefully drifting, just like Bradley had described that time long ago when he and his little brother performed the drowning experiments and got close to their dad.

death a concept invented by man for his strange purpose

∞ ∞ ∞

A MOUNTAIN LOOMS AT the Equator of a strange world in a desolate galaxy on the edge of the universe. In truth, the colossal mass should not be there. The highest pinnacles are eternally snow-capped. A million billion suns could not melt the ice. I exaggerate. Nonetheless, between these peaks stretches a vast, arid plain blanketed in velvety talc, a delicious dust, which would squish seductively between the toes should any creature walk there. Boulders of surprising size, shape, colour and texture litter the surface. They bring to mind grazing herds of migratory beasts in search of water. They could also be mistaken for monuments to past civilizations. From this distance, the rocks give rise to speculation; how did they get there, where did they come from and why were they forsaken?

It has been said that once upon a time, a life form climbed near the summit and that the carcass remains preserved – freeze dried in a small crevice awaiting resurrection by its imagined god. What else? Creatures crawl the lower slopes, forever looking up, struggling always to reach the sublime air.

A WOMAN IS BAREFOOT, dressed in animal skins. Her hair would make a splendid nest for homeless mice. The soles of her feet are thickly calloused, so much so that leather boots would be a waste of hide. The woman looks into the setting sun and shields her eyes with one hand. Below are savannahs and jungles and then an ocean in the far distance. A few clouds drift over the land below. She sits beside a round rock. Her rock is not merely round, but a perfect sphere, precisely a meter in diameter, neither a millimeter more nor less, a black surface polished as smooth as the finest marble from antiquity. A closer inspection reveals that her possession contains embedded jewels. These jewels sparkle brightly, not a reflected light as one might imagine, but colourful pulsings from an inner source of perpetual energy. She rubs her sore back and moans, the resigned whimper of a tired slave. Her name is Margaret.

She takes a twig from her hair and writes on the earth, 170,064. The number represents her steps from the base of the mountain to the present location. Margaret has never come this far, never achieved these heights until today. The feeling of accomplishment is almost unbearable, a joy that hurts. The number is so large: 170,000 was an objective set years ago and now that it has been surpassed, she will have to set a new goal. The woman has always kept track of her movement. With her advanced mind she has learned to count each of her footsteps, measuring progress and egress, adding and subtracting, calculating to the step exactly where she is on the mountain at any time, night or day. Her clock is internal now, resilient like the beat of her heart.

Margaret has chosen this spot to camp, as the incline is hardly perceptible. Even if her rock should dislodge, say from an unlikely earthquake, it would only roll as far as that shallow ravine down there, over to the right, squint, it will help. No no, look farther to the right, where she has just come from, only 123 paces from yesterday's camp, where the number 169,941 has not yet eroded, beyond that tall prickly cactus plant, to the left of that colony of seven ant towers where earlier she had rested and watched the red ants pack off the larvae of the black ants - though larger and more numerous, the adults seemed helpless to stop the blatant robbery of their young. She, in fact, had tried to disrupt their long lines as they made off with the booty, but the determined red ants reformed their columns as though the interruption hardly mattered at all.

If by chance Margaret's rock breaks free during this coming night, she judges it would catch in that thicket of gnarled and stunted trees where water flashes and floods, following the luminous electrical storms from the far heights above – where she has never been. As a manner of speaking, if push comes to shove, then the loss of a day would be negligible. Margaret has time on her side, so much so, that fooling with the ants does not fill her with guilt. As is obvious, guilt would only be a warranted emotion if time had both beginning and end.

Even so, she wedges her rock with a branch so there is little possibility it can roll away. The branch looks and feels petrified - striated, brittle, hard and cold - on short notice the best material available. As an added precaution, she collects insignificant stones scattered over this resting place, their congruency flattened and distorted, again the best material available. She braces the branch with these smaller stones and then tests her rock with a slight shove. Safe.

If Margaret had companions, she might have enjoyed a celebration of her feat. Days earlier, she would have let her friends know by dropping subtle hints that an important moment was in the offing, and "wouldn't it be nice" to think of ways to mark the occasion, but only, she would caution, "if it really comes to pass." Her imagined friends might have planned a ceremony, mainly with speeches and song, rhythms pounded on their breast plates and tapped on their own rocks, and the sprightly maidens might have danced around the fire, provocatively heaving their shadows at the coming darkness and crashing their voices against the silent mountain. They would have danced with abandon like zealous pagans shouting at the top of their lungs, and taken the rare and simple liberty of enjoying one night from eons of others. Food and beverages would not play a role in the festivity as those things hardly exist here. Maybe sips of clear sweet water from the small stream nearby. These fanciful thoughts had come to her over the last few days, while she pushed her rock and counted her steps.

The day is ending. Margaret builds a fire. All is well. Let's enjoy the view, the wonderful sunset, and her rock sparkling more brightly as the light fades. Let's have a good sleep. Perhaps dream that we are part of the celebration.

UNKNOWN TO MARGARET, MARLENE has also completed her journey for the day and set up camp over the next rise. Like Margaret, her apparel is hide and fur, and her feet are unshod as well. Her rock is a slab, exactly one meter by two meters by thirty centimeters deep – coarse grey granite. A monolith that hums. Her rock is not a roller like Margaret's, but a flipper and flopper. A slider and plower. She has become expert at raising her slab to vertical and then encouraging it to free-fall towards the sky - uphill. Always she carries a sturdy pry bar, a black mahogany pole, both as an assist in the raising maneuver and a brake for that moment when her rock concusses against the incline and inevitably tries to slide back. Thankfully, due to its propensity for stasis, her slab rarely goes far. Marlene has friction on her side as well as tortoise resolve. The delightful combinations of friction and resolve have taken her a long way. Unlike Margaret, she is not a counter; she has no idea how many times she flipped her slab today or yesterday, or the totality of flips in her lifetime, and no idea where she is on the mountain. Still, even though she doesn't keep track of her progress or know where she is exactly, Marlene experiences moments of setback.

Sometime she loses control of her slab. These uncontrollable days occur when concentration is not what it should be, or when she is unable to apply the brake quickly enough. On such occasions, the rock will slide backwards or even flip, but thankfully, soon will hang-up on roots, depressions, large obstructions, or tree trunks if she is below the tree line. The more dangerous times are when she slowly and carefully traverses old animal trails along winding ridges, where there is no easier route possible. At sharp bends in the path, the hazards increase. Over the decades, it has happened many times more than once, that her humming monolith tumbles into the emptiness and the valleys and depths below.

After a good tantrum, she will retrace her steps to the lower sections of the mountain and eventually find her slab, locating it by the humming sound or by the detection of minor vibrations in the earth. Then will follow months, even years of depression, energyless days and nights, long contemplations on the futility of purpose, progress and hope, before she rediscovers the dying embers of her ambition. Then she dusts off her slab and begins anew.

It has been this way always: these women never give up.

Marlene has often wondered what it will be like as she nears the steeper sections. Will she be able to devise a new method to scale the sheer slopes other than the flip and flop routine? What other tool might she use besides the mahogany pry? Can the vibrations in her slab be used to advantage or are they simply a pleasant sound, a beautiful aesthetic amidst the despair of life? What if there are no trails? What if progress is fully vertical all the time? These worries occupy her mind off and on through the days and nights.

At all events, these are not worries for this late afternoon. She enjoys this part of the day the most; a cozy fire, a vast panorama of plains and jungles below, and to the West, an unnamed ocean that greets the sky each night. If this were

another time and another place, she might have a stiff drink –
for medicinal purposes only.

When the sun has gone and the stars appear, she will put
her ear to her slab and listen to the gorgeous hum. She will lie
on her slab and let the gentle vibrations enter her body. Her
aches and pains will fall away. What more could one ask?

HAD THE TWO WOMEN known of each other's existence,
instead of following their usual routines, they could easily
have met half way between the two campfires. Given the short
distances involved, perhaps 200 hundred meters at most, they
could have thrown caution to the winds, as the saying goes,
abandoned their rocks, temporarily of course, and walked in
the direction of the other, both women advancing 100 meters
only, no more no less, neither with advantage nor disadvan-
tage. Neither woman would distance themselves from their
rocks more than the other as these rules of approach and
retreat are understood intuitively and need no reinforcement
through acquired knowledge or training. Each woman would
approach the other at a similar and casual pace, there would
be no quick moves, no swerving, no hesitations, no breaking of
the crystalline spell that has been cast in this unusual scene.
One can imagine that they will notice each other at about the
same time from their respective positions and give a greeting
wave before setting off for the mid point. Every effort would
be made to make their wave seem spontaneous and cheerful.
Margaret and Marlene are tired, but not so tired as to skip
this opportunity for a good chat. The fact that there is still adequate daylight would surely favour this outcome. The sun has
miles to go before hissing into the distant sea, their campfires
burn nicely, will not require replenishing for at least fifteen
minutes, and there is no visual obstruction across a no man's
land like a forest of tall cacti. Between the women lies only an

open space on a slight incline so the possibility of the unexpected becomes next to remote. Given this perfect moment in time, the wonderful weather, the peace of the quiet evening, the mutual need for human contact, it seems that the conjunction of these events, and others not yet imagined or required, is a conspiracy orchestrated by the mountain itself.

We can progress farther with the hypothetical meeting and imagine that everything goes to plan. Perhaps only minor variations exist. At the midpoint of no man's land, Marlene stands rather than sits, thereby preventing the shallow rise from intercepting her line of vision to her slab. Instinctively, she is constantly alert and listens for its faint hum. Her anxieties will wash away as soon as she hears the pleasant sound. As for Margaret, who has just completed her 100-meter approach, exactly, we might add, there is no need to stand like her newfound companion. She may sit at the midpoint - remember she has been on her feet all day – and she could face downhill to watch that the fire doesn't go out, or for that matter, that her own rock continues to sparkle. Now both of them can watch their chosen territories and prize possessions while they each face the other and talk amiably. How convenient that neither needs to experience the discomfort of turning and craning one's neck. Margaret needs only to lean a bit to the side, or look between Marlene's legs, to insure that all is as it should be. Though Marlene looks down at Margaret, she only needs to lift her head to see her slab. Everything appears perfectly okay.

For starters, their conversation necessarily would centre on introductions: I'm Margaret and that's my rock, Jewel. Marlene turns and looks downhill in order to see the beautiful rock. She says, What a nice name for your rock, and then adds, I'm Marlene and that's my slab, Monolith, Mono for short.

Marlene points up hill and says, Can you see it just over the brow? Margaret decides to stand. Now she can see the rigid, ground-hugging, rectangular object. How different from her radiant globe. Wishing to be gracious, however, she says, What is it that I'm hearing? Is that lovely humming sound coming from your slab? I knew I heard something earlier but had no idea what it was.

Marlene is so pleased that her companion can hear the vibrations. Not wanting to hog the whole stage they play upon, Marlene says, That's quite delightful how your rock sparkles and I can see that they are simply not reflections from the flames in your fire or the sun either.

As is so often the case, once the formalities of an introduction are complete, new acquaintances fall silent for long moments. These women both realize that carrying on a conversation is not easy, indeed awkward, especially when one is so out of practice. Marlene is the first to think of something to say, Isn't it an interesting coincidence that our names start with M? Not believing in coincidence, Margaret replies, More like extreme odds. Now we have moved onto a subject in which both women excel, but for differing reasons. Margaret is on familiar territory because she is both a counter and calculator. As she rolls her rock from day to day, and rests night to night, she doesn't just count her steps, as mentioned earlier, but performs other numerical exercises. She counts the breaths she takes, heart beats, pebbles on the path, and she counts the number of days without rainfall, hours, minutes and seconds for the sun to reach zenith, and days for the moon to wax and wane. Since she has an excellent memory, she stores these sums in her head so that she can manipulate them later. As if all this measuring were not enough, she can enter the realm of higher mathematical theory calculating the height of every ridge and every peak. In her spare moments, simply for the exhilaration of a meaningful mental challenge, she calculates the decimals of pi in every direction toward infinity. She has gone as far as 5065 decimals, but detected no pattern in any sequence of numbers, yet. Margaret calculates the time for light from the sun to reach the mountain by manipulating formulas, like say, t equals *distance* divided by *velocity,* and then wonders, as an after thought only, would the light from the sun feel odd if it traveled at a different speed? Now that Marlene has brought up the M controversy, Margaret reflects that an impressive problem has been introduced requiring the knowledge of not just present M beginning names, but an inventory of all M names forever into the past as well as into the future. One can only imagine that Margaret's propensity for manipulating numbers is nothing more than a diversion, a diversion which occupies her mind while she toils on the mountain, a diversion which is unlikely to bring any real benefit, especially when one keeps in mind the grand scheme of things, which, incidentally, she has never calculated. Nevertheless, it is fun when you meet someone who poses these problems.

Marlene has had time to reflect. She says, I don't believe odds have anything to do with our names starting with M. In fact, I shouldn't have characterized my earlier remark as a coincidence, because I believe everything happens for a reason; therefore, coincidence, chance, luck, all those notions are really just masks for a design that already is thoroughly in place. What we really should do is consider that our M names are a sign – a sign for something yet to be discovered.

Now we come to Marlene's forte. For her, signs are everywhere in the universe and she is proficient in reading them. The stars, the detritus of animals, tea leaves if she had any, or a jumble of sticks. Just the other day she came across four beaks of small birds, different beaks and different birds, but beaks nonetheless, all pecking at one weed grass. Analysis of these signs gives meaning to her life. This isn't just fun, these auguries help her plan her day and determine which route to take. One might venture the thought that she could be useful to the recalcitrant gods at the top of the mountain if they ever remember she exists.

The women approach the conversations with caution. Perhaps they suspect their chat could become confrontational with each of them occupying an intractable frame of reference. The one mind relies on the tools of mathematics and logic to define her position on the mountain, whereas the other chooses the tools of superstition and intuition and cherishes the conviction that the world of the mountain speaks to her in an infinite variety of possibilities. By either one of the two – coincidence or design - the women balance on a fulcrum from the far ends of an exceedingly long spectrum. So, instead of reinforcing their position on the fulcrum, they look to each other's attire. They pretend to have just noticed, and Margaret says, Is that a wildebeest robe you wear? Yes, but I really like your patchwork of gazelle, ibex and giraffe. When they finally learn to trust one another, they might find that serious talk is easier and continue with the M debate.

BUT WE GET AHEAD of ourselves. More likely, we have gone astray. Taken liberties. Indulged in nonsense. Given the impression that we glimpse the future. Let's go back to the beginning, as any other forward movement would never get us there. To sum up, we have two women unaware of each other, two unique rocks, two campfires separated by a stretch of no man's land, and the scene unfolding on the midlevel slopes of an immense nameless mountain. Suppose that Marlene, who was up hill of Margaret and concealed by the rise, decided to wander just a few steps from her camp, perhaps only to relieve herself, or simply to stretch her aching limbs, and if she had walked over the brow, she surely would have noticed the jeweled, pulsing, perfectly round rock and the campfire. God knows what would go through her mind at that moment. One can assume that she is not simply going to shrug her shoulders, as if to say, here's another awe-inspiring rock, there's another campfire, here are the most unusual things I've ever seen in my entire life, therefore, I think I'll just go back to the camp now that I've watered the good earth, and I might just as well pick up a few sticks on the way to rebuild the fire. No, now that we have regained our senses, we see her crouch from her strategic position, look quickly in every direction, and check two or three times that her slab hums peacefully. Since the sun is setting and chooses to shade one part of the hillside before another, Marlene also chooses to move to the darker section of terrain where there happen to be fallen cacti trunks, other uninteresting rocks and small outcrops to hide behind, none of which were mentioned earlier. Her tread is light; she knows not to step on loose shale, or a twig for that matter, which under these dry conditions would sound like the electric clap of a Zeus, for instance, and wake even the sleepy lions on the savannahs below. Luckily her apparel blends perfectly with the colour of the earth and the few golden tussocks of grass that somehow manage to survive at these altitudes blend in nicely. Marlene moves imperceptibly like the cheetah seconds before the pounce. She carries her dark mahogany pry.

One can conclude that if Marlene saw only the sparkling rock and small fire, then she failed to notice Margaret, who earlier heard a hum and smelled smoke and had approached the other camp in a long sideways sweep under the cover of the ravine we had described earlier, which continued to wind its way up the mountain. So the scene is really quite different than we earlier imagined; both women suspect that another lives on the mountain, they are curious to investigate the rocks, yet uncertain about whether or not to take defensive or offensive actions.

Unfortunately, neither of these very real possible scenarios materialized. Both women were so hopelessly tired that they fell asleep by their fires and dreamed. Incidentally, they dream nightly, always remember their dreams and then cogitate with these visions, fantasies, hallucinations and nightmares during the day while they push, roll, flip, kick or drag their rocks. Margaret incorporates her dreams into her calculations, whereas Marlene uses them in her analysis of signs.

Curiously, Margaret's dream this night isn't about counting and calculating, but turns to thoughtless excretion. Metal objects: even liquid mercury, tungsten, the rare metals plutonium, palladium and uranium, common zinc, corroded and green copper, brass, tin, bronze, silver and real gold, not fool's; these tumble and pour from every orifice. A magnificent letting go, which happens so quickly and thoroughly, she is unable to count their abandonment from her being. A disturbing dream.

And even more curious, Marlene's dream is one of transformation. She is Lucy, a small naked woman crawling on all fours, who hears a voice, "Walk upright," so she obeys and it is easy. Lucy leaves tracks for all time in the volcanic mud of a dried creek bed. The rest of the dream is walking, just walking and walking and walking towards a tall mountain.

AT DAYBREAK, JEWEL RESTS near the number 169, 941. During the night, the petrified branch had snapped and Margaret's rock rolled into the ravine precisely where she had calculated. Now we see her beside her rock, weeping. Her grief is a surprise given that only one day's progress has been lost. And her crying is a surprise because she has never cried before. Her elbows rest on her knees and her hands cradle under her chin. She stares at the distant pink morning ocean. Her rock brightly sparkles yet she seems not to notice or care.

As for Marlene, she heard a crash during the night but thought it somehow part of her dream. She rises late, quite tired, one might think from trudging through volcanic mud. She remembers the long track of footprints ran straight for the mountain just as though Lucy were a compass herself, so Marlene takes her dream as a sign. She surveys the route ahead and decides to go straight over one rise and then the next. This part of her journey looks easier. She reminds herself that she has been wrong before, but that is no reason to give up on the scheme she has chosen to guide her life.

Grieving Margaret feels a slight quake in the ground while she stares out over the distant nameless ocean. At each shudder she also hears a thud, but is too disheartened to investigate the tremors or sounds. She has lost 123 steps and feels as though she starts from the beginning, even though a quick calculation confirms that her penultimate depression is a gross exaggeration.

PERHAPS ONLY A MILE or two below Marlene and Margaret, Meredith had a restless sleep. Her dream was about flying on a giant featherless bird. She had woken frequently, whenever she thought the bird would collide with the mountain. Unnoticed, sometime during the night, her rock got itself perched high in the crotch of a tree. All she could do was laugh when she saw it at daybreak. Meredith's rock is porous and pocked with holes, close to weightless and looks like a brain. There are times when her rock gets up and walks and that is funny. And other times when it hovers or flies and that is funny also. She keeps her rock on a long leather rope, but the tether had snapped while she slept and *Rock of Holes* floated into the tree. Now Meredith worries about the Ballentyne Journals lodged inside her rock. And that isn't funny.

Appendix I

Selection from **Passport Home**
by John Ballentyne

1

frostbite on Kilimanjaro
frostbite at the equator
when i returned
the rock of holes
had floated away

2

a remote village in Afghanistan
a moonlike land
the still air
defiant and hot,
the ragged road
deep in the day's dust,
billowed, while i walked,
filling my sockless boots,
and the fine velvety talc
seductively squished
between the toes

i ate a pomegranate
while i walked,
and spit the peel and pulp
onto the dusty road,
to which adhered,
a seed here and a seed there

as the red juices dripped from my chin
i noted behind,
a frail old man,
squatting and naked
retrieving the discards,
hardly concerned that my detritus
was coated in the dust of the road

i gave him the remains
of the fanciful fruit of infinite seed,
and these many years later
wonder,
did the fanciful fruit of infinite seed
cause him to grow inside,
an eternal garden?

3

In the rasping voice of his Father
Jesus commanded,
"roll the rock away."

His angels thought it absurd to wake the dead
so far along the road
to ultimate decay,
for that matter,
why give life back at all
they asked amongst themselves,
yet Lazarus left the cave,

no reason other
than the rock was rolled away.

St. Michael was the first to see
the sadness in the aching heart,
as he watched the man walk
the streets of Bethany,
in the sun's blinding light,
the soulless man,
stumbling over his stinking feet,
his skin pale and hanging loose forever more.

St. Michael said to Jesus,
"Have you not a soul to give?"
and the other angels
thought it a good question,
but their Lord answered
in the frail voice of the Holy Ghost,
"A soul once given
cannot be given again."

St. Michael, now frustrated,
said to Jesus,
"I know that, but
what about another soul
an unused soul,
is there nothing left in inventory?"
and the other angels
thought it another good question.

Their Lord answered,
giving a long and tedious explanation
in a searing voice they had never heard before.
"It wouldn't work,
don't you know

it wouldn't work,
this is not unusual and
he is not singled out either,
if you look closely
you will see that many
have the Lazarus affliction,
and the malady will increase
as we move the clock,
move the clock,
move the clock."

4

a rock got up and walked
voices got up and walked
the shepherds got up and walked,
they each carried a distinctive crook,
their unique signature,
and used it they did,
we heard the solitary taps
on the red earth road

later they danced in circles,
and musicians played,
the mandolin balalaika accordion,
the shepherds danced and twirled
and kicked a chair,
only because the chair was there

now time has moved,
the shepherds have lost their sheep,
this was long ago
when mist hovered over the animals,
the time when
the flock disappeared,
whilst a squashed sun

hovered low on the horizon
concealing the retreat

but look closely,
the immense flock
ruminates in blue pastures,
their fleeces white as snow,
they are not lost
they are not lost

Appendix II

Christian Brothers of Ireland: Official Statement - 1998

"OVER THE PAST NUMBER of years we have received from some former pupils serious complaints of ill-treatment and abuse by some Christian Brothers in schools and residential centres. We the Christian Brothers in Ireland wish to express our deep regret to anyone who suffered ill-treatment while in our care. And we say to you who have experienced physical or sexual abuse by a Christian Brother and to you who complained of abuse and were not listened to, we are deeply sorry. We want to do much more than say we are sorry. As an initial step we have already put in place a range of services to offer a practical response and further services will be provided as the needs become clearer."

Appendix III

ON SEPTEMBER 14, 2006, a staff member of the Cortes Island Museum, while sorting through boxes of old artifacts and uncatalogued archives, found journal entries from a diary kept by Mrs. Melissa Holmes of Mansons Landing, now deceased. The Archive Program has as its purpose the acquisition, description, and preservation and storage of those documents (fonds), maps, photographs, letters, journals, audio tapes, and videotapes which serve to shed light on the history of the island and its people. This ensures that the valuable threads of the past contained in the documents of community groups, local and provincial associations, businesses, schools and families are preserved and put in an order that can be accessed by archivists and viewed by researchers, families, authors, school children and the general public. Many thanks to the Museum for permission to use excerpts from the Holmes' diary.

August 22, 1947

"Breezy and cool. Looks like fall might be along early.... Gerry and Freddie went up Waddington Channel yesterday prospecting on the East Redonda side. They came back this afternoon and Gerry said they only found traces of copper. When I asked him what he had wrapped in the towel he said none of your business. I made it my business after he went to bed. He found an old pistol that was completely rusted with the handle rotted away. It'll take me forever to get the rust out of the towel."

August 23, 1947

"Looks like I was dead wrong about fall coming early. It was 75 today and the radio said we can expect 3 more days of it…. Gerry looked it up in the encyclopedia and the weapon is a .36 revolver from the 1800's. He told me it didn't shoot bullets, but patch balls, whatever they are. After a few ryes he said they found it in a cave under rocks and rubble along with a skeleton. I told him we had to make a report to the authorities. He just blew up because he knew they'd want the evidence. He thought the body and gun were so old nobody would care anymore. I didn't agree, but what could I do?"

Acknowledgements

WITHOUT ENCOURAGEMENT AND SOUND comments from my manuscript readers, this work of fiction would still be in draft form. Thanks to Carol Tidler, Yvonne Kipp, Dana Davis, Christian Gronau, Aileen Douglas, Ian Ross, John Preston and Monica Nawrocki. Many thanks to Richard Trueman for photographing, elements of interior and cover design, and computer support. Special thanks to Ruth Ozeki for her friendship and belief in the importance of this project. Andrew Weil, Bill Gaston, Rex Weyler and Ruth Ozeki, I so appreciate the testimonials. A very special thanks to my good friend and Go partner, Rex Weyler, who slogged through numerous drafts and supplied the necessary and brilliant analysis when he should have been putting more *Green* in the *Peace*. A father's delight, love to my remarkable and wonderful children, Lisa and Michael Gibbons, who made particularly insightful suggestions. Then there is Denise, my superlative wife and best friend of fifty plus years – you pushed, you supported, you loved. As it shall always be.

Note on Sources

1. "The evening redness in the West" A sub-title from Cormac McCarthy's novel, *Blood Meridian*. Page 8.
2. "the remains of the day" Title from Kazuo Ishiguro's third novel, *The Remains of the Day*. Page 13.
3. "the doors of perception opening wide to the marriage of heaven and hell" A mix of titles from *The Doors of Perception* by Aldous Huxley (1954) and the poem, *The Marriage of Heaven and Hell* by William Blake (1793). Page 18.
4. "IT WAS LATE SEPTEMBER when the leaves come falling down." Adapted from the lyrics by Van Morrison, *When the Leaves Come Falling Down*. Page 24.
5. "There was nothing really to concern one's self about, really." An adapted line from a Raymond Carver short story, *Will You Please Be Quiet, Please?* Page 57.
6. The voice of Bradley in the chapter titled, **1950**, was inspired by *Paddy Clarke, Ha, Ha, Ha*, by Roddy Doyle.
7. In the chapter titled, **December 1954**, the lyrics from *Sailor's Lullaby* were taken from the CD album, *Catch the Light* by Rex Weyler. Page 88.
8. In the chapter titled, **1956,** the eulogy, *R.I.P. The Shipmates of the Arrogant*, was altered from a magazine clipping in a private archive.
9. All quotes from Arthur Rimbaud in chapters, **1961** and **1964 May**, are taken from, *A Season In Hell and The Drunken Boat* translated by Louise Varese.
10. Elements of style and voice in chapter **1961** inspired by Witold Gombrowicz in his books, *Cosmos* and *Pornographia*.
11. Elements of style and voice in chapter **1994** inspired by W.G. Sebald in his books, *Austerlitz*, *The Emigrants* and others.
12. Elements of style and voice in chapter ∞ ∞ ∞ inspired by the novels of Jose Saramago.

Images

Pencil drawing of *Georgie's Rowboat* by Lisa Gibbons. Private Collection. Chapter **1923-1928.**

Fisherman and The Siren by Knut Ekwall. Public Domain. Chapter **1945**.

Evening Walk by LeRoy Jensen. Private Collection. Chapter **1997**.

All other images, including photographs, letters, etchings, logbooks, calendars, Christian Brothers of Ireland apology and magazine clippings belong to private archives or are part of the public domain.

About the Author

Photo by Frank Vitz

Norm Gibbons has lived in the Desolation Sound region for the past forty years. He has a background in social work, shellfish aquaculture and business. He studied Creative Writing at the University of Victoria, British Columbia. Presently, he is retired and lives on Cortes Island, where he continues to write the *Edge of Desolation* trilogy.